SO IT WENT
LIKE THIS

Praise for C. Spencer

On Second Thought

"Hello, chemistry! Madisen and Rae had chemistry in spades and it radiated off the page. They also had these lovely moments of nonsexual intimacy that were fuelled with love and affection…Great story. I really hope we see more from these characters in the future. I'm looking forward to checking out what's next from C. Spencer."—*Rainbow Literary Society*

Truth or Dare

"*Truth or Dare* is an entirely fun read. When *Truth or Dare* reaches into the realm of the erotic, it excels. Such scenes are sexy and palpable; they're striking and tense…and there's much solace to be found in the book's snowed-in, relaxed atmosphere and pleasing plot. This book is a must for fans of multiple-character structures and shows like *The L Word. Truth or Dare* is charming with its stories of queer women falling in and out of love. It is smart, funny, and romantic—the perfect read for a snowy night in."—*Foreword Reviews*

"*Truth or Dare* is a thoughtful, intimate, slice-of-life story that delves into relationships and the intertwining of lives. It's a must read for those who enjoy unique and well-done character work and a multiple-character structure that allows for a more expansive look at our humanity. Because of its depth and many layers woven into this work, I know it's one of those books that will offer something new with each read, so it's a story I'll revisit many times."—*The Lesbian Review*

"This is a great story for a debut novel. One that quite honestly, I wasn't expecting. This is more than a romance novel. I think it's a Lesbian Romance and Drama novel. Great debut novel and I can't wait for what's next from C. Spencer."—*Les Reveur*

By the Author

Truth or Dare

On Second Thought

So It Went Like This

Visit us at www.boldstrokesbooks.com

So It Went Like This

by

C. Spencer

2023

ISBN 13: 978-1-63555-971-2

This Trade Paperback Original Is Published By
Bold Strokes Books, Inc.
P.O. Box 249
Valley Falls, NY 12185

First Edition: March 2023

Credits
Editor: Ruth Sternglantz
Production Design: Stacia Seaman
Cover Design by Inkspiral Design

Acknowledgments

I never know where a manuscript might go when I start out. There's just an impression, a vague idea. In this case, perhaps it was our dependence on social media. A remote inn far away from it all. Our chosen family. And soulmates. Because I wanted to somehow in some way delve beyond meet-cutes and try to convey that soul mate connection. That familiarity, that innate intimacy. That instant attraction. Fused with insane giddiness, with hope, with blind trust, with inevitability, destiny—and with the brilliance you feel once you find her. That, to me, was the challenge I wanted to undertake in writing *So It Went Like This*.

I want to thank Len Barot for allowing me the opportunity to write my stories and share them with you. Along with the talented team she's pulled together—who've pulled this book together. Like Sandy Lowe, who asked all of the right questions and offered the patience of a saint as we cycled through several cover iterations before reaching the one I felt comfortable with. Not to mention the hours behind the scenes by those combing through and pulling together, proofreading, typesetting, and managing production. And especially, my editor Ruth Sternglantz, for her wisdom, vision, and continual reassurance—along with the creative freedom she's always offered me.

But more importantly, it's you for picking up this book for whatever reason, for those who've read earlier titles, and for those who've lifted me up along the way—a Thank You does not seem enough. And of course my kid, who named a main character and who is crazy proud to have a mom who writes the kind of books she's not allowed to read. And last but not least, gratitude to my wife, without whom this book would not have been written.

Don't give up on the fairy-tale romance.
Dreams do come true.

CHAPTER ONE

But in Any Regard

Kennedy

I'm opening up my legal pleading template—multitasking with a can of Blue Bottle cold brewed coffee—when that calendar alert glides across my screen to let me know it's quarter to two and time to leave. And suddenly, it dawns on me. In the eight months that I've quietly slipped away to see my therapist, not once has a colleague asked me where I've been, though I know they talk. They being Faith, Olivia, and Emmy, better known as The Clique.

You'll often find The Clique in the copier room gossiping, perhaps justifiably, during a heated bout of collating, stapling, and three-hole punching. I use the term *justifiably* only because, inside the span of however many years it's taken this modest law firm to expand from two names on its letterhead to four, we've been host to our fair share of scandals—from your run-of-the-mill personality skirmishes to an accountant's mishandling of equity (only to be discovered by Ernst & Young), topped last year by one highly unexpected affair involving our top partner's incompetent son (because nepotism) and one of our anchor clients, incidentally outing them both as gay. News that didn't land well with the partners, which would be why I tend to keep a low profile here at the office.

Still, the fact that they've never even hinted once about my absence leads me to believe—or perchance hope—that they might secretly be anguishing over the not-knowing part, which feels oddly satisfying. Either that or they've presumed, erroneously, that an unwed thirty-five-year-old woman like myself, not having found Mr. Right, must undoubtedly require therapy to deal with her abstinent ill-fated slide into spinsterhood. Not that I would discourage this level of misperception. In fact, I might be guilty of encouraging it, dragging Seth along to all of those plus-one socials at the office, given most require a higher proof of alcohol than the company is willing to serve.

Seth being my neighbor slash trusted confidant. He also happens to be a highly believable faux heteronormative armpiece. And while his fresh-out-of-grad-school bearded poli-sci flannel aesthetic doesn't quite mesh with my Brooks Brothers Red Fleece, The Clique assumes we're entwined romantically.

And boy am I glad he's charmed them. Because trust me, it's often the smallest of personality clashes that will make or break one's career. And once you're on their bad side, you're under the bus, especially when you've landed a position of marginally higher status, following a promotion from legal secretary—an equal—to paralegal, which they consider grandiose. A bump I fairly earned thanks to hours and hours of overtime and my worthless college degree in liberal arts, not to mention the good fortune of working for a highly encouraging female attorney who just so happened to have been in a similar predicament, she being a theater major turned unfulfilled trial attorney, clearly lured by the paycheck. The NYC transplant who longs, still, for her lost Broadway roots, for sight lines and curtain calls. For gay theater culture. For her rainbow urbane life, which I now channel or epitomize or somehow substitute for. A longing that has led to an office friendship, to mentorship, and to advice that is always accompanied by an unspoken yet clear hint that not all the partners are as accepting as she.

Which brings me back to therapy.

Because therapy was supposed to help me deal with that—with The Clique, with professional closeting, with my newly broken heart (which I'll get to later), and with life in general. Perhaps I figured that talking with someone impartial and schooled in this sort of thing might help me navigate and avoid career sabotage. Even avoid sudden heartbreak. That whirlwind. That emotional trauma I seem so ill-equipped to handle. You know, hone my intuition, read intentions a little better, and quit falling for players. That's to say, stop falling for the archetype I seem so hopelessly attracted to. You see, therapy was always about them—about their problems. It was never supposed to be about me.

"It's crazy that you never show emotion," I tell her, settling back into the couch, one that's too firm for my liking. And maybe that's the intent. As if to say, don't get too comfortable. You're on the clock.

Her look, as stoic and sincere as ever. "That's because I'm not supposed to," she says.

"But you must feel something," I say, shaking my head.

"I feel a lot," she tells me, which seems sincere. "But I want you to think of me as a blank slate. Imagine I'm anyone you need me to be."

"That's impossible," I tell her. "You're not anyone. You're my therapist."

And, sure, I'll admit that through the course of several months, I might've opened up to the possibility that there could be a few areas about my own—how would I put it—characteristics, my behaviors, that might need examination. Analysis. Not repair per se, because we're not flawed. But there are unresolved issues that might need to be resolved. What I'm trying to say is therapy might have more to do with me and less to do with The Clique—or Léa, my ex.

Because who knows, something might've happened long ago, which led to a longing, a yearning, an attraction to all I can't have. To girls I can't have. For this reason or that.

"We're not here to talk about my feelings," she tells me. "We're here to work through yours in a safe environment." Her boilerplate. "Things you might not feel comfortable discussing with someone who's caused so much pain."

"Safe," I scoff. "You're referring to Léa." Léa, who on our first encounter, hopped onto the hood of my car and asked if she could take me someplace.

Where? I said.

Someplace, anyplace, she said.

That was the only time I told her *no*.

"I think we should talk about Léa," she says, "and others."

"I can't pretend you're Léa," I tell her, snickering.

"What would you say to her?"

What would I say to her? "I'd say a lot, though it's for the best that I keep my mouth shut. So I don't get angry."

"You're angered by her." She nods.

"Of course I am. I mean, not always. Not now. It's been eight months. I feel betrayed. She betrayed me. But it's not her fault, right? It never is. At least, logically, it takes two."

"Tell me about her betrayal."

To stall—or no, I really just don't want to talk about it. Because it always leads to this, which is unbelievable. As my gaze drops to the pitcher of herbal tea on the table, her dainty cups, saucers, not the stuffy kind but, instead, mismatched in a way that works. It's emblematic of how she is, or at least how I imagine her to be, off-hours. The yogi who grows weed in her backyard and wears Birkenstocks with socks. So much the opposite of me. Which is precisely why we click.

Anyway, I pour myself a cup of tea. Then I lift my gaze. But you know what amazes me? How anyone can maintain their silence and patience the way she does, and for this long. "Léa led me on in a deliberate way, in a selfish way, and it worked for her at the time," I say. "She got me to open up in ways I never could before...with anyone. And she rejected that."

"Could that have been sincere at one point?"

"Why would you ask that?" I say.

But again, she doesn't offer an answer. She just stares at me, as if to say, *You tell me.*

"It wasn't that long, was it?" I say. "It wasn't long enough to dwell like I am. It lasted a few months. Do those relationships count? Does it count when you don't live together, when you don't exchange rings, when you don't die in each other's arms?"

"Yes, it does."

"That's what I don't understand. Because it meant so much. It meant everything. She changed me. I don't know what to take from that."

"You say it wasn't long," she says, "though she asked you to marry her."

"She didn't ask," I say because it wasn't a question.

"She said she'd marry you."

"Exactly." When I exhale, it's so heavy, as if a dam has held everything back. "Why'd she do that? Why'd she act like I was her world, only to walk away? Was it me? Do I give off that vibe that shouts unbreakable? Come fuck with me. I'll be fine," I say. "I'm more afraid than I am mad. I'm afraid to trust. Like I might not have it in me anymore. Like she took that from me."

"Trusting anyone is frightening," she says.

Right, but if I don't? If I hadn't. "I want to think she loved me. But you don't leave the one you love. You don't cut them off."

"*You* don't," she says.

"I couldn't have."

And have I mentioned the notepad? She's always jotting stuff down on this notepad, like now. And I wonder what it says. It's probably her grocery list.

"What is love to you?" she finally says, gazing up, expectant.

As I twirl the tea in my cup. "What is love?"

"Yes." She uncrosses her leg, leaning forward.

"Are you asking me for a dictionary definition?" I say.

"I want to know what it is for you," she says. "It can be different for everyone."

"Are you saying she loved me in her own way?"

"I'm saying I want to know your way."

"My way," I say, "is that it feels so incredibly powerless."

But she doesn't break her gaze. "So love, as a feeling, is powerlessness?"

"Definitely."

"Why does it make you feel powerless?"

"Well, it's powerful, too. I felt powerful."

"Did you feel this *with* her," she says, "or *for* her?"

I guess I've never thought of it that way. But I am. I'm thinking about it. "I felt that way when I was *with* her. But I'm not with her now, and I still feel it. What does that mean?" She just looks at me like, *Keep going.* But I'm leaning over my cup thinking about *with.* Thinking about *for.*

"Why don't you finish this sentence for me. Perfect love looks like—"

"Romeo and Juliet," I say definitively.

"And why'd you choose that?"

"They were soulmates," I say, wistful.

"Yet *Romeo and Juliet* is considered a tragedy," she says. "It has an appeal. But that portrayal of romance is generally thought to be youthful."

"So you're saying it's naive?" I say. "Can I counter that? Because I tend to think that, as we age, we get worn down and scorned and settle. And that's something I refuse to do." She's silent again, which probably means that I've said the wrong thing. So I finish my tea. "I'll take one thing back," I tell her. "You asked if I felt love *with* her or *for* her—Léa. But it's like, she didn't need to do anything for it to be there. I couldn't *not* feel it. So what does that mean?"

"I'm going to answer you with a question," she says. "Could you love her enough to let her go, to see what happens?" But those tears are welling again. "You don't have to answer that right now. But I hope you'll think about it. What it is to love. And what you want from love. And what kind of love you give." As she glances at her watch. "I'd like to talk about that."

"Next week?" I say.

She nods. "Next week."

CHAPTER TWO

A Farewell to Grace

Logan

Six weeks. Tops.

Beyond that, things get a little complicated. It's like a glittering promise of potential, an unspoken arrangement that inevitably entails a soupy breakup ballad and that reassuring *It's not you, it's me* adage playing over and over again.

So why'd I break that rule? Who's to say.

Perhaps something about Grace felt unstoppable. Not that I'm waffling. Besides, a few months of monogamous sex are easily replaceable with some of the more exceptional kind. Not that Grace wasn't exceptional.

And trust me, I'm not torn up over this. Far from it. I'm better off channeling that energy at the office where I can do work that actually matters. Like balancing this Hot Pocket with my inbox during those few precious hours after the engineers have gone home to their aproned wives and chemicalized lawns in cul-de-sacs, while I, to the contrary, happily forfeit domesticities for a slice of peace. And for a night I've already committed to Tanner.

From: Tanner Walters
To: Logan Carlisle
Sent: Friday, June 15, 06:02 PM
Subject: TGIF

I have an insatiable craving right now for a Brandy Alexander, and you're written all over it. Let's meet up at that new blues dive. It's called Rue B, previously known as Belstaff. :(Tragic, I know. We'll commiserate or commemorate or who knows. I've heard all good things.

XOXO,
Tanner

P.S. Alone. Please and thank you.

Tanner being this hot mess of a train wreck. A beautiful train wreck, that is, radiant and exquisite and effervescent, with that youthful exuberance and naivety few women are able to maintain past their eighteenth birthdays, though she's just turned thirty-three. And as much as she's tried to make friends outside of me, especially at work, she's cursed with that blond Scandinavian air that makes most women resentful. Even though gay men just love her.

And here's my theory about that. I think somewhere in the back of their minds they're thinking she's amusing. She's amusing enough, entertaining enough, to toy with momentarily. And that attraction never ceases to amaze me. Because, as soon as they come in contact with her, they're in love with her.

As are women.

Myself excluded. Reason being, Tanner's my nearest and dearest friend. And I'm perhaps the only real friend she's got, the only one that counts, at least, aside from a string of casuals she's met on Tinder, Instagram.

I texted Tanner my response. *Grace won't be brought.* ~ *L*

Tanner replied, *Is this a farewell to Grace? Such a cause for revelry. With bated breath. XOXO, Tanner*

Plus, Tanner is, like, the only person in this world who unequivocally gets me, though it's odd given we couldn't be more dissimilar, Tanner being a fierce magenta alongside my matte gray. But not in a dark cloud way. Hmm, let me put it this way. Tanner once filled me in on the fact that, back in high school, she was voted most likely to drop her phone in the toilet. And while she's lavished in gifts and floral arrangements from admirers, I'm more likely to ink a girl's name on the sole of my shoe, then forget about it. But honestly, I can't remember the last time I had to win a girl over. Nor can she. They fall at her feet.

But where was I? Right, so as much as Tanner gets me, she can also get to me at times. Which naturally segues into our most recent episode of life at a heterosexual cocktail bar and this bad habit she's picked up since we lost our gay hangout, that being her tendency to dump drinks on the laps of lecherous men. Because you know how it is for girls like her—lechers are relentless. They'll mill around and circle like sharks until their crotches are swimming in gin. Which is why I'm here. To zen her. To low-key her tinsel, her glitter.

On nights like this, when the scene downtown is brisk, promising, the bouncing girls, the reticent boys, and their meet-cutes all act as if this was early spring and not June—but still New England with that sweet scent of cigar lingering in the air as I round the corner of an old brick front and make my way in through propped doors where it's lush and loud, transformative. And this is where Tanner pours out of the shadows, this raging Scandi blonde with pale blue eyes and red lips, coming at me like a whip.

"I told this girl I met online how you're into straight-passing girls like me," she says, buoyant though not quite inebriated. "But not me."

I settle onto a stool at the bar, which is brimming in suits, *that* crowd, as in not quite my crowd. "I'm sure she took that wrong," I say.

She settles in beside. "You look devastating, as usual," she informs me. Which makes me smile. So I turn away. "I cannot believe they've replaced our one and only Belstaff with the likes of this."

"It'll be missed," I say. "But there are more important things in life than a wardrobe."

"More than missed. It's who you are—functional, hard-wearing, with a dash of rake corduroy." She chuckles.

"Is that how you see me, hard-wearing?"

"Don't forget rakish." She has the cutest damn grin. "So now we're forced to shop on a dot-com, which is sad given the number of girls I've picked up at that place. That shop appealed to the hottest clientele."

"It was largely guys," I say. "Which does not a crisis make."

"Why do you never allow me my crisis? Your go with the flow," she groans, "is maddening."

"How was work?" I ask.

"Logan," she says, "I'm not cut out for this digital life. Kiosks and self-checkout and automated phone attendants and bots. I was born to be waited on. I was born for atmosphere, for a certain je ne sais quoi experience. Which is vanishing before our eyes. This"— she gestures around—"being the exception. Local bistros, non-chain cafés, exorbitant coffee shops, and niche cocktail bars—but who'll I meet here? Don't concede. When gay culture is being relegated to a computer screen exclusively, which says everything about my dating life."

"So now we get to the real issue," I say. "This has nothing to do with my wardrobe and everything to do with your sex life."

"It's so, what's the word for it, depressing."

"I won't swipe an app to find a girl," I say.

"That's easy for you to say," she says, pinching a twenty. "You look the part." Now tossing me some serious side-eye.

Which I toss right back. When the bartender swings by, I order a Black Cat Stout, open a tab.

"Brandy Alexander, please."

And he pops the top, slides a coaster, takes my card. "You'll adapt," I say, sidetracked by my phone for the umpteenth time since I left the office, though it's not work.

Opposite us are booths that are tucked in tight and darkly lit. High carved wooden backs with their rich velvety drapes bound at either end leave diners shrouded in privacy aside from one discernable hand that's feeling the rim of his whiskey glass. In the next, those curtains are drawn, secluded from plates topped in fried plantains, po' boys, trays.

"The other day," Tanner adds lazily, "I was reading every single message she'd sent."

"And why would you do that?" I say.

"I'm a glutton for punishment," she says sullen. "Or maybe I'd misread the first time. It's hard to interpret conversations the same way after a break."

I nudge her knee a bit with mine. "The hottest love," I tell her, "has the coolest end. Socrates."

"I really like that," she says. "Listen to you. You're so deep. This would be why I adore you. I ordered a bra, though, to cheer myself up. In red. That's to say, I ordered black."

"And it came in red?" I ask.

Her finger runs along her brow. "I sent it back. They emailed this thing. A label, you know? Which one must physically print and tape and transport to the post office during normal business hours because I don't own the proper tape. I own Scotch tape for gifting, that's all. It was such an ordeal for an article of clothing, one that couldn't have weighed an ounce. And given the price, you'd think they'd send a courier. On Saturday. To my door."

And all the while she's talking, the space bustles with geeked-out servers in black who blur in and out of corners. The walls are plastered with autographed headshots of unknowns. Faces I should know but don't. And there's that girl over there. I rest a foot on the rail. "So," I say to Tanner, "why so averse to red?"

"I'm not averse to red," she says.

"I happen to favor red," I say with a wink.

"On me?"

"Absolutely on you."

"Did Grace wear red?" she says.

"Grace wore white," I say, "most often."

She smirks. "How virginal of her." I shake my head, thinking *not quite*, a thought that has to be written all over my face. "And that's why you went back, isn't it? No, I mean, honestly, why did you?"

"Get back with Grace?"

"Yes."

"She's a good bottom," I say. But it wasn't that. I don't know why I said that. I told Tanner what she wanted to hear.

"And you're a good top," she says.

I arch my brow. "So I'm told."

"Have you ever fallen for a girl who's just not what you're usually into," she says in a voice that's aching for something. "It's like, at first, it's refreshing, so you give it a try. Like maybe it's best that you're not into her. She's safe. Which feels good. To be unafraid. To be in control. Though, in the back of your mind, you know it'll never work. But, still, you want her for a time. You want her no matter how ill-suited it feels. And you hold on to that delusion for as long as you can. But it always fades away." She's effectively described every single girl I've ever been with. Then her gaze shifts off across the room. "Imagine how many prospects we've passed right by because we were too busy deluding ourselves," she says, gesturing around.

To that girl over there on a stool, who's eyeing me, her skirt hiked.

"I must have *available lesbian looking to be your first* written all over my face," I say.

She elbows me. "You do, actually. Go teach her."

I glance back. "Don't tempt me."

"You do so love those curious girls."

As I signal the bartender. "Did he ever bring your drink?"

"I'm still working on my first," she says.

"Another Brandy Alexander, please."

"You remembered," she says.

"And this surprises you?"

As we watch the bartender do her thing, the crème de cacao, the cream, with ice, and just before the shake, which is quite the presentation, she reaches across, touching Tanner's arm. And they exchange words. Before she's sliding back down to her stool.

"She doesn't seem your type," I tell Tanner.

"She's not," she says with this sort of side nod. "I sent a drink over to your admirer on your behalf."

But that very thought generates such a head rush. "That ought to frighten her off."

"You're really into playing standoffish, aren't you?" Tanner says, then peers up from over the rim of her drink. "So where'd we leave off?"

"I believe she was taking you on the requisite gondola ride," I say.

"Which was followed by mad, gut-wrenching breakup sex, though I hadn't realized what it was at the time," she says. "I enjoyed that end a bit too much. You know how I get when I'm angry." And there's that smile again. "So, Grace," she says, "was cordial?"

"Not cordial," I say. "More...sad."

"She was in love with you."

"She wasn't in love with me," I say laughing, thinking she didn't even know me.

"I wish I had your intuition."

"I wish I had your wherewithal to stick it out," I say. But what I've never really understood is why she keeps falling head over heels for girls like that, the one she's paused on her screen. But it's hard to warn her. She refuses to see it. She refuses to acknowledge the signs.

There was a time, I can't remember when, but I know we were young. Not college young but nearly. That period in your life where you still think you're better than everyone else, but you know you're not smart—or at least not as intelligent as *they* are. They knew politics. They knew art. They knew everything. So, we were at this thing, what was it, a few people. A small, private affair on a high floor on a sparkling night with trust fund girls tucked into the kitchen and zipped into pencil skirts and prepping lemon shortcakes and crepes and tarts.

But around the sofa was a group of intellects discussing philosophy or literature, topics that baffled me. Topics I didn't understand at the time but tried to pretend that I did, alongside uptight gay men, aesthetes, in slim trousers and formfitting turtlenecks. And everyone was holding champagne and carrying on as if they were tipsy, though we never saw them drink. Their glass, like their phone, was merely a prop they could hide behind.

Whenever we went out like that, we'd stay briefly and say a few words to the host and then head home and talk behind their backs as we drank freely and ate calzones across from one another on Tanner's small Ikea table before collapsing across her bed. In other words, we only went to make appearances. To seem social. To grow our network. It's not that we enjoyed it.

Except this one night when Tanner met a girl. A tall, plain-looking girl who walked with a certain swagger, the kind that makes you seem more confident than you actually are.

"I want to break convention," Tanner had said.

"By doing what?"

I remember watching the two of them and feeling envious of what they had—or at least of what they seemed to have, which was this natural chemistry. Indescribable, really. A familiarity layered with apprehension, with nervous laughter. It just felt off to see, after I'd been with more girls than I could recall, but we never had that.

And, to be honest, I hadn't wanted that until Tanner had it.

"It's like I'm obsessed with her," she'd said. "Maybe that's it."

Before making that move. Before slipping along the arm of that couch as if engaging in their conversation, their politics, their art, but still with that look of objection in her eye as if to say, *Take a picture. It lasts longer.* Before squeezing in and practically falling onto that lucky girl's lap.

Later that night, I fell asleep in Tanner's bed as she recapped their entire conversation from start to finish. And a few days later, she confessed that they were in love. But she doesn't fall in love the way I do. She loses control. She loses her mind.

Tonight, throughout our next drink, she goes through a similar recap of her last. She tells me about their breakup, their sex. She tells me about one crazy-ass night, a marvelous night. She tells me about their travels to Italy. But somehow we wind up on, "Maine," she says, slapping the table. "I'm taking you to Maine."

"What on earth is in Maine?" I say.

"It's the Fourth of July," she says. "I need to be around my people. We need to celebrate around our people."

"All right," I say.

"So you'll come?" Except, now who's crowding up against me? Ahh, right, she sent over a drink, didn't she? On my behalf. I feel myself blushing. And let's just say this girl is hot but not ruin-my-life hot.

Though she's mouthing words I can scarcely hear, so I lean in.

"Never has a girl bought me a drink before," I finally hear. Which makes me smile. "I do like being a girl's first."

Chapter Three

Actually, No

Kennedy

I arrive at my therapist's office feeling, oh, I don't know.
"I called Jaime," I say, then tent my hands over my mouth.
"And this is an ex?"
"Yes and no," I say. "It was casual." No response. "We slept together. Once. Not recently. We weren't actually in tune with one another, which we never discussed outright, just that I wanted to be friends." But she's doing that thing again with her ring where she twirls it around on a finger. And I've found that, as much as she tries to seem neutral, small gestures like this can slip through on occasion. So I'm trying to be mindful of that. Observant, attentive. Because they do mean something. "She apparently met someone," I say, disheartened.
"That's news," she says.
"Yes, it definitely was."
"And how'd you feel about it?"
"I felt nothing," I say, "astoundingly. Finally." Which is true. "I mean, I shouldn't be possessive, right?" And next she gives me this look. One I wouldn't call disapproving or anything like that. "I started the conversation off with something generic like *Catch me up*, that being last Friday after an insufferable week at the office for obvious reasons." All right, so it wasn't *insufferable*. Which means I'm falling into that therapy trap where I exaggerate every minute

detail of my life as if it's clinical. "Which went well. For some time. You know, catching up, that sort. And then she went on about work, something about internal rate of return, which just glazes me out. It always loses me. Nothing out of the ordinary. Anyway, eventually, as you might've guessed, I slipped and mentioned Léa in passing, and after that, the line goes completely blank. *In other words*, she said, *you broke it off with her.* Not exactly, but that just sort of spiraled, and long story short, she said something to the effect of *If you keep coming back to me, if you keep calling whenever things fall apart, I might begin to think you're in love with me.*"

"Is that how you feel?"

I squeeze palms between thighs as I'm crossing a leg. "She seems to think so."

Followed by a long pause that I'm not compelled to fill with more rambling rationalizations.

"But what do you want her to think?" she says.

Which loosens me up, not that I feel insecure or uptight, just judged. Though she's not judging me, logically. Never has. Maybe I'm judging myself. So for the next however many breaths, I think about how I could possibly answer that without incriminating myself. I mean, here I am, midthirties, with not a female friend to my name. With the exception of my therapist, who doesn't actually count. And one quasi-ex, who I return to as some sort of romantic insurance policy because she's so incredibly nice. And because she's always been there for me on a rolling six- to eight-month basis. And then there's Seth, the lugubrious hipster neighbor, who's great and all. No, he really is. I adore him. It's just that we have a very different connection. He's very much a guy.

And then of course there's Léa, who's not speaking to me. After months and months of *You hang up first. No, you. I love you, too*, she's vanished, plunging me into some sort of existential shock, which I'm just now beginning to crawl out of.

"They're not serious," I say. "I asked. And she wasn't sure. So that's one good thing."

"Did you tell her this?"

"That it was good?" I say. "Yes."

"And how'd she respond?"

"She brushed it off."

"So she didn't respond either way," my therapist says. But I'm thinking, a brush-off isn't exactly a nonresponse. It's something. It's like leaving the door open just a crack, which felt empowering—which still feels empowering, not that I share this. Instead, I make my way across the room and glance out the window, feeling a bit confined. Stifled. Or perhaps, misunderstood.

I guess what I'm trying to get at here is, for the first time in however many months, my therapist's questions feel off. Like, heteronormative. Or heterosexist. And I don't know how to explain that without offending her. That we trend toward friendship even when it's off. "Can't I dial someone up from out of the blue and talk about life and it not mean anything other than simply Hey, I happened to miss you? And maybe I wanted to talk." But she doesn't respond. "Apparently not...because it was all thrown back at me with *You don't miss me. You miss her,* as in Léa."

"Might that've been defensive on her part?"

"Were I a threat, which I'm not," I say. "Except, eventually she offered to come over. And when she did, I'll admit, after that right there, it felt good—like I had her. Or like I could have her if I wanted to. And believe me, I thought about it. Or at least tried to convince myself of it. But then she started in about that girl, which I didn't like. Not that I explicitly told her this because, by then, sure, maybe it would be."

"Maybe it would be—?"

"*That* might be leading her on. Which wasn't my intent. I'm not here to split them up." She's pressed a loose fist against her mouth, thoughtful. "The flattery, though, is nice," I add. "But it wasn't how Léa said it. It wouldn't obliterate me. She couldn't hurt me to the point of doing *this* week after week. Which felt hopeless more than anything," I say. "Like, why'd I even call?"

"You wanted that," she says.

"I wanted to feel consumed again by anything. I wanted to live inside of it, to lose my mind over it. But she's never been that. Which is why I said what I said, earlier. That I felt nothing. I felt platonic. It was like, why can't I feel it? Why can't I feel a thing?" Anyway, I'm back on the couch now.

"But you knew that going in," she says.

"I knew that, right. So why'd I do it? I guess, even though I knew logically that none of this would get back to Léa, in the back of my mind, I think I wanted it to. I wanted her to know. I wanted her to feel as if this was her last chance—because maybe it is."

But when I tell my therapist this story, how desperate I felt, how I held back, and how I didn't do it even though I could've, easily, she hits back with, "Our time is unfortunately up," ending our session with—how'd she put it?—"We might be on to something."

Still, the fact that she ends our session on such an abrupt note feels reprimanding. It feels like mother, reproving, when in fact I need her approval. But in the end, I didn't get that from Jaime, and now I hadn't found that in my therapist, either.

Which doesn't matter, anyway. Because, by the time our next session rolls around, I've somehow convinced myself that I was being irrational and unreasonable and that my response was not logical. And that she wasn't disapproving. That she wasn't chastising. That our time was simply up.

And as opposed to dredging it all up again, she delves into something about boundaries, instead, about sacrifice, circumventing Léa until the very end.

"We have fifteen more minutes, right?" I say as I process my thoughts.

And without even so much as a glance at her watch, which is right there beside her, always, she says in this gentle, affirming tone, "Yes, we do."

"Because I have one more question about Léa," I say. "And then I'll move on, I promise." So next the sting of emotion, and why? I'm thinking about it again. I'm saying it. And of course she's looking at me in that same nondescript way Mother had when I came out to her, as if she knows exactly what I'm about to say and lacks a positive response, lacks reassurance. Or maybe I'm just projecting. "Here's what I've been thinking about. What if I allow myself to let her go? How do I know that she won't come back?" Because that's really what's holding me back, isn't it? The finality of it all. "I can't put my life on hold," I say. "I guess I'm afraid I might."

"Put your life on hold?"

"Yes. It's like I'm holding back in hopes she'll change her mind—as if she's confused, momentarily," I say. "Like it wasn't her decision. I mean, how'll I know if it was a kinder, gentler way to go but still, in the end, a break? Or one she'll soon regret? And then what? What if I've moved on? Then there's more collateral damage. Like maybe she just needed space or time, and I'll give her that. To process." But she just sits there silently listening. "I know what you're thinking."

Now she's leaning off the edge of her chair. "What am I thinking?"

"You think I'm a fool. You think I'm fooling myself." But as opposed to expressionless, she's shaking her head in an unusual display of bias. "You don't?"

"No."

"Then tell me, why'd she blur those lines?" I say. "Did she want me to wait? Could she ever, eventually I mean, someday, maybe be okay with the whole *gay* thing?"

"Think about why people might blur those lines," she says, which is not an answer. "She left you and, all the while, insisted she's still in love with you. So now it sounds as if you're trying to regain some sense of control over a situation that—"

"That I can't control. I guess," I say. "But I don't feel like I'm trying to control anything. Trust me, I don't want to control her. I want to understand her and do the right thing and not hurt anyone else. Not regret anything. Not regret moving on. Because unlike her, I do consider the consequences." I shift in my seat. "If she finds someone else," I add, "I'm done."

"Why do you say that?"

"Because I could never go back after that, which is something she cannot comprehend. She cannot comprehend what she's done."

"Why are you so certain she'll find someone else?"

"Because she will," I say.

"And is this the type of person you want?"

"I don't know," I say. Because maybe I do. Maybe…if it's her.

"I'm noticing something about you," she says.

"What are you noticing?"

"It's as if you live out there in the future—in some hypothetical tomorrow—as opposed to here in the now."

"Don't we all?" I say.

"No."

I don't know how I feel about that. But it's okay because our time is up, which is fine. And I am emotionally drained after this one.

So by five, I'm treating myself to General Tso's and fried rice from a local Chinese dive, which has zero atmosphere despite it being the world's best takeout. And then I get home, and I slip out of my shoes and curl up on the couch cross-legged in work clothes while listening to a rather intense podcast on surround sound. Which reverberates throughout my studio, one studio of millions they've carved into an old industrial building, the kind that's scooped up and converted into luxury condos by wealthy tycoons for the likes of the eternally unattached, the childless bicoastal executives, some academics. Think minimalist meets nuanced sophistication. Lush landscaping. Lake views. Commutable convenience.

"This week in *The United States of Anxiety…*" I hear as I crack a fortune and read: Good decisions come from experience. And experience comes from bad decisions.

I pin this to a corkboard on the wall, where I've also stashed a handwritten recipe for Ricotta-stuffed handkerchief pasta with pesto, because Seth is delusional enough to think I'll make this one day, along with a gift certificate for Ralph Lauren and two embroidered patches I bought from Strange Ways, one referencing a song an ex sang to me and another that simply reads *Nachos*.

Except, also on this board, I'm now realizing, is this strip of photos, this strip of me and Léa, the kind you take in one of those sexy little marketplace booths, which I might unpin. Which I might even demote to the status of kitchen drawer. And maybe, later on, I might demote to the status of box-I-use-to-store-things-I-shouldn't-even-have-anymore.

After dinner, I bring my glass of Lambrusco with me into the bathtub where I sink down and wind down before climbing in bed with a book because comedians have become best sellers and because I need more comedy in my life. And as the rest of the world shuffles in and out of dressing rooms or sits through five-thousand-calorie desserts never to gain an ounce, or so their Instagrams say, I read.

Thinking...Instagram. Because imagine me now trying to convince myself that Léa's Instagram is not my life's breath, that it can't fill this eternal void of her absence. That knowing what she's doing on an intermittent basis throughout my day is not in some way essential to my not nearly as social existence. My phone is all too reachable, which is not in the least bit helpful, as I open the app and gaze at her outings, her people, her grill skills, and her cheeky, cheeky grin. And as I seek to comprehend why a picture of her cat in an open cupboard, of all things, can resurface so much pain.

So maybe here's where I fall apart, with all of her stupid, silly games, her running away, and seriously—Instagram? Is this what I've succumbed to?

Thinking as I close the app how badly I need to get on and get away and forget about her—and find me.

Which leads me straight to Google, as I launch a desperate quest to find something coastal, somewhere gay, and maybe a little cultured and chic, only to unravel a slew of unsavory results, which I attempt to whittle down by means of an elaborate scheme of rankings, of bookmarks.

And then, then...

The Port Nob Guest House

Described as...

Boutique luxury meets award-winning hospitality at our secluded seaside bed and breakfast set amid the panoramic coast of Maine. Escape to our beloved centuries-old inn situated on fifteen acres and offering eight handsomely appointed private guest rooms, each impeccably renovated to meld tradition with modern convenience. Balancing vintage aesthetics with eclectic decor, guests are treated to clawfoot tubs in every room, complimentary Bliss spa amenities, in-room fireplaces, along with specialty coffees and imported teas and wine and cheese, and libations from our very own cellar cocktail bar with orders for porch, beach, and room-side service...

Made only that much better with...*Superbly gay owned and operated.*

So I stare at my screen, musing. Because who doesn't need this in their life?

Wondering, though, if I've sufficiently reached take-a-vacation-alone years old.

Anyway, the very next day, I book my stay, and hence begins a string of plans for my impending beachside solo-cation, my enthusiasm bubbling over and so intense that it fundamentally distracts me from the obvious until I reach my therapist's waiting room, where I'm sedated by hypnotic flutes that harmonize with her zen wall of water, bringing me nearer to comatose by the minute until she steps out of her office to greet me. And I'm set once more on her couch.

"Where would you like to begin?" she says.

"I guess I've been thinking," I say, "how strange it is that some of the most influential people in your life can just slip in by chance unexpectedly, without even knowing the seismic effect they'll have on you. Without knowing how much they'll change you. It's always so random, life."

But her response is just a rather passive nod.

"You know who I'm referring to," I say, swallowing hard. "I've been thinking about what you said. And I need someone who wants me. Who'll talk when she needs to talk, when she's afraid or overwhelmed or confused or elated or any of those pretty or ugly things we all go through. As opposed to seeing other people to confirm whether or not I'm *it*. Because why is that even a question?" I glance at the door. "I would've done anything for her. Anything in this world to be just hers, right or wrong, unquestionably. And if that has to end, she should let that end. She should let me go, eternally and positively, without stringing me along in limbo, waiting, wishing, hoping that someday, you know, maybe. Maybe she'll want me. When?" In her silence, I pour tea. "Did you make these?" I say, noticing a plate of heart-shaped frosting-covered cookies. She nods then gestures. "I enjoy baking," she tells me. And I guess I'm just taken aback by this news, this glimpse into the human side of her. Of her at home. So I take her up on that offer.

"I'm glad you do," I say. "These are pretty amazing, and incidentally, you cannot squash my love of tragic romance."

"I didn't know I tried."

"It's just that, in a way, our loves are set up to be tragedies," I say in a hint-hint but nonoffensive way. Because we're not the same. We're just not. "There's always something out there that's holding us back or telling us no. That's penalizing us, that's separating us. That's belittling us. Threatening us. But I don't know. I could use a little less tragedy in my life. I mean, couldn't we all? Maybe we all deserve a happier ending. And I guess I'm just fighting it all to allow myself that."

CHAPTER FOUR

The Dirty Sex Rule

Logan

Tanner's already on Tinder. So I'm pretty sure she's looking to abandon me at any moment. Which is fine. We do it all the time.

I just hadn't expected *eventually* would be at, um, checking my phone, ten o'clock. Nor that she'd be this geeked out over what she's now coining our restorative self-care road trip, a concept only a Corporate Wellness Coordinator like herself could conjure up, leaving me solo at Rue B hitting on some girl I've supposedly bought a drink for.

Not that I mind. It's bound to be a night.

But, jeez, this crowd, exuberant and shouting and smashed. Think Rolex wristwatches and five o'clock shadows. Those vapid lipstick stains.

"I work," she's telling me, "in advertising," as her fingers comb through thick Barbie doll hair now falling to frame her face.

"And what does one do in advertising?" I ask, leaning in.

"I convince people to do things," she says, placing her hand within taking distance, within leaving distance. Which I'm about ready to do.

"And you're good at that?" I ask.

"On most days," she informs me. "Or so I'm told." Her lips are now smashed against that cocktail glass.

"Persuade me to do something," I say.

"Oh, that would be easy."

"And why is that?"

She chuckles. "Because you already want it." And that smile, it's nice. Except that's not all I'm into. First impressions being innocent debutant. Harmless, likely, though there's hubris in the midst of it. You hear it in her voice. You see it in her stance, detached—the kind of girl you just ache to break down. Anyway, Tanner taps my shoulder, slips away. And then, "You're someone important, aren't you?"

"Would you like me to be?"

"You carry on as if you are," she adds. "So I'm thinking you're the type that could go on and on about fascinating things I could never comprehend."

"You wouldn't want me to," I say, blushing. Because she's more like out of my league. So I scan the crowd, one that's getting stodgier and stuffier by the minute. Picture a Wall Street cigar lounge where executives schmooze in cuffed-up button-ups while sipping their dry martinis.

Take this guy, for instance, who—noting her glass is half-empty—has the gall to barge in as if we're friends because he knows damn well that we're not. And not only that, he's almost perversely intrigued by it. Which is about to set me off. As I lean in and explain to him that, "We're in a private conversation, here," with a tone that catches his eye. And then he dawdles off. "So, where were we?"

"Where would you like us to be?" she says, her expression oddly enthralled.

"Oh, don't get me started," I say, bottoming my drink. And here's where I weigh my options. "Listen," I say, "I've got an idea. Are you in?"

So we take a walk, her laughter leaning in as we near that downtown fountain, which I find, on most days, far from dramatic, tonight being the exception, owing to this haze illuminating its mist. Its glow is submerged, quivering, wavering, radiating spray that's now coating our skin, that's obscuring those two over there—his modish spectacles, his trousers smashed up to her tweed, her thighs twisted to bury his roaming hand.

My own sunk deep into pockets.

And we take a seat, but, really, what I'm thinking is *Is he her happily ever after, or somewhere in-between? In response to her broken, her ghosted, her guarded, or have they found their end of the road?* Covetous like newlyweds. Enmeshed in their chic yet scholarly vibe, her tight tights, her tie-up oxford flats, commanding in a way you'd expect on an academic dean. Or perhaps an editor in charge at one of those stuffy women's magazines you scan at checkout. *Good Housekeeping.* Or *Real Simple.* When all she really wants is to edge up into *Food & Wine*, into *Sports Illustrated.* Into *Allure.* But she wouldn't fit in there, either. She's more *The New Yorker.*

While I recline alongside the glossy pages of *Vogue*, beside "Cool Girl Hair That's Unfussy," beside "Hot Lips, Colors That Bite," while she indulges me, her lips now close enough to kiss.

And then, "Imagine how many drowned wishes lie in that fountain," she's saying, bending over one knee after it's been crossed. "And what would yours be?" She glances back.

"My wish?" I say.

"You're not one to bother with those," she tells me.

"Why not?"

"You're not the delusional type," she tells me. But her posture is somewhat off. "Or I should say, I'm not the delusional type. I just like to have fun."

"Am I making you nervous?"

"I think you're hoping to," she says. And next she's smiling to herself.

"Hey, come here," I say. Then she tucks beneath my arm and it's, well, nice, which goes on for a while until I get that kiss. And then I walk her home.

It's dark, and there are shadows and coddled light as we pass that loud crowd gathering at the entry of the all-night café, past low iron gates that curve and mold around low ferns and tall trees. Until she's shuffling for keys. And she asks me up.

And I walk her in. And we wait until the elevator drops, which has that low-lit mirrored gold reflection just inside. Dazzling.

In any regard, I watch her back and forth, her come hither. Her self-conscious and staring. Her hand tucked neatly into mine. And this kiss—God, this kiss—within a deep, echoed space. As we near the seventh floor, her front door.

And yet, she's still fully dressed.

So I lean across the counter, eyeing her twist, her grip, her pull, her lips still ruddy from that kiss—as she's discussing *I don't know*. Elsewhere, well, there are books piled high on crates. There are midcentury stands and tall corn plants. And there's a faux-sheepskin shag rug over boards that creak as I search out a view through a narrow pane that's washed in evening light. And next, she's handing me a drink.

Then heels balance her body weight as she flips through vinyl, drawing music from its sleeve. Meanwhile, I sink down deep into her sofa.

"What do you like?"

I guess that depends. On who, on why. But sure, why not. Since my mind's not on music. It's not on reruns, either, or some show she's been binging all week or politicians or any of the stuff she's been talking about.

"Just a little something," she says, as crackles are forming a tune. Sinuous. Shameless and erotic. As she takes a seat beside.

As I absolve myself in this drink. "This is good," I say.

And she says, "I like it, too." But I hadn't meant the song. "When I came across you earlier tonight," she's telling me, "I thought, this girl has such style." And her eyes are intense. I set my glass on her table. "And then I wondered, what would she be like?"

So I take the drink from her hand, and she gives me this look. "Would you like to find out?"

Which is to say, I'm balancing on the couch, one foot on the rug, her breath like a plea at my mouth, my hand up her shirt, where she's apparently wearing no bra.

But I keep thinking, why is she moving my hand? Why is she moving my hand down, down—

"Here—right here—like this."

Breathy and staccato like that. I mean, is this not a bit insistent? Is this not premature? Though it's hot, since she's already wet.

I'll bet she read this in a book. You know, "60 Sex Tips to Tempt." Or "The Dirty Sex Rule," dog-eared in her issue of *Cosmo*.

Until she's busting out of her shirt, and I raise it up and over her head, and we fall like that to the floor, clutching, swelling, knees widening, fingers gripping the couch as I'm edging down. As she's lifting hips, wave after beautiful wave. Through the crackle of a record's spin.

Afterward, as I'm kicking back on her couch, as I'm finishing off my drink, as she's shimmying up her skirt, she tells me, "I've never been with a girl."

"Well," I say, "now you can say you have." And that'd be my cue to leave.

CHAPTER FIVE

Boozy Brunch

Kennedy

Nothing is more quintessentially me than devoting all of last week to planning and packing and provisions only to overlook the single most crucial element of any road trip, the iPod, leaving me stuck in the car for hours on end listening to radio static as opposed to a good playlist. Say, Songs That Make Me Question My Life's Choices. Either that or an audiobook. Anything to get my mind off one hundred forty-two miles of mind-numbing roadway, hulking and wooded and potholed, leaving me desperately alone in one of those *GPS don't fail me now* moments.

And still, I'm repeating my maxim—that silence, that unreachability, that desolation and isolation can be restorative, therapeutic even. And that intermittent radio static is akin to the silent hum of that little white noise machine my therapist always sets outside her door.

Last week, my therapist and I were discussing—what was it? The breakup, guilt, my plethora of coping mechanisms? I'm not exactly sure. Just that we were diverted into a rather candid discussion about dreams or, put more accurately, sexual fantasies.

Can you recall your earliest, how would I put this? Unrequited attraction. That was it. That's where it began.

And I said, *Maybe fourth-period history, my teacher,* who must've been in her midtwenties, whereas I was fifteen. Not that I hadn't crushed on friends as well. I had. It's just that friends largely consisted of Kathleen, and those thoughts typically coincided with underaged drinking in the back seat of her car.

I'd like to hear about her.
Kathleen?
Not just yet. I'd like to hear about history.
You really want to talk about it? It kind of makes me feel bad. Because it was terrible. Horrible, shameful, then. It's just that it wasn't actually apparent to me why that was. I was trying to block it out. And yeah, she was brilliant—in that plain-Jane, modest, unexceptional sort of way. That's what I held in. I used to be so good at that, at holding it all in. But I mean, don't get me wrong, she was straight. It's just that, in my heart of all hearts, in my mind, how could she be?

I guess I was just really surprised by her behavior toward me. So, yeah, it was just that, a dream I had with her in it. I didn't understand it. Because something about it—it all felt wrong. Hmm. But yeah, it was such an illusion. Not really, just much more intense. And yeah. That guilt hook. Mm-hmm, it can be. Very, very unsettling. I guess that's a lot of pressure I put on myself.

The radio kicks in.
WSAD-FM: *"It's a holiday weekend. So we're bringing you our best deal."*
GPS: *"You've arrived at your destination."*
My destination being a big old estate skirted in one of those sweet wraparound porches now teeming with people, handsome people. Precarious people. Intimidating people. Superior and utterly unraveled people. And they're all just hanging out with one another, as if we're at home base, were home base set against a white beach with waves of that pistachio-colored grass, though elegant in a high society way. Panhellenic and queer. A slippers down the hallway vibe. I mention this only because it's probably one of the most insanely elegant inns I've ever seen.
And it's everything I'd imagined.

Minus a single glimpse of sunshine.

So as opposed to my original plan of checking in then checking out my room, where I could strip down to my bikini and perhaps unwind beachside along the seductive swoosh of the sea as skies drag me into a lush Orange Julius night, instead of that, I'm accosted by a downpour of rain as I frantically gather belongings that are stowed on the passenger seat of my car—this empty water bottle and my phone, my crumpled-up bag with napkins, and that wrapper, which I should've just left in the car, not to mention more luggage in the trunk—only to drag despondent wheels along sand toward a charming porch where charming men are charming one another, you know, mingling, ruffling wet hair, and running about.

My own hair drips as the screen claps shut.

So, wow. You know what this place reminds me of? It's as if, at any moment, Nicole Kidman is going to slide down that banister wearing some steamy negligee then start dancing or acting wild, and we'll all dive right into that outrageousness. Except Nicole's not here, just that lingering hint of excitability, to the overture of some glammed-up drab instrumental that's piped into their surround sound. Baroque would be my guess. Dramatic and grandiose—and that scent of everything's so wet.

And there's that guy over there who's making his rounds. Poised in the way one must be when balancing mimosas on a circular tray, each with a slice of fresh orange slit over its rim. And that girl, that girl over there slouched and downcast and immersed in a game of cards. Consumed in a look of stern conviction, which he gallantly interrupts.

Meanwhile, I'm standing in this doorway staring because we're all sequestered inside. Eavesdropping on talk of condominiums and kitchens in Puerto Vallarta because something happened to happen.

And just then, she glances my way. Which has me swirling in dizzying wonder.

So I drag my luggage over to the couch and pick up a magazine. There are several from which to choose. But I select a creased and well-worn copy of *Cook's Illustrated*, which I read without actually reading, peering up. Eventually, though, the concierge pops over to offer me a drink. "I still need to check in," I mention as I'm taking a sip.

When somehow, imperceptibly, hot girl materializes beside me, and concierge has darted away. I smile in disbelief.

"Hi," she stammers.

"Hi," I manage to say as she zeros in on me.

"You're laughing," she says, and her voice, my God, her voice, "but you're not refusing me." She looks amazing. "Logan." Her grip strong, but her hand supple. "You seemed a little bit lost a second ago," she says with her head slightly cocked.

So color me officially self-conscious. "I guess I *was*—in a way." She seems almost too competent, too composed. "What's that you're playing?"

"Cards."

"Cards," I say, only to sink back into myself. Because I'm remembering my shirt, which is drenched. I'm remembering my hair.

"Have you ever met anyone so incompetent as to lose at their own game of solitaire?"

I peer up at her. "I don't find that incompetent."

"Sure," she says, unconvinced, before we silently finish our drinks. Her gaze, unflinching. Her lips, simply edible. "You know," she adds, "they charge an arm and a leg for these."

After which, I must look, how would I put this, calmly alerted. "But he just handed it to me." And I'm thinking, *He doesn't even know my name.*

Next is the matter of her laugh, which can only be described as humble, unassuming. "I'm just messing with you," she mouths.

"Are you?" I say. And then we exchange this look. "It worked."

"Only question being," she says, her voice dripping in sex appeal, "how well?"

I can't even tell if it's the drink or her that's intoxicating me. "You must be here on holiday?"

"I'm here to support a friend," she tells me. "To console her."

"Which means you're an awfully considerate friend."

"Oh, I wouldn't go that far," she says.

"Then how far do you think you would go?" I hint as I shut my magazine, leaving it on my lap.

She laughs quietly. "I've always been a fan of their sauces."

"Do you cook?"

"I enjoy sauces," she tells me. Then peers up at me, inquisitive. "That storm's paid you no mercy."

"Yeah, yeah," I say. "At least it's not cold. Though I should maybe cover up."

"No." She shakes her head, appreciative. "Not at all."

So, um. "Do you think they've forgotten about me?"

"I'll go find someone if you'd like."

"Oh no, I just came at a bad time," I say. "He's probably with someone else."

"He's probably just passing out towels."

"Which makes me low priority," I say. "But that's okay."

Eventually, she leans in, achingly so. "Perhaps they'll offer an upgrade. You know, to make up for lost time."

"But this drink," I say. You. Sitting here. With me. "This whole place feels like an upgrade."

"The rooms are much nicer," she hints.

"Spacious?"

"That depends—"

"On what?" I ask.

"On your definition of spacious," she tells me. "They'd rather we lie out there," giving a nod toward the shore. Then we smile, gazing at one another for the longest time.

But I keep fidgeting, I am, with my hair, pushing it back. Fingering it. It's soaked. "Is that your plan?"

While her palms run along the lengths of her thighs, which are nice, by the way, as in grippable and— "I can't say I have a plan," she tells me.

"So you just go with the flow?"

She shakes her head, grinning. "You don't?"

"Of course I don't," I say. "I have a plan."

God, she has this way with her eyes. Attentive. Inquisitive. "Do you always?"

"I haven't thought too deeply on that. But yeah," I say. "For the most part."

"And how's that worked out for you?"

I shrug. She's challenging, no doubt, which I like. Softened only by her apparent interest in me. "There's a reason to go on vacation."

"A reason isn't a plan," she says.

"I can't disagree."

"Tell me about your reason," she says.

"My reason, let's see. I was hoping this could keep me out of trouble," I say without going into too much detail. Because what should I really share? "Why does one go on vacation?"

Her gaze is piercing, purposeful. "Why do they?" she says. But there's something about her questions that make me want to spill. Which I won't, I know.

So responses are what I'm pondering, safe ones, and topics, when the front screen claps, drawing my attention over there. And when I finally come back to her, she's still considering me. "Your go with the flow," I say. "I suppose you might be on to something."

"I suppose you might be, too." She smiles, then shakes her head.

"This seemed a good place to disconnect," I say.

"So that's why you came?"

"Sort of," I say.

"That's admirable of you."

"And you're here for a friend?" I add hoping to sidetrack this conversation.

"I'm here for my friend."

"But what about *you*?" I ask.

"Me?" She laughs, big.

"Yeah," I say. "*You.*"

"I could never disconnect," she tells me, rather amused.

"How come?"

"People need me," she says.

"And you enjoy that?"

"Sometimes," she says. "It's nice"—peering at me—"to be

needed." But there's something in the way she's saying it. In the way she's leaning into me, greedily. In the way she's smiling at me mercilessly, peering down at my lips for one, two, three seconds. Only next, she's changing the subject. "You keep looking at those two over there."

"Because he looks like a GANT runway model," I say. "I was admiring his outfit."

"What part of it?" she says.

"All of it," I say.

"Want to hear their story?" she says.

"You know them?"

"No," she says. "What I do know, though, is that they were an item not too long ago. And then, somehow for some odd reason, it crumbled into bits."

"And you know this, how?"

"I was sitting right over there," she says, nodding in that vicinity.

"Eavesdropping," I say.

"Eavesdropping, playing cards." She rubs her brow.

"You smile at their heartbreak," I say.

"Who said heartbreak? It's just a breakup."

"And how would one separate the two?"

"Easy," she says. "What I'm wondering is, what would make that pair come back after all that? This is apparently their place. It's where they met. And they revisit—year after year after year. Why carry on, though, after a split?"

I peer over at their slack expressions, rapt attention erasing any distance they may've had. "Could be anything. Regrets. Opinions—"

"Opinions?" she says, prompting.

"You know, other people."

"Like, in what way?"

"I don't know," I say. But I do. "Disapproval," I add. "Maybe."

"And why would you listen to other people?"

I shrug. "Some do."

Her eyes fly open. "I don't."

"Well," I say, "some do."

"Do you?"

"Not really."

"So in essence," she says, "you do."

"You seem very strong-minded about this topic," I say.

"Because I am."

"I don't listen to other people," I say. "But I've certainly known some who do."

"Maybe it's just regrets," she says. "Those are the worst."

"Have you done a lot you regret?" I say.

"Not lately."

But that's when the concierge comes back. He's ready to check me in. He's reading off terms. He's reading off rules, deadlines. Until it's time to head up, which prompts this whole back-and-forth *What's next?* sort of thing on the couch.

And I would like to say I'm not falling. As we do this awkward dance.

"So, maybe I'll see you around." And it's just in the way she says it. Humble. Unassuming.

"I would like that very much."

CHAPTER SIX

Friday Forecast

Logan

I guess you could say it was around two, two thirty, midday, by the time we got in—that's to say, when Tanner made her presence known to the concierge. The concierge being this cute dirty-blond kid prepped out in Nantucket red who introduced himself as Aiden. He's the guy who checked us in. He's also the guy who brought us to our rooms, narrating the entire time and brimming in faux pleasantries. You know, the kind of back-and-forth that's meant to make uncommunicative guests like me more demonstrative.

Like Tanner, a girl whose exaggerated *oohs* and *aahs* extended well into his line-by-line on the weekend's events, which were described as novelty, as celebratory, as sparkling in drag—before he rushed off to the tune of, "Hope to see you there!" only to leave behind a bottle of chilled rosé, which was tucked beside an exorbitantly marked-up wine list.

As soon as he left, we fell back on her bed laughing and ate lunch at a table alongside an inoperable window—her suite being essentially a replica of mine though nicer with a laundry list of extras and loads more space, a welcome box, Bliss spa amenities, a Nintendo Wii with yoga, a distressed brick fireplace, and a minibar. She's also landed herself a king-sized bed, rivaling my queen, along with a sitting area, her space being divided by a whiskey-colored futon made of leather. A suite designed for entertaining or socializing, not sleeping. A space that felt endless and smelled of fresh linen, in stark contrast to the gloom and doom outside, which was befitting her mood, befitting mine, befitting a conversation that had grown stagnant and tired lagging two hours of crammed legs in my car.

So as opposed to talking over one another as we normally do, we dined silently on grilled Reubens snatched up at a mom-and-pop just a few miles back. Me, skimming a booklet on state tourism while daydreaming about craft distilleries, about sailboats and ATVing, about lodge life and snowmobiling as I popped open a bottle of mineral water, the kind with the resealable swing top, and shared my bag of kettle chips. While Tanner snapped her iPod into the docking station, navigated to the most appropriate song, and sucked down a Diet Coke.

After lunch, I went back to my tiny room, one affording little more than free Wi-Fi along with this welcome box of sunblock, a pair of flip-flops I'll never use, and some crazy-ass Turkish towels, which I hang over the shower curtain before jumping in, thinking nice touch, but not exceptionally practical or absorbent once I get out. I'm still sporting wet hair while I slip up a pair of jeans and text that I'm ready to head down, assuming I'll get back an enthusiastic, *Let's go beach.* But instead, she stalls. *Call came in.* And then another: *Half hour?*

Which is why I've made my way downstairs to the common room—abandoned—to, you know, people watch, bide time. Or just become one more brooding girl in the midst of solitaire while a salacious crew of muscular men scuttle about in their various shades of Vintage Vines—and where mimosas are being served liberally on trays that sashay past conversant tables and out doors, onto a rain-coated porch, where mist is clinging to their skin.

Meanwhile, I'm over here at a table shuffling cards and contemplating why I never bothered to learn any of the rules when I had a chance. Yet as I recall, it's only a matter of hearts, spades, diamonds, and clubs cascading down in rows with stacks of seven—or something like that.

Eventually, though, I'm sidetracked by a cart that's being used to roll out cupcakes, artisan style and topped with wood-grain and camouflage candy saucers, confections that are carefully arranged to form an appetizing tower, a display that would normally capture my interest except...this girl who just walked in.

And let me pause right here to say that I tend to rank women based on their hot-cute ratio. Take my dental hygienist, for example, not that I'm into her or anything. She being the weighted blanket sort. You know, the type who'd tote freshly baked biscuits over to dear Aunt Edna before bustling back to make a.m. service at the church, which happens to be an actual conversation we had during a recent cleaning. The weighted blanket thing, the Lands' End monogrammed toy dog carrier thing, and talk of buttermilk biscuits made from flour versus my spoon-popped can.

But I mean, sure, who wouldn't dream of flipping that sort of a girl, you know what I mean?

The thing is, every girl can pull off cute with a few cleverly timed giggles, the well-pinned hair, the perfect etiquette that upholds absolute control over her spotless life—sparkling and bouncing with energy and zest. But it's rare to encounter a girl who can pull off this, let alone do it so well.

I mean, for starters, she's decked out in a now sheer—that's been too rain-soaked—shirt, my guess being white linen, buttoned down to reveal a string bikini just beneath that, dare I say, scarcely covers a thing. Fresh-faced and poreless, with a body that's dripping in just the right appeal.

While I'm tucked back here in a corner pretending I can play and contemplating whether kings top queens—or is it vice versa? As I drink a mimosa. Because you don't want to look. But then you do and, when you do, you notice something new. Like the wet sheen glazed across her lips and that ripe look that feels somewhat unsettled. One that's easily becoming my mood.

So next I'm ineffectively wrangling my mind around spades and aces and jacks as opposed to some illusory dialogue that I might be having with a complete stranger and, all the while, credibly convincing myself that I might actually pull this one off. Except

I've yet to play a card. And I need to make a play. But my mind's blank as I think about threes, as I think about twos.

Because here's how this might pan out, that is, once I've made my way over under the guise of—what?

Which is where it all falls apart.

Where the scene fades to gray and I glance up and she peers my way, like that. That thing we just did. But isn't this where I swing by, where she gestures me over, where I take a seat and, well. You know the rest. Which even I know wouldn't work. It's never going to—it's preposterous. Because I have nothing of value to say. And because that look she just gave me right there was a little slice of nothing. And besides, who in their right mind would insert themselves into a girl's washed-out entrance?

Although, if anything's going to happen, it's going to be me making the first move. I'm certain of that.

Which is why I'm thinking, just do it. Don't think about it. Don't script it.

Just go there.

And that's what ushers me into this final scene, the one where I half-heartedly introduce myself.

So where was I going with this?

Given the fact that, not even halfway across the room, it dawns on me that she might've come with a date. Or a friend or a spouse. Or someone who's likely outside at their hatch juggling all sorts of duffel bags—because who comes on a trip like this companionless?

And why hadn't I realized that until now, at essentially the point of no return, as I'm taking a seat? Not that we're close or anything. All right, so, maybe we are a little close. But in my defense, I might be a big fan of *Cook's Illustrated*. Like, how would she know? And she just so happens to be near a stack of periodicals.

Which means it's achingly obvious to her by now what I'm about to say.

And what was that again?

So as opposed to my making eye contact, "Logan," I say as I gently rub the back of my neck.

"Kennedy," she says, amused.

Then over the course of the next suspended minutes, as I watch her talk as if eavesdropping, I'm finding out just how insatiable I can be. Until I'm offering myself up like hors d'oeuvres. Her words having misguided me, having eluded me, while my mind's conjuring up fantasies about a girl who's been talking me in circles for miles, framing come-ons with innuendos, clearly hopeful I've misread—as she slips the spine of her magazine up the ledge of the table without breaking our gaze. And all the while, my mind's beginning to envision the shape of her body, the feel of her lips against mine as that drink slips over her tongue.

You know, the kind of impulsive thoughts one would expect to subside once she's gone. But, instead, they've only ascended until I'm filled with an elated sense of sadness, a reaction I hadn't expected and one I'm trying to hide from the likes of Tanner after she's bounced down, coiffed, breaking my meditation, my confusion, with such utter banality.

"Please tell me you're kidding," I say to quiet her down. Because she's overreacting.

Yet the look on her face, arresting. "I need debauchery."

"At this harmless inn?" I laugh, nudging her knee with mine. "So who kept you?"

"Hallie," she tells me. But my mind's not on her work. *I feel unsteady coming out of that.* It's not focused on my phone, either, or any of those never-ending chats. *I'm beginning to get the feeling that everyone leaves eventually—sob, sob. They'll just fade away.* As I tip a stack of cards then shuffle the deck. *It's just a lot right now.*

"All of this over a silly little gift?"

"Logan, I need you to practice your active listening skills for, like, ten minutes," Tanner snaps. "It's a gift that she bought for his girl, his paramour. And she's quitting."

"Hallie?"

"Yes. She's quitting over this. But here's what I can't figure out. It's like, you fall for a sort of archetype who happens to be ambitious. And maybe you're too young or naive or incapable of comprehending that level of commitment, to marry that level of ambition. Which can radically change your life. It couldn't have always been like that." When she turns her head, I tuck a label back under the neck of her shirt. "But that's the choice she's made. So now, she's got to realize—I mean, she must realize—that she's sacrificed her own potential to build his up—to bolster his image, to tell his tale," she says with a one-dimensional look on her face. "But I guess that's something, right? That sort of thing matters. She matters. So maybe what I'm trying to say is what would motivate someone to stay like that? After what he's done. In perpetuity. Now that she's abandoned, not physically or financially but, you know, emotionally. He's left her. But maybe she doesn't see it. Maybe she doesn't realize her worth. Now that it's gone, *she's* gone and has perhaps lost sight of all that potential she once had—or could've had—on her own. For occasional pity sex with a philanderer. For bragging rights at her high school reunion. So yeah, maybe I'm just a little sad about that." So after I figure out my play, I peer up at her.

"I need something to drink," she whimpers.

"It's still early for that. We'll get one a little while later," I say.

"You've had one," she snaps.

"And I should've saved you one," I say. "I apologize." But I was otherwise distracted.

"I need to stop going for ambitious girls," she tells me. "I couldn't handle that."

I bend over the table to make a move, then sink back down in my chair. "Why do you care so much about other people?" I say. "You're not them."

"No, I'm not. But I'm thinking I've had enough. I've had *enough* heartbreak. I've had enough letdown. And I'm not even married yet. Getting hitched should end all that. It should be your happily ever after," she says.

"There's always going to be a trade-off," I say. "It doesn't matter who you're with. And please don't say this is all you guys ever talk about."

"I guess it is in a way. Along with her hating the gifts, the buying of gifts and hiding of gifts, and knowing when the wife calls in. Incidentally," she adds, "one can learn a lot about oneself through other people, in the way they make mistakes."

Which brings me back to Kennedy, to that linen shirt wet against bare skin, which isn't at all relevant but it's on my mind. That shirt I was aching to peel off. Not even Tanner can bring me down from that ridiculous high. This sad, sad sort of high.

"She's quitting."

"I know she meant a lot," I say. "But you'll always have me."

"You can't talk at my desk," she says. "You can't join me for lunch. You can't leave for a fifteen-minute walk when I'm pissed off."

"You can call me."

"As if you have time." But her laugh is not a happy one. "I doubt I'll ever find *the one*."

"I can basically guarantee that you will."

"And you?" she says.

"I can't adequately deal with life as it is," I say. Then I try to shift the subject. "So, what was that gift?"

"It was a bottle of perfume," she says as if this was a personal failing. "Do you realize that every bottle of perfume I own is a gift from an ungrateful ex? Every single one. It was ingenious, really. It's like associating a girl with a song. That shit never leaves you. It haunts you," she says, now sitting upright in her seat. "Today, I'm wearing Cameron." Then under her breath, "Dear God, does it make me miss Cameron."

"Then stop wearing her," I say.

She tosses her hair. "I can't. I have an entire bottle of her. And she's expensive."

I glance up. "Well, you smell really good. And, about that affair—" I say.

"What about it?"

"You have no idea how hard that is, getting ahead. So don't judge. Cut a little slack."

She taps my hand lightly before getting up. "If you say so, boss."

As we step outside under the shelter of their porch. As I take a seat on the bench. And as Tanner presses her body firmly against that rail—lackadaisically, pensive, mischievous.

"What types of things do *you* talk about?" she asks.

"At work?" I say. "You, sometimes."

Which prompts another hair flip. "I want to be your secretary," she adds with a cute glance back.

"Which would be highly unethical," I tell her.

"How come?" she says weakly.

I smile, musing. "Where are you going with this?"

"I have absolutely no idea," she tells me. But we burst out laughing, regardless. "You tell me where you'd like it to go."

I stare a little while at the ceiling. "Maybe we should go for a walk," I say.

So she heads over my way, bends over, whispers alongside my ear, "Debauchery."

"Which you're not going to find here."

"I can find it anywhere."

CHAPTER SEVEN

Postcards from Barcelona

Kennedy

This can't possibly be where he said I'd find those towels, beach towels, this little enclave? Which is a questionable description of the space. It's more of an archway into…I can't even call this a room. Perhaps a nook for daydreaming or, you know, that first sip of coffee in the morning while gazing into your lover's eyes after a night of…I'm not even going to think about it. And besides, this window, this breeze, this view is everything.

"I'm sorry," Logan mutters, brushing up against me. And I just, I just can't. Breathe easy. Just breathe easy. Yet all I can focus on is that slow moving hand down the back of her neck, that bicep. "I came up for something—"

"A bar of soap?" I joke.

"Yeah," she says, "I'm all about soap," sarcastically…or flirtatiously—one can only hope. Because she is still keenly intent on me. And that scent she's got on is not helping matters in the least.

"They said I'd find some beach towels, larger towels at least, somewhere in here," I say, which sounds like I'm ill-prepared. "And extra soap. But I can't seem to find either."

"Have you looked here?" she says opening the obvious, as in a stout and sturdy armoire. Which holds, lo and behold, linens. Soaps. Supplies. Coffee pods. Tea packets—*mmm*, chamomile, my favorite. All organized and orderly and arranged. Along with a courteous little tent card right up front that reads, *Please help yourself.* Which I do. I'm snatching a pack of rum bath salts and this beach towel. Only to raise my brow at this cold brew soap, which I read out loud. "Enriched in shea butter." One of those samplers tightly wrapped in its thick, neat sleeve. Thinking she might like this.

"Cold brew," she questions, "as in coffee?"

I shrug. "It's exfoliating."

"Yeah, no," she says, choppy, just like that, in staccato.

"Oatmeal?" I ask. "Driftwood, tobacco, leather?" Handing her a few. Or more like succumbing to a rush of nerves. "Here, you take your pick," I say. Still, she takes the latter. And when she does, her hand brushes up against mine, intentionally so. "I like your smile," I say. And there it is again.

"Are you flirting with me?"

"Maybe." She *is* using it a lot. I glance around, if only to conceal those nerves. First at that painting on the wall. A man in a stout black cap. A woman wearing the same. Then just below is an iron table that's round and topped with a nice little task lamp, on either side, an austere upholstered chair.

Her arm brushes mine. "A bit tight in here." She's blushing, apologetic.

"If you're planning to host a party," I say.

"Or this." Her gaze holding mine.

"What? Illicit encounters with strange girls?" I ask.

"Are you saying I'm strange?"

"I'm not saying you're strange," I tell her, "just interesting."

"Is that a good thing?"

"It's—" I pause, feeling clumsy. "It's a good thing. Yeah."

"And how *good* would that be?" She adds, "You know, on a scale of one to ten?"

"One being—?"

"One being, well, not desirable."

"Not desirable," I say. "Well then, I'll give you a solid nine."

"Just a nine?" She feigns discouraged, downcast. "Not a ten?"

"I think a nine is pretty good," I say.

"Yeah," she says, relentless. "But it's not a ten."

"All right, then, I'll give you a ten."

Which pleases her. "So you think I'm a ten?"

"When coerced," I say.

"I don't think I'd need to coerce a thing out of you," she says, and when she does, she grins in such a defiant way, which is melting me. The sheer tenacity. Because my mind's still back on *coerced*. If only I were thrust up against that wall, her grip around my wrist. "So what else do we have here?"

"Beach towels," I tell her, coming up from behind.

"And?"

"Well, what exactly were you looking for?"

She turns to me and, in midmovement, "*You*, I reckon."

I laugh. "You reckon?"

"Yeah, sorry," she says. "I don't know where that came from." She's rubbing her forehead. "It looks like they have a few of those logs in here. You know, the stuff you fake in a fireplace when you don't need heat." And then, "Bet it's nice up here, midwinter."

"Bet it's *cold* up here in the winter," I say, cognizant of how formal, how calculated, I seem to be in comparison to her.

Next she's handing me a pen, a pad of paper, a postcard. *Greetings from Maine* the card reads in bold red script. "Anyone you care to write, you know, back home?"

"You mean those people I'll be seeing in just a few days?" I joke.

"Or nieces, nephews—"

"No siblings," I tell her.

"Same here," she says. "So how about that gay second cousin twice removed? He probably sends you postcards from Barcelona because he's bitchy as hell confined to that small bungalow in the Midwest. So he winters somewhere warm to stay bronzed—the restaurant hopping, the globetrotting—if only to add to that never-ending stream of reviews on Yelp, on his Airbnb."

"All right, so I do kind of have that."

"No way," she says. "I was just making that up."

"Well, it's not Barcelona but Cozumel. And not the Midwest—more like Asheville, North Carolina. And I could not tell you our lineage. Aside from the fact that it's far, far off. Though he does adore me."

"Who wouldn't?" she says, pressing a postcard up on the side of that armoire, a side I can't see from this angle, before jotting something down.

"Well it would've been nice to have known him when I was younger," I say, wistful. "So who are you writing?"

"You're awfully—" She shakes her head. And next she's tucking it away with the rest—or at least shuffling it in.

"What?" I say. "I'm awfully *what*?"

Her voice is gentle when she answers. "Curious."

"Well what were you writing?" I say.

"It's a secret."

"A secret, eh?" A lump rises in my throat. "And you're awfully—"

"What?" she insists. "I'm awfully what?" But her eyes are unstoppable. "I'd love to know what you think of me."

I swallow hard. "Charming," I say.

And there's that laugh again. "You think I'm charming?" And I'm imagining this radiant glow on my face, this heat, as her hand runs, again, along the back of her neck. "I think you might be," she says with a pause, "the most beautiful woman I've ever met." My lips pressed tight, I shake my head. "If you don't mind my saying so," she adds. And just accept it, Kennedy. Accept a compliment and leave it at that. Which I do. "Well, yeah," she's saying. "I'm sorry to interrupt."

"You're not interrupting," I say.

"I just wanted to drop by," she tells me, "to see you."

"You didn't come by to see me."

"Well, no," she says. "I came by to get this soap."

"You came by for something else," I tell her.

"My sunglasses," she says, "which are back in my room," nodding in that vicinity.

"So, your room's right down the hall?"

"How convenient," she says, "for all those nights I'll need a beach towel," as she's sucking her lower lip. "Everything I need, right here."

"It *is* rather convenient," I say, her gaze still locked on mine. "So here we are," I add.

"Yeah," she says. "Here we are."

CHAPTER EIGHT

Swept and Stormy

Logan

Well, it's tight, which might be why it's so warm in here. Or it might be what she said just a minute ago. *Here we are.* Holding me, drawing me in like this. Not that we've said a word since, but still. She's here. Staring at me. Smiling unapologetically. Stringing me along. Because outside, or at least right here by this window, there's a nice calm breeze. Or make that a somewhat stormy breeze, it's picking up, one that might possibly stall our plans. "I feel as if my hair's still wet from the last one."

"It looks pretty dry to me."

I can hear my voice quiver a bit as I say it. But she doesn't say anything back. So eventually, I'm diverted to that line of paint just beyond her shoulder, a line that's dividing a wall, a dull gray shade across the lower half and a flat cream painted just above. It's the same cream they've used down the hall. But right here, just under that line, are two vacant chairs. It's where I take a seat, hoping she'll join me. And she does.

"Well...my hair isn't typically this," she says. As in beachy? Shiny? Wind-tangled? Light-streaked? "I did not expect this much rain. And of course it stopped the moment I got in."

"How's your hair normally?"

She fingers it. "Not clumpy like this."

"Not sexy like this," I say, correcting her.

She drops her gaze in a modest way. "Not this unmanageable."

"So you prefer manageable?" I ask.

"I prefer manageable, yes."

I lean in, entranced. "In everything?"

Which makes her look everywhere but here. "In some things," she says. "Not all."

"What should be unmanageable, then?"

"You're all about tough questions," she says.

"And why's that tough?"

"Because, because," she's saying, her tone slightly agitated yet still agreeable. "Why don't *you* answer that question?"

So I repeat it. "What should be unmanageable? Well sure, there's lots. Thoughts should be unmanageable. Women should be unmanageable." Then after a long enough pause, "Sex."

She shrugs, amenable—then gradually breathes in before letting it out as if contemplating what I've just said. "Okay. I'll give you that. You're better at this than I am." Her shirt's evocative, suggestive. Though I'm fighting that urge to glance down. "A summer storm," she adds. "*That* should be unmanageable—if I'm not in it."

"And what else?" I say, encouraging.

"All those birds that sing when the sun comes up." But she keeps searching me for approval.

"What else?" I say.

"I don't know." She shrugs.

"You *do* know," I say.

Then eventually, with a hint of...what? Trepidation. "True love?" But those are questions I'm not about to ask. "Just not hair," she adds abruptly. "Or at least not *my* hair."

"I think you're unreal," I say.

Which she ponders for a little while. "I think the next time you see me, I'll look much less of a mess."

"Next time I see you?" I ask, piqued.

"We're here for a couple days, aren't we?"

She has this soft warmth about her that's clearly doing me in. "I see." And that's the way we stay, smiling, eyeing one another.

"So," she says, stringing her words as if backpedaling.

"So—?" I counter.

"So we'll run into one another," she says. "I figure, at some point."

I can feel my brow crunch. "Are you always this worried about your hair?"

"I'm not high maintenance," she says, "if that's what you're thinking."

"So you're always this way."

"What way is that?" she says, defensive.

As my eyes narrow in on her. "Naturally stunning."

But she's blushing. "I'm not stunning."

"Have you looked at yourself in the mirror?" And can I just pause right here to say she has the most pleasing laugh. "Not that I mind high maintenance."

"All right," she says. Then she tucks her hair behind her ear.

"I feel like I'm making you uncomfortable."

"No," she says.

But when I stare at her too long, she turns away. "I'm not?"

"You're not making me uncomfortable."

So I lean over myself, peering up. Wavering. As I flip a couple of those cards I have in my hand. "So," I say in this lingering way, "what are you running from?"

"What do you mean *running from*?" she asks.

I glance again at her sidelong. "You came to an inn on your own," I say. "So I figure, you must be escaping something."

"It could be purely recreational."

"Is it?"

"No," she says. "How about you?"

There's a touch of thunder rumbling in the distance. "I'm always looking to escape."

"Care to elaborate?"

And I must say, we're stuck in some serious eye contact. "For me, it's generally work. So I guess I just needed some time away."

"I don't have that kind of a job."

"You're lucky," I say.

"What do you do, then?"

"Computer hardware. Research. Design. I manage a bunch of people. So let's just say engineering. What about you?"

"I'm a legal assistant," she says. "Well, actually my new official title is paralegal. Which is nothing much."

"Why would you say that?"

"Because it has nothing to do with my degree."

"And what's your degree?" I ask.

"Liberal arts." She smiles remorsefully. "So is this your first time?" And I'm not oblivious to the fact that we're both ignoring that storm. Or I should say, she is. "I mean, I've never been before. Here. At this inn. I've never been to this town."

"Yeah, me neither," I say. "So how do you like it so far?"

"It's very…posh," she says glancing around. "It feels as if they had a lot of money and a lot of time and passion and it's all very exacting. Very comely."

"And I guess they're really into this holiday."

"But for some reason, it doesn't feel like a holiday," she says truthfully. "Though I'm not patriotic. But I'm up for a bit of nostalgia."

"Nostalgia," I say. "Are you referring to those black charcoal snakes that wreck your sidewalk?"

"Why do you seem the type," she says, "who would do precisely that?"

"What, kiddie fireworks?" I say. "Because I am. Oh, oh, and that confetti cannon."

"We always went to the lake. I was never allowed near fire. That was for professionals," she adds in a motherly tone. "So instead, I got Pop Rocks."

"Those can be fun."

"I feel as if I might've missed out."

"Trust me, no loss," I lie. "Most are illegal anyway."

"When a minute ago," she says, "your face lit up."

I answer with a smile. "It's not fireworks I was thinking about." But now, she wants to know. "It was another thought that came to mind."

"And what kind of thought would that be?" Kennedy says.

"I feel as if I shouldn't divulge something like that," I say.

"This sounds scandalous," she says.

"Could be."

"Well, maybe you'll share that later on," she says.

"Maybe," I say, "when we see each other again." But my gaze keeps drifting toward her lips. "Why do I feel as if I could talk to you for hours?"

"I feel as if you would definitely be overdosed by then," she insists. But I don't think I would. "So if you were back home right now, what do you think you'd be doing?"

"Is this your roundabout way of asking what do I do for fun?" I shake my head, grinning. "Whatever you want it to be."

"I'm sure you're not interested in hearing about my weekend errands," she says.

"I'm interested in whatever you have to say."

"What do I do for fun?" Kennedy reflects. "I never know how to answer that, though I'm asked quite a lot."

"A lot?" Ahem. "By women?"

Then, in a tone that implies she's stating the obvious, "Usually."

"So you must frequent certain places," I say. "Because I'd never take you as…gay."

"Yet you did."

"Because you're here." But my voice of course just cracked. "Which eliminates one crucial variable."

"And what are the others?" she says.

"Well, um, I don't see a ring."

"No." She laughs. "You don't see a ring."

"So, what's the deal?" I say. "You must have some deep-seated psychosis or something like that. Because I cannot for the life of me understand why someone like you would be available."

"Let's see," she says, "why have they left—"

"Wait. Someone *left* you?"

She grins, nods. "And vice versa."

"Then let's get into those reasons," I say.

"Well, one deal breaker involved baking," Kennedy says. "I'm not a kitchen girl. And she needed a kitchen girl who could bake warm brownies on occasion."

"Could she not measure?" I say.

"She thought it would be romantic," she tells me, feeling along her lip. "To bake together. I don't know, whisking eggs and all that. Every once in a while. I guess that was *that* important. There are always so many incongruities." Incongruities, I ponder. That's one way of framing it. "How'd we get on this?"

"I don't bake," I tell her. "Though I've ordered stuff online, if that counts? I mean, I've always thought that was the purpose of bakeries."

"Thus eliminating one more crucial variable," she says.

"There would be very few variables keeping me from the likes of you," I say.

"Are you like this with every girl?" she says.

"Like what?" I say.

"I don't know," Kennedy says. "Charming." I laugh. And we stall and delay. Delay and stall. But I'm running out of excuses. "Well then, I'm keeping you too long," she tells me. "From your sunglasses. Your soap. And besides, I really should unpack."

"If you must." I pause for a moment, glancing down—and that's what I forgot. The postcard advertising Maine. With its white sailboat and a seagull soaring past, which I've memorized by now. In black ink on the white side where you're supposed to print their name. *I like your smile, too*, I wrote. Which Kennedy reads on her way down the hall.

Chapter Nine

Try Not to Try

Kennedy

It's not as if I hadn't expected single women here. Because maybe I had. Vaguely. In the back of my mind. Though in none of those musings could I have ever anticipated someone so…you know, and that whole exchange we had back there.

Which has left me crazy shaken up. It's dizzying. I feel ditzy. In a lost my mind sort of way. Even worse, it's still with her, my mind, doing unspeakable things against that wall. In the hall. Right here on this bed as I lie back in various shades of undress and let my mind get lost inside of it—inside thoughts that I would not even share with a beloved journal had I kept one, which I don't. Though my therapist insists I should. *Journal, journal*, she keeps at me—about how it can bring such inner clarity.

And isn't that the whole purpose of this right here, this trip, to find inner clarity? To live and breathe clarity, as opposed to longing for that mess in my past. And as opposed to longing for someone new to fill that gap. You know, flying solo for a little while versus getting swept up in fleeting dreams like these trailing two miniscule encounters. My God, what am I doing?

What's worse, in the process of losing my mind, I seem to have lost my phone as well, which is bizarre given it was just in my hand a minute ago. In fact, I distinctly remember unplugging it from its charger when I got out of the car, as I gathered my things, as I carried it in—and please don't say I've left it down in that room, which would not even be subtle.

Sitting up, though, it appears I've already hung up a few things on the garment rack over there before setting my keys on that table. Which is where I leave my phone, always, right beside my keys—so I can find it—along with my wallet. Except I was absent-minded, preoccupied when I set those clothes out to dry over…There. There it is!

In any regard, had I expected to see anyone like that, it would've been more along the lines of hyperabsorbed newlyweds strolling along the shore in matching Athleta swimwear to the accompaniment of "All I'll Ever Need" as clouds part to form a rainbow just above. Because, and I'll die on this hill, Independence Day has got to be the most romantic holiday outside of Valentine's Day. Which I know, I know, is going to make me sound trite, envious even. But I'm not, I swear. I'm happy for them. Thrilled.

Equally thrilled, however, for my relationship detox.

This being a uniquely atypical resort for the likes of Maine, so no duck boots or antlers or sheepskin or hair-on hide as I might expect. Instead, it gives off a more cathartic, reflective, restorative vibe.

Albeit out-of-the-way inaccessible.

That's to say, one could not sport up a few blocks were they in search of a quaint dining establishment as a change of pace, or a cool local ice cream bar. Nor would one find civilization nearby should they, say, inadvertently forget to pack Excedrin PM. And as riled up as one might be, this place is certain to trigger insomnia.

So I was talking with Seth the other day and *Did you know*, he said, that of the entire US population, a mere 4.5 percent actually identify as lesbian? Way more for Gen Z, but that's sort of robbing the cradle at your age. I mean, it's miraculous you've found anyone at all.

Gee thanks, I said.

Sure, he replied. At which point, he served up a generous portion of jalapeño poppers and guacamole, so I temporarily forgave him, though he was lax at reading the room and kept on about how it's been flooding airwaves and socials and so on. *It* being news about this survey.

In any regard, we ventured to assume that perhaps half— or nearly half—of those who identified as lesbian were likely in love or otherwise committed, which limits me even more. Not to mention you're all so geographically dispersed, he told me, adding an underhanded shrug.

Which is to say, the probability, statistically, of my running across anyone even remotely my age, let alone of my persuasion and—you know—of her caliber, is next to unbearable.

Logan, who just has this air about her, this quality. This attentive indifference, I guess you could call it. With the kind of conviction that every girl who's ever tried to come on to me has hoped to pull off. But they never really do. It's never authentic. It never, ever comes off naturally.

And they're never so in sync with my words that they could use them, could play with them, could toy with them, with me—which has left me weakened and more than willing. As I recall the classic lines of her face and the way she observed me, intent on me and moody, motionless, as if she was unpeeling every layer of defense I've ever had, every edge, until there was nowhere left to hide. Her voice as cool as chilled Lambrusco on a hot summer's day, aching and devious and leaving me feeling such feelings, such longings for a girl I will predictably never have.

Which is what I'm still grinning about as I make my way along the pier with plans to finish the novel I brought along, as if one could possibly comprehend someone else's thoughts on a page at a time when I'm far too absorbed in my own.

The only pier I've been on other than this was large and commercial and offered the reward of a restaurant at the very end for those of us who ventured that far out. It was meant for people watching, for bench sitting, for wandering unnoticed through clustered conversations as aggressive gulls swooped down to catch their next meal. And as tall boys rebelled beyond *No Skateboarding* signs only to thunder past the occasional fisherman, clipping couples who might've been strolling or who might've been squared up against coin-op binoculars to see—what exactly? What were we looking for? For a bite of shanty food, the aromas of which could tempt lovers long after they'd been served frothy beer mugs with red plastic trays piled high in all things battered and dipped.

Now that was a lot of commotion, but it was not unlike this, which is quiet and personal. But the ocean's always liberating, centering—as I gaze down at the shallow surf, braced against its rail, absorbed in its rhythms, that low muffled breeze, its deep marine scent and its weathered wooden planks that escort me toward its end where it widens into a sitting space for two.

Which feels as if I'm a world away from shore, from that crowd now gathering around that taut volleyball net. Making me wonder if that's her, tossing their serve—a sight that's ignited another warm flood of fuzzy, of floating.

After several minutes have passed of that, and I still can't say either way, I open my book to find the sun has a glare with such intensity that it's blinding my white page, rendering this book unreadable. Making me wonder if this might've been the worst possible idea I've ever had.

Not that I wouldn't enjoy a sunrise from this very same spot, which is something I'll need to add to my bucket list of things I plan to do. That and coming to terms with a few of those nagging questions that keep rummaging up.

Like why is it, when girls follow their hearts, they're considered juvenile, impulsive, naive? Yet those of us who are vigilant, who pause, who refrain, who think twice and move slowly with caution are thought to be bitter, jaded, confused? I'm thinking not just of Léa but others as well.

The thing is, girls want what they want, regardless. They'll take what you give. She got what I gave her, freely. I wanted that much.

Which always comes at a price.

But why do I even try? When I'm always bending to their likes. When I'm folding into her mold. When it's never about me, about mutuality, reciprocity. It's one-sided, always.

It's a question I find myself immersed in deeply when Logan stops by, as she takes a seat, and when she does, it's as if I've been stranded on the side of a highway with cars whooshing by, unsteady. Or sucked down beneath that thick flood of waves. As if this was imagined, motionless as I listen. Not listening. Not thinking. Not here.

I've often rationalized my many short-lived yet wildly intense affairs with, well, a healthy dose of naivety. Of stupidity. That girls drop pretty promises and then run off while I'm in a field of grass far behind, searching and scouting about with hopes of scooping them up. Until she's down on the ground alongside me, doubting me, seeing the real me. Leaving me.

Because short-lived is synonymous with failed, with never good enough. As if the good ones carry rings.

Which is not to say that I'll throw caution to the wind with this. But I think I might need to loosen up or lighten up. Or live right here in the now without analyzing so much, without worrying, without planning or knowing. Without having to know. And without having a goal.

CHAPTER TEN

Act I Scene 2

Logan

"How is it photos of you have amassed more than a thousand likes," Tanner says, glued to her never-ending documentary of our lives otherwise known as Instagram, "whereas mine barely halve that?" She's reflecting on a series of shots that she's posted of me as I waited at the car as part of her road trip anthology. And another of me carrying out our gas station cardboard tray of chili dogs. Before lying on my back on her hotel-cornered bed as if beckoning her over.

Meanwhile, we shift our little heart-to-heart to a boulder overlooking a few buff boys as they artfully contend in a rather competitive game of beach volleyball along the shore.

"For the record, I have no desire to compete with you for Instagram likes," I say, shading my eyes from the sun. And why Tanner feels so compelled to broadcast our lives to complete strangers, I'll never know.

As for me, I'm incognito. My theory being, the minute you post anything on social media, you'll have one ex adding a comment to which another ex replies and soon enough they're comparing notes. Or worse yet, hooking up. Likewise, I'm not exactly keen on the concept of watching the chronicles of said ex as she moves on. Not to mention hours and hours of deletions after we split.

"But imagine us a couple," she says, rather randomly.

So I turn and look at her dead-on, bewildered. "And—?"

"It's just that our combined likes as a couple could make us the most popular pair in history."

"I hardly view instafame as reason enough for anyone to, you know, romantically partner up."

"Is that right?" she says, adding a questionable grin. "Speak for yourself." But now I'm thinking she might be taking this little photo-sharing hobby of hers a bit too far. Either that or perhaps I'm witnessing firsthand the ramifications of celibacy, three weeks' at that, otherwise known as her breaking point. Anyone's breaking point. "Vacations like these are social media gold," Tanner informs me. "They want to be you, that unreal you. Take Venice, for example, our delays, our balcony, quaint canal luncheons slumbered into breakfasts in bed, espressos in handsome pottery as I lounged in lingerie and that view, our playlist, our breakup—each carefully choreographed in a carousel series of three."

"And this pleases you?" I say.

She throws back an ill-fitting grin. "One must focus on the bright side of each catastrophe."

Perhaps. But there's something to be said about privacy, about boundaries. About the experiencing of life as opposed to the invention of one. Which is something I'm trying to explain to her as I brace myself over knees in an attempt to situate myself on this boulder, which isn't exactly comfortable—it's a rock—and then something catches my eye. I glimpse at Tanner, who's glued to her phone, before peering far, far out past the shore as I slip my sunglasses down to the edge of my nose.

Being that, this girl couldn't possibly have made herself more difficult to approach, and holding a book, at that, the most *don't bother me* pastime of all. Which I'm thinking, given her unapproachability, might indicate that she's into one of those risqué titles that would make a girl blush were I to, say, catch a glimpse of its cover. Which makes me want to do exactly that.

I mean, something tells me she's not the sonnet type. Nor Anaïs Nin, nor one of those quasidepressive feminists who read Plath. Nor trash of mass appeal, but perhaps. Or I might take her as a bit highbrow. Clearly more paperback than Kindle. Perchance provocative but with a touch of distinction, with credence. Or, say, a rare memoir, a reserve one might grab for its margin notes, its inscription. That jewel of the used book shop that you fast recognize as a one of a kind. A keepsake. The archive.

"But you're so ambitious otherwise," Tanner's saying, still clearly in some sort of twisted social media rivalry with me. And next, she's brushing sand off her knees and gazing in the distance, pensive, daydreamy, through a pair of honey-colored shades. "You're not one to be topped."

I glance over at her, piqued. "When you put it that way," I say. Before I'm back at that pier.

"What do you think?" she says, posing provocatively in her suit. "Am I suitably dressed for the role of soul searcher?"

"If that's what you're going for," I say.

"I plan on leaving this place fully transformed, a groovy, voluminous new me." Her voice grows sexier the lazier it gets. "You know what," she stresses, cuddling in, "the whole time I was in Venice, I was thinking about you, wondering what you'd think. About this, that. About all of it."

"And why do I doubt that?" I say. Moreover, why is my mind now strolling those streets alongside her, taking in scents of sugar and vanilla at the pasticceria. Which mingle with the pizzeria next door, with its crumbled brick and spinning dough amid the sounds of floating hearts and accordions. That gondola, Instagram.

"You should've come along," Tanner says, while sliding a thumb over her phone.

When in fact, my Venetian experience would be closer to a fleeting Vespa ride panning lush countryside with the chest of a girl built like Natalia Bonifacci smashed against my back. Just add a Negroni. I glance intently at Kennedy off at that pier. "I'm not the best companion," I finally say with a slow grin and a thought that must be fleeting across my face.

"Well, I happen to think you are."

"When I get you likes on your Instagram," I say, glaring.

She glances up at me. "We should come again." Next she slips bare toes into cool sand.

"I hope you're not referring to this when you say *come again*," I add, gesturing around.

"It can be our annual thing, our escapism"—she beams—"and once we're married, we'll bring our gorgeous wives and we'll drink and swim and sun. People do that, you know. So don't say no. Won't you consider it? When I ask?"

It takes me a moment to respond. I mean, it's the kind of relationship we've had but not in that way. With the exception of a weekend excursion last summer, when she wanted to meet some girl from online who just so happened to land a trip on business to 3 West Club in New York from—Texas? Tennessee? It could've been Toronto. And since Tanner knew zip, zilch, zero about navigating, I offered to tag along, not the wisest thing I've done, though I did enjoy a rather hazy evening at a bar in Lower Manhattan. And while that trip might've resulted in a breakdown over boozy ice cream at Tipsy Scoop and an amorous Uber ride to an ice skating rink, a girls' weekend it was not. "Someone's been gleaning friendship advice from the likes of talk radio," I say.

"More like someone's been gleaning life advice from the likes of Bumble." Tanner groans.

"I thought you were all about Bumble," I say then nudge her with my elbow as if to say *Hey, cheer up.*

But she lowers her voice. "You know what she said to me?"

"Who," I say, "gondola? Your ex?"

"She told me I felt familiar. She said our sex was routine, vanilla." Then she flips her hair, incensed. "While we were at this place, this insane sort of well-born marketplace, where we had milky double espressos alongside waifish well-to-do wives who had nothing better to do with their lives than fantasize about us. Then afterward, after this deep and highly emotionally intense interaction we'd had, she just casually wanders off—under the pretense of paying our bill—and I lost it. I waited, sending her text after text after text, which she deliberately ignored. So eventually, I took off, and she found me at a nearby shop. And she took me by the hand and found a changing room, and she asked me to undress. And when she kissed me, as she touched me, she said I looked sad. She thought I looked so striking sad. She wanted me that way. It's like she seriously got off on it."

"Are you saying she's into anonymous sex?" I ask.

"It's more than that," Tanner says. "It's almost like making up. You know, we had a fight."

"Which she started intentionally," I say.

She sighs, shaking her head. "But she was so good. I mean *it, it* was so good after that. I can't even explain why."

"Perhaps you might consider girls offline"—or at least off Tinder, off Bumble—"where it's less, you know, superficial."

"How could you say that, when offline is the epitome of superficial," she tells me with absolute conviction.

"Because she sounds like a complete narcissist," I say under my breath. Which should've been the end, right there. Had I known.

"Oh, you don't even know the half of it," she adds. "Because those photos she had over her bed, turns out the whole time she'd been fucking me beneath nude portraits of an ex taken some six years earlier. Which of course she disclosed rather openly. And that's another thing," she tells me. "She had the audacity to say *I love you* when disclosures and details like that and figuring it all out takes time. Which I did not reciprocate, thank God. Though that should have triggered ingenuine bells—or exactly that, desperation. It lacks everything. As in, maybe she just wanted someone, and I happened to be in that mindset at the right time."

"I happen to like your mindset," I say.

"And that's always the thing," Tanner says, sneering, sarcastic, "they always love my *mind*."

"Perhaps the key is to stop short before the fall," I say. But again, my mind's right back on Kennedy. "Enjoy it for what it's worth. Enjoy it for what it is."

"If only I could," she says.

"I won't fault you for wanting what you want," I tell her. "But don't go there. She wasn't everything."

And next, she's giggling. "But she was something else." Now reclined, Hollywood style, knees up. "My life would be so dull without you."

I'm glancing over a pair of sunglasses. "You could do so much better than me." This day is brilliant, briny, almost teal. With a scent of slight seaweed and kelp in the air. And I'm thinking the only thing missing from this scene is a surfboard propped in the sand.

"Perhaps I'll find someone better than you," she says. "But I *have* to use you in the interim."

"I'm fine with being used," I say.

"I'm glad someone is."

And you know what else this scene needs? A classic VW Bug. In something like Habanero Orange. With lovers over there on a towel, making out. And one of those shacks back there that should be decked out in some of those triangular flags made of felt. Where the *U* in *M A L I B U* is squished and compressed at its point.

To go with those predictably choreographed waves along with its audience of beach chairs covered in umbrellas that are angled just so over suntanned legs that extend in an orderly row.

Except, right beyond that is the pier that I keep coming back to.

I run a hand down the back of my neck, and I try to pretend, as I should, that I'm just a spectator at the sidelines of their volleyball game. "I could never get into all that," I say as I do.

Tanner's adjusting the straps of her bikini. "I know, it's all hot and sweaty and *eww*."

"Not to mention that sand," I say.

She smiles, but she doesn't respond. Instead she goes back into herself, reclining and closing her eyes, sunbathing-style. As I gaze at her mindlessly, that cherry-colored mouth and those wrists now crossed overhead. But then my attention shifts back over to their game, zoning me out completely.

It's not until quite some time has passed that she's sitting back up. "You've given me a thought."

"Please say I didn't."

"It's too late, doll, you did."

"But you were working so well on your tan," I say.

"And you see, Logan, that's the thing. You're so dreamy athletic and far too humble. But girls love that in you." I'm pretty sure the reason Tanner's been the one constant in my life is that she finds *dreamy* in just about everything, and that's no exaggeration. Right now, though, she's back on her phone and I'm hovering over—I'm spying, pestering as I vie for a glimpse of her screen.

"Oh my God!" she says, then elbows me.

And I say, "Who's she?"

And she says, "She followed me back."

"She's definitely your type," I add, resigned.

"You say that with such contempt." And next she's asking about rules, about positions, and so on and so forth. About volleyball. "I think I'd do well at that," she says, following the arc of the ball.

"Of course you would." Then she stares at me in that you-must-know-what-I'm-thinking way. Because she's now itching to play. "It's just, what, a bunch of diving into sand. Not to mention that serve you see right there, it kills the heel of your hand. Trust me, I speak from experience. And besides, they don't seem to be recruiting."

"Dear Diary, first day on holiday," she narrates, flippant, tugging a rogue strand of hair, "and Logan's the biggest drag."

"You'll do anything for likes," I say. And her eyes widen. "Well, for the record, I won't be joining."

"C'mon," she whines. "Seriously. Do I need to spell this out for you?" I gaze at her, like, where is this going? "You take me for such a fool. You're so ready to walk down that pier." Which I'm sure puts the most guilt-ridden grin on my face. My God, I feel flushed. "So, what do you say?" She's even nodding that way. "Do you think she's single?"

"She most definitely is."

"So you've conversed?" she says.

I flutter my eyes at her. "We have."

"Why does it feel as if I'm missing a major piece of this puzzle?" But she's glaring at me accusatorily.

"Because you always are."

And next I'm stringing Tanner along with what should be a reasonably convincing argument as to why we're not going to intrude on their volleyball game. But she could not care less. She's already stood up, peeled away her coverup, and flashed me a backward glance.

As if I'm even dressed for this. I'm not. Try loose jeans, which are far from bendable. But still, I make the serve, which is killer, remarkable given I haven't played in how long? And look, not to brag or anything, but overall, I'm not half bad.

Not that I can say the same about our prima donna who, in an attempt to spike the ball, collapses to her knees—and that right there (don't ask) takes me back to Lauren, like the worst flashback ever. Lauren with that pile of hair that kept falling in my face, not to mention the palest skin imaginable, which practically glowed in the dark. And while Lauren was no Olympic athlete, damn, could that girl block. And argue—which at that age was love. So, sure, we might've had a thing—a tight, tense, orgasmic thing that steamed the back seat of her car.

"I think you've made an impression," Tanner says, intruding on my thoughts. But she's not mad. She's just had enough of me for one day. "What have you done to that girl?" And she's gesturing again at that pier.

"Why?"

"My God, she's been staring at you."

"Yeah?" I say, clearly posturing. "So, did I look good?"

"Go ask for yourself," she tells me. I shrug, glance back. "You won't be missed."

But in any regard, let's fast-forward because Tanner can be persuasive. Make that impossible to the point of insular, once she's found her perfect crowd.

And next, you'll have to imagine the sounds, the sights, the sensations as you're making your way along wide, rickety boards, which seem to be the only real barrier separating me from the sea below, just to talk to a girl you've somehow grown mildly infatuated with. And not only that, this dizzying uncertainty that always accompanies heights and this need to contain yourself, and all the while, you're racking your brain, trying to figure out what you might possibly say this time around, as if anything might impress her.

So maybe it's a healthy dose of apprehension or something like that. But all I see are sun-drenched shoulders and a taut bikini that's peeking beneath. Enough to make me pause, hang back, waver. Second-guessing. Make that, succumbing beneath the worst flood of an adrenaline rush that you could ever in your life imagine. As I take my final step.

And with that, she glances up. "Um, hi," is what I say.

"Hi."

"It looks like your clothes have dried."

And when Kennedy smiles, I watch her lips. "I was hardly presentable."

"Sure you were," I say as I wrestle impatience, reluctance, euphoria. "I'm sorry," is what I say as I crouch down beside her. "I didn't mean to startle you." She wrangles with her hair in this wind as I take a seat beside her. Then my gaze drifts down to the sea.

But I sense her eyes lingering on me. She leans in close. "It's really not that deep," she says, mirroring my grin.

"So, this place," I tell her, "has sort of a sordid past. Did you know that?" Meanwhile, I'm trying *not* to focus on how focused I am on her lips. "That is, we could be sitting on the very shore, roughly"—this nonsense is not enhanced by my nervous hand gestures—"where they fought the first naval battle of the Revolutionary War." As her lips part into the prettiest grin. "And then, you know, during Prohibition, this right here, this inn, is where you could come and get a good shot of whiskey. Except now, it's pretty much puffins."

"Puffins?" she says, intrigued.

"We could see them, that is, if only I had a boat."

Her smile straddles the line between mildly apprehensive and curiously engaged. "But if you did," she says, "have a boat…"

"If I did," I say and then we're silent for a little while. "If I did, I'd ask you out."

Kennedy folds her sunglasses and sort of hooks them down her shirt, a move that sinks my attention to an inappropriate spot. "In that case, I wish you had a boat," she says. "Because I just might accept."

"How could you not?" I say. "If only for the puffins."

"I'd like to see these puffins."

"It's like a penguin meets Toucan Sam."

"Toucan Sam?" she says, her gaze lingering on my mouth.

"Please say you like Froot Loops?"

"I do." And those eyes, my God. "I'm thinking you know a lot about this place."

"Yeah, well." I lean close, softening my voice. "I found a few brochures they left in my room." Her laugh, exquisite, roomy. Ascending, gut-wrenching. "How's that book going? And what sort of things do you like?"

"What sort of things do I like?" she says, bemused.

"To read," I emphasize.

"I like this," she says.

"And what is this?" I ask.

She smiles at me. And as she does, my gaze finds the hollow of her neck, that weightlessness of her hands. And the way the sea's haze is reflecting across her face when she says, "Nice serve back there, by the way."

"You saw?" I say like a fool.

And then she says, "I love the scent of the sea."

"And what else do you love?"

"I love thunder, warm air, summer. Stargazing. Which makes me pretty cliché," And when she talks, it feels as if I've been sucked into a ballad on loop. "What do *you* love?"

"Well, for one," I say, "I love whatever it is you're wearing." Which, based solely on the look on her face, has won her over. "And summer grills," I say. "Pub food. Stargazing. I guess I'm pretty cliché."

And then she says, "This is important stuff."

As I smile at her, achingly. "Is it?"

"This friend of mine," she says, "he makes the best pub food. I bet you would like it."

But as I lean in, all I can think is, Let's stay like this all night. "So tell me about your friend."

CHAPTER ELEVEN

Opening Lines

Kennedy

How hard would it have been for her to steer our conversation back into vague territory with something like *How do you like your job?* Or *Interests, hobbies?* You know, something predictable and stereotypical. The type of *nice to meet you* questions that reveal nil about oneself. After which I could share an anecdote that offered precisely that—yet one that would still pique her interest.

Like, say, last week's client interview, which began innocently enough when a beautiful, milky-skinned academic, who I guess you could say was in her late-thirties early-forties, wanders into our office unscheduled. And then came her story—just, wow.

But I know, I know. Client confidentiality. Which limits my range of *How do you like your job* topics to…what? The Clique? To our not quite tipsy enough for this Halloween potluck last autumn? Or to our fascinating new Fitbit tracking program that's been put into place to keep insurance premiums at bay?

Equally as riveting, come to think of it, are my non-occupation-related interests and hobbies. Because what do I have? A highly pampered Siamese kitten, a desperately adoring neighbor, and a nefarious habit of online shopping on Friday nights beneath crisp linen sheets after one too many glasses of Cabernet Sauvignon have rendered me incapable of comprehending my newest novel.

But instead, tragically, Logan delves into *Tell me about yourself.* And while this might seem innocent enough to anyone who has not been on the receiving end, I can assure you it's not. In fact, it's quite possibly the most open-ended question one could ask. Because what do you even say? My first thought being, right, so, I'm the type of girl who falls head over heels for girls who ask me...*that*.

Given here I am, a serial dumpee whose only good fortune in life is that I've been gratefully gifted the deed to my aunt's lofty loft, where I've been known to spend more time with my neighbor and his snickerdoodles than I have in relationships. And why? Because I've rarely been able to delve past their maybe-we-should-commit mark, though I'm apparently marriage material by the third date. All of which I blame on an upbringing that's left me internally conflicted and swaying between *Please love me* and *Don't you dare try*. The latter of which is currently winning me over by a pretty slim margin.

"Let's see," I say, hesitant, wondering how can I project interesting and sophisticated though not stuffy? Self-reliant and independent though not romantically clueless. And calm, rational, sensible versus out of my mind, which is how Logan's making me feel.

And that's not to say mislead.

Though why am I always doing this? Projecting perfection. Projecting pretty. Bending until I'm them. Until I don't know who I am.

I settle on, "My favorite shirt is a threadbare Harley-Davidson jersey I purchased at the age of twenty-three because it felt edgy at that time, and which no longer suits my present-day hoping to be professional because I'm well into my thirties aesthetic." I wait anxiously for a reply. "Still, I can't part with it." And adding apologetically, "I don't know what that says about me."

She leans back, poised against the rail. And, listen, I'm not going to say that I don't like the look she's just given me. But it's making me feel vulnerable. And gullible. Whereas she just emanates cool.

"Did you bring it?" she says. Which I can barely hear because I can't stop fretting. "I'd love to see you in it." And you know how, when you're imagining that best-case scenario right down to the made-up dialogue you're going to have with that dreamy girl, and how, in your mind, it's flawless and how she says exactly what you want to hear—all of the stuff that never happens in real life? It's happening. Which feels surreal. And next Logan says, "It tells me you're sentimental." Her hands are so strong and supple. And I keep fantasizing about them on me. "So," she says, intrigued, "do you ride?"

But I'm pretty sure I'm laughing out of nerves at this point. "Edgy, I'm not. So would you believe I studied them as an undergrad? It was more some youthful exuberance drawn to an iconic brand," I say. "So, wait, are you saying you have?"

"I have, once." I love when her voice sinks down like this. "It was a friend of a friend of a friend. But it wasn't a Harley. She was showing off a new vintage Indian."

"So now I'm wondering, did you like it?" I ask.

She glances away, then back, pensive. "I like threadbare shirts, if that's what you're asking." Which has caught me completely off guard.

So I need to change the subject. "You know, there's a big show right here in a few days," I say.

"Is that what you'd like to talk about?"

I force myself to pause. "Why do you seem the type who would try anything once?"

"Because I am."

Then I don't even stop to think. "I seem to attract risk, apparently."

"And now that I'm intrigued—"

"Don't be," I say. "It's just that I'm frequently coerced."

Logan meets my eye then smiles. "Which could mean you like to be coerced." Which is quite the leading question. Not to mention, merciless. I turn my head and feel myself blush. But now she stares me down. "Maybe we'll continue this later?"

"I'll assume," I say softly, "that we're discussing the type of risk inherent in, say, rock climbing."

"I guess I won't be asking you out for that." But it's like a ping down deep in my gut.

"Or escape rooms or kayaks or anything like that," I add,

lighthearted. "But that's not true. I enjoy rivers, creeks, observing. It's just that I wouldn't step foot into one. And I have no desire to float down one. Though I could be coerced into boating," I add, turning away from her gaze, "were it out to spy on puffins."

"That could be arranged." She draws back the front of her hair. "I do love that you're coercible." With this slow, sensual sort of gaze.

"Not easily," I say.

And that grin. "*Mm-hmm.*"

But then we're on to something new. Like the towels they brought to Logan's room. And how she needs to unwind after work. And how someone was doing something—and now she wants to, too. Which is fascinating, appetizing, she's gushing about its nooks and crooks and alleyways. And all the while, I'm staring at the movement of her lips, ruddy. At her legs, cocked. Her fingers, blunt.

"Because there's nothing that could beat the pub crawl you'd get in London," I can hear her saying. "But that's been eighty-sixed by Tanner, who'd rather we do *this* till we die. She is determined to live a rather sheltered life."

I don't know if it's okay to smile this much. I don't know if it's scaring her away.

But next, she's wanting to know more. And we go back and forth like that until I'm rambling about my commute and how I was filling up my tank and reading some lines of instruction on that small touchpad, and how I was made to endure some guy's curriculum on horsepower, on handling, an exchange that ended abruptly and one that left me feeling, "Well, you must know how that feels."

She tells me she does.

Which is hard to believe given the next word out of her mouth is, "V-6?"

"If that means it's reasonably fast," I say, "yes. Though I went with this car for style."

"But fast is always good," she says. Fast is always good, I muse. As she meets my eye then smiles.

"It wasn't just that, though," I say. "This place had such déjà vu. It reminded me of this girl I'd known in high school, one of those now confined to socials but then best friends, Kathleen. And come to think of it, she was always like that, too. She always needed to try something new. So she'd get me out on these epic day trips—unforgettable. And there was this one stop, this country shop out there in the middle of the boondocks. The kind that has everything you'd need, you know, wine and farm tools and chicken feed. And one of those soft-serve windows out front. And brownies wrapped in cellophane. Cider doughnuts. Fruit platters and bouquets and every kind of cheese you could imagine with bins and bins of local apples. And there were pies alongside postcards. And two dusty cans of spray paint in the worst and most unpopular colors you could imagine. But of course, they had pink. So she bought a bottle of cheap Barefoot Fruitscato with her fake ID and a can of hot pink Krylon. And we took off with the radio cranked up and the top down and found a riverbank and ate cheeseburgers under some backcountry bridge because Kathleen had fallen in love with some guy." The air was as damp as this. And those insects, the creak of that tree. "And this stream kept rushing by. And we took Polaroids of each other to the soundtrack of *their* song," I say. "At some point, then, she shook that can and climbed up and onto my shoulders, and look, it's still up there on that bridge if you drive by. *K + J.*"

She smiles, then turns from me and…this is hard to describe. But she gets this look that fades the instant she's facing me again. "You had me at backcountry bridge," she says.

"You know what the funny thing is?" I say as I cover my mouth. "They hadn't even gotten together. He wasn't into her."

"Unrequited love," she says, and that just hits in a way.

"She eventually asked him out," I say. "It's sweet. That they're actually still together." I glance back at the inn. Those lights, once crisp, once creams and browns and butterscotch, now blur right into a thick fog. "I'm so sorry."

"Sorry?"

"That I've kept you this long," I say. Now that we're blanketed in a film of marine fog. And I'm reminded of where we are. Of who we are, strangers. While Logan's shaking her head.

Which is confusing, isn't it? Not just this day but this pretty little distraction I've found. I wrap my arms around myself. "I suppose we should start to head back." And all the while, her hand's been inches from mine.

How had we gone from *Tell me about yourself?* to this right here?

But it's how you feel, my therapist would say.

Which is not encourageable. It's more like improbable. But isn't everything.

And I am, aren't I? I'm wanting her. Regardless.

Too wrapped up in illusions, in absolute delusions. Because this could not end right. "What was that again?" I ask her, leaning in.

"You said we should maybe head in. And I said, I can't really say that I want to." Except when she says this, it stirs up those nerves again.

"But you know, that convenience store," I say as we're helping each other up. "I couldn't just pump gas," I say. "I couldn't even think, what between Mr. Horsepower and that low-budget ad that kept shouting at me in a loop *Come in...Go grab some...Tasty flavors.*"

"Tasty," Logan says, chuckling. And when she sucks her lower lip, all I can think is, How would they feel against mine? as we gradually amble back.

"You know what?" I say on a whim. "I guess I don't want to head back, either."

Chapter Twelve

Parting Is Such Sweet Sorrow

Logan

I was actually supposed to meet up with Tanner a good half hour ago. But here I am wandering back, late as usual, pausing periodically, or at least Kennedy is. She's stopped just ahead of me, her elbows braced against that rail when I come up from behind, fixed on that photogenic smile. As she laughs about something else I've said.

She has this soft sort of laugh but one that's overflowing with sheer exuberance. One that captivates me. I almost tell her so.

But even if I had, every word would've been drowned beneath this wind, which is cutting and raw. Ridiculously overstated—much like my mood, this sort of bravado that feels too good in the moment, or at least until it's been chased with a hefty dose of doubt, of uncertainty and humility. Until I'm slipping, slipping. Drifting. Adrift and yet, somehow, I'm where I want to be.

Just kiss her already.

Except here I am standing beside her, rigid. Clueless. Focused down on that sand as she slips a foot between rails.

Then somewhere in the midst of it, in the midst of my hesitation, this indecision, I seem to have—for lack of a better line—I seem to have challenged her. Into a double dare. Into a winner takes all. And now everything's just a blur. With her racing and me chasing down the pier, her eyes darting back, her gaze shimmering, and that smile beaming, pounding, pulsing, my feet leaping, landing—as I attempt to catch my breath.

I swear, she's like a dream, glancing up, as if windswept hair were smudged in acrylic, in oil, smeared, malleable. Into the faintest ivory. Into a wilt of copper, frost, as I extend a hand because *I've got you.* Her shirt slack, revealing, slips down into my arms and then is smashed against my chest. Her cheeks still marked by the wind, lustrous. So near that I catch the faded hint of spearmint in her voice. "Fast is good," she's saying. Then she returns a look as if to say *Take me, you've won.* But it's not really a race, is it? Though I do feel as if I've won.

Except then, after steadying ourselves, we just sort of move right along, cordial.

"So, I never really asked what you're reading," I say.

Her grin, half apologetic. "It's a classic," she tells me.

"And it's about—?"

"Well, right now, it's sort of slowish." She shrugs. "Maybe it's just a big buildup."

I laugh. "I see."

"But it has me intrigued." I look at her, inquisitive. "It's good," she adds with a dreamy expression on her face. "Involved but really, really good."

I peer over at Kennedy with her half-cocked grin as we near the door, which is now ajar with traffic moving in and out in both directions, some folks now crowding around a banquet that seems to have a pretty sweet spread—you know, the cheese, the grapes, the pecans, the fancy fanned apples (and those are not Ritz Crackers) next to little condiment cups of jam—amid the faint thrum of a soulful soundtrack, one that I deeply appreciate but can't quite narrow down, not the artist nor the era.

Which is where I'd expect to find Tanner reclined forlorn on a chaise lounge quasi-conspiratorially, martini in hand. But instead, she's mingling graciously, engaging herself in not one but a handful of social circles all at once.

Hence instead of making a beeline to appease her, I take Kennedy by the hand, and we duck behind a rather immense bookshelf, and she's lolling against the side, hair clinging to her face, expectant, expended. "I hope I'll see you again?" I say, but my voice, which shakes, betrays me.

As Kennedy fondles the key to her room, her eyes shift between mine. The dampness in the air has now settled above her lip. Her breath so close I can almost taste it. A thought I'm really getting into when my phone goes off.

Tanner: *Parting is such sweet sorrow.*

"So," I say, thinking *shit* as I peer back and catch Tanner still thumbing her phone.

Tanner: *Not to kill your mood, Romeo.* ;)

"I'd better head off," I say, feeling a repressed grin. Feeling repressed. "And make good over there, you know?" Stalling, hesitant, as she tries to duck past me with eyes that just don't want to leave. "Wait," I say, clipped, tugging her in, and she lifts her gaze, and for a moment, in a flash, it's like I've forgotten what I was going to say. Though I know what I wanted to do. Everything feeling so easy. Even this kiss, which is slow, sinking.

"So," I say once we break away, "what if I got your number?"

After she heads upstairs, I catch up with Tanner, who's lounging against the bar beside two guys, and who's now oblivious to me. So I barge in, not bitter, mind you. Not seething in the least. When she lifts her drink and gestures. "This is Paul," she tells me. "And this is Woodward. They're not together, but they'd like to be." A comment that prompts a bout of restrained laughter. You know, the inside joke that makes the outsider in me feel momentarily unwelcome. At least until they sail off into what could very easily be their own private production set, the pastel-pink rom-com, the quaint coffee shops and crumble-topped baked goods, the musical soundtrack. Tanner, the matchmaker, their orchestrator, who might as well be holding a big buttery bucket of popcorn. Then she starts in about that lesbian couple over there in a *Shh, don't look!* way and how they've propositioned her.

I order a craft beer, something called Dead Zone. "As in both?" I ask, intrigued.

And she's all about it. "Both."

"But I thought you preferred the girls who were, you know, a continent away and unattainable. Or at least virtual."

"It's not cheating," she tells me, hushed, rationalizing, "not technically…when it involves both," expecting I'll agree with her.

Meanwhile, I'm watching our bartender twist, snap, grin. "For you, it's not cheating," I say.

"I've been talking with the boys," she informs me, "and they're under the impression that queer women are just too uptight about these things," her tone reminiscent of a 1950s home economics film. "You're not asking for a ring, they said. You're asking for a good time."

"I would agree."

"And I deserve a good time."

"You do—"

"*Single* is not a journey," she resumes with full-on air quotes. "Single is a destination—and I need to make the most of it while it lasts." And all the while, she's eying me as if I were the key that's holding her back.

"Certainly," I say, "if they're single."

"And they are," she eagerly informs me. "Not that I'd consider it otherwise, you know, were we back at home. But what happens in Vegas, as they say."

And I'm thinking this drink is substantial, almost espresso, roasty. "Follow your heart."

"My heart is always wrong," she says, disgruntled. "I'd much rather follow yours."

"Well, this isn't my decision to make," I tell her.

"In any regard, they *did* offer. And they happen to be…" She fades off, with a quick glance back.

"Yeah, they're hot." Like, both. Like, maybe not one or the other individually. But collectively, sure.

"And it's, like, they seem to know what they're doing," Tanner says in this far-off way. "It's like they've done this before."

"But doesn't that bother you?"

"Logan," she laments. "I need to feel appreciated."

"I appreciate you," I say. "Even when you're rebounding."

"I know I am," she says, then smiles, ingenuine. "It's not a sad thing. But it's not happy. It's a numb thing."

"It's going to break you," I say.

"No," she says. "But it might break them." And next, she's back to rationalizing. Insisting. So I'm back to checking my phone to the backdrop of her ramblings about *self-awareness* and *inevitability* and *intimacy* and...*Tic Tacs. I forgot them. Do you have any?* But I have no messages.

"It's good that you're weighing your options," I say.

"But you don't think I should."

"I think you should do what's right for you," I say.

Which is funny—because sometimes Tanner acts like I know what I'm actually talking about.

"She was a head trip," she says, "but still the only one I'd go back to."

"And knowing her," I say, "you'll likely get that chance." I glance back at those two now tucked in a nook in the corner. Two who clearly don't know what they're in for. "You know what'll happen, though. One'll fall madly in love with you."

She glances over my shoulder, piqued. "Which one?"

I bite my lip. "Which one would you like?"

Only this time, we both glance back, nonchalant. "That one," she says. "I definitely favor that one."

The guy beside us pops a cork off champagne, its bubbles now dripping over the bottle's rim as the sky melts into a pale aqua blue, dim lights filtering through.

"All right then," I tell her. "Go make that happen." I tuck my phone under the table, checking, thumbing in Kennedy's number.

Me: *I just wanted to go down on record saying that I very much enjoyed what we just did.*

But it takes a while to click send, to stop toggling, toggling, I keep toggling. And then Tanner gets up—"I'll be right back"—to leave as we're handed the dinner menu.

Kennedy: *Likewise.* :)

Me: *And I'm hoping you might come down and perhaps join us.*

Me, again: *Or I could come up.*

Then Tanner gets back with a plate full of ripe grapes, wheat crackers, spreadable cheese. "A nice, light beachside hors d'oeuvres."

And I appreciate the thought, but... "I'll check out the menu," I say, "thanks."

Kennedy: *I was settling in to read.* But she adds a smiling emoji. And a bathtub emoji.

Me: *With the beach right down here?* So of course I add a winking emoji, something I fucking never use.

Me, again: *I know this might sound ridiculous. But I was wondering if this might be an appropriate way to ask you out?*

"What are you doing?" Tanner says, intruding.

"Nothing," I say.

She takes a bite. "Whatever happened to *Girls come to me?*" Which is antagonizing. "Maybe I should head over there and talk to them." And meanwhile, she's ordering a Flirtini.

"Tell me everything they said."

"It was unprompted. Sort of. Cloaked in the middle of *You're really beautiful* and a bunch of other things. Unusual, really, the way she kept at me. That's really the best way to describe it, unusual."

And, anyway, I'm listening, I am. To Tanner. She's just the diversion I need right now and just about the only thing that's keeping me from cringing over the fact that I haven't heard back. Yet another text to remind me about an appointment that doesn't even occur until later next week. One that offers a *Type STOP to unsubscribe* option. So I do. STOP. And as I'm typing this, as I'm feeling this, Kennedy's shown up.

Except I don't actually realize she's shown up until I hear Tanner's rather long-winded *Pleased to meet you.* And then I hear Kennedy. And that voice...and of course I'm offering up a seat and we sort of ponder this plate of cheese and I hand her the menu, half hoping Tanner picks up on my cue and excuses herself—for something, anything. Which she does, eventually, says she's off to get a plate of cheese.

Meanwhile, my knee's slipped between Kennedy's, slightly parting them. "I really didn't expect for you to show," I say.

"I can't say that it was on my agenda this morning," she tells me.

"So what convinced you?"

And this look she gives, dear God. "I couldn't say."

"Well, I'm really glad you did," I say. "Can I interest you in a drink?"

"I'm interested," she tells me. Which is how everything flows with her, so easy, the tipping of our heads, more sidestepping, until I'm leaning in—hardly aware of her lips, of mine, of how they brush one another. "I think you've lost your friend," I hear with her mouth pressed against my smile.

As I settle into my seat. As I settle into her. "Tell me..." I say.

And she asks, "What would you like to know?"

So I tent my hands. "Everything."

CHAPTER THIRTEEN

My First Warning Sign

Kennedy

I remember sucking down that drink but still with every intention of making my way back up to my room early enough to finish reading that chapter. Or, I don't know, something.

Anyone nearby would've backed me up on that.

"I'd better go," I'd whispered.

But I was more focused on that navy cotton twill shirt, the one she'd cuffed to the elbow, a heavy curb chain bracelet around her wrist, brass, like something you'd pull from an engine. Her skin, bright. Her phone lit on the bar. An orbit of voices around us.

Logan was making a face that seemed to be asking *Am I doing all right?* So I smiled back to tell her *Yes.* And when she leaned in to me, I inhaled her—fresh, intense, like cut wood yet salty-sweet. Bergamot? Invigorating. It made me forget who I was. I'd never felt that.

I'd really better go, I said again. But I knew it sounded weak, and my voice felt broken.

Because I'd said it, but I hadn't meant it. It was just easier that way. I imagined walking away from her, self-conscious and unsettled, regretting that decision to leave. Knowing she'd be watching me. And how twisted that was, how infatuated I'd become, only worsened as she fingered down the length of my thigh—as if she was pulling off paper from a gum wrapper, ordinary. As if she touched everyone like that, and maybe she did. Afterward, lounging back, taking a slow drink as if nothing had ever happened. As if she hadn't made me feel utterly lost and disoriented. Meanwhile, everything around me—the candle flickering near my phone, the couple over there on the sofa—had dissolved. They hadn't even mattered.

A little while later, we decided to leave our empty glasses and go for a walk. Logan held the door and then hopped down the steps and ahead before reaching back and feeling for my hand, her grip loose as if it might slip away at any moment had I not held onto her. But still she wanted me near. It was so in sync, so intuitive, not just in the way she fit in my hand but in all of it. That moonlit shore. Glittering waves. That slow and steady roll. The air clear, damp but not motionless. Sulphury, briny. Unlike the surf, which felt ominous, threatening. But of course, we didn't go there.

Instead, at the waterline, she bent over and cuffed jeans and we wandered barefoot on sand that felt firm, reflective, only to settle back into the kind that you sink into like a beanbag—warm at its surface but cool where you buried your feet. I can't remember what we talked about. I just remember her voice and wanting to hear it. Wanting to hold her interest the entire time. And I did.

But that's when my drink kicked in. It softened my mind. It made thoughts linger. Musk. Salty-sweet. That hint of bergamot. And she kissed me slowly. Like she was trying to draw some sweet secret out of me.

And maybe she had. Almost mollifying like that—mingling like something veiled, like some sort of understanding that was all our own, unhurried. I really shouldn't do this, I thought again. But then I stopped thinking at all. As if a million years of wanting had fused into a single moment of bliss.

And besides, her hand had already diminished between that crease down the center of my thighs. I had already parted my knees. And I already sensed a tinge where a finger had touched beneath that cotton band between my legs, which felt carnal. It felt like yearning, not love, not affection, but something so lascivious, erotic. So I wasn't thinking *Someone will see me.* I was thinking *Put them in me.* She reached behind my back and I let it snap, her thumb shifting my bra.

As the tide rolled in and out. And that's all I could hear, some words, some soft, soft whispers like that in private, encouraging me. I was lying on my back with sand mixed into every strand of hair, my knees on either side of her and bent, her breath in waves, my pulse, that gust of wind up my shirt. And still with every stitch of our clothing technically on.

Eventually, though, we were racing back to my room. But I'd fallen behind, still buttoning up my button fly, and Logan was just ahead, back-walking, looking me over then tugging my wrist, drawing me in, pressed tight, wrapping me into a kiss. Because the night had grown that unstable.

Before we'd reached the door. Before we'd fallen in, a thin breeze, a glint of light streaming in as I followed her through the room. As we tumbled down on my bed, so clumsy. So presumptuous, she was, tugging and tugging until all our clothes were scattered along the floorboards. Only to crawl up me, between me, down me.

Her breath between my legs rippling through me like those waves of light along the ceiling. Until that fleeting thought that if her mouth were to touch me there, I'd come.

And that happened in glimpses. Like pure white-hot euphoria. Disorienting. Focused and tense and tight. My skin heated, flushed, and that pillow I'd kicked to the floor, my legs quivering, and that rushing, rising, building.

Afterward, we were lying in the dark, spent, the swell of her chest beneath my cheek. Cool sweat on my skin. Cotton sheets twisted at my hips. "What else do you like," she'd asked me. But I hadn't expected conversation. I had expected, as it happens, that she'd have a change of heart. That this would be where we would part.

"I liked *that* just now," I told her, breathless. And we laughed and talked for hours. About that and this. About what we did. About wanting to do it again. About finding time and about friends. About *what excites you?* About crème brûlée and *mmm*, as she gushed and gushed about my body, uncovering it, admiring me, her lips teasing me. Caressing me.

But it's not anything that would've seemed significant to anyone outside of ourselves. "Like ten or eleven months would've been the longest we'd stay." And the way Logan looked at me, as if she hadn't devoured me already. "Which made me the intriguing outsider at the start of each school year."

"Intriguing is how I'd describe you," I said.

And she kissed my grin. "I reinvented myself constantly."

"I didn't reinvent myself until college."

"I didn't stop until college," she told me. "It's like a love-hate thing. Not having that past—or more like, not having someone there to remember it."

"What was your major?" I said.

"Materials science."

And then I asked, "First kiss?"

"She was straight."

"Sorry," I lied.

"Don't be," she said. "It didn't need to last."

Which was my first warning.

Which I ignored.

Why must you make things difficult for yourself? I could imagine my therapist saying.

Not difficult, I'd say. *I'm older, wiser. So I can't keep overlooking such things.* And then I'd wax poetic about *love and how it has to be coupled with things like forethought and logic and prudence.*

But this felt purely physical, she'd tell me in a gotcha way.

To which, I wouldn't respond.

So I asked Logan if she's online. Not that I wanted to connect. Okay so maybe I'd like to connect. "So you've managed to avoid it all this time," I continued, envious.

"It's a bad habit of mine."

"Of yours? What's that?" I said.

Her voice seeming casually cautious. "Not being an early adopter. And don't read into that."

While I peered up from her chest. "How should I read it?"

"Just that it's gotten me in trouble," she said.

"What else gets you in trouble?"

I felt her fingers tickling up my spine. "My impatience."

"Disastrous," I said in jest. "What other quirks should I know about?"

"Royal blue," she told me, "is my least favorite color."

"And what else?" I said.

"Nothing I care to share."

"Oh, come now." But I didn't sound like myself. I sounded so natural, so gratified. Quietly exhilarated. "It's not as if we'll ever see each other again."

She groaned, wavering. "How do you do this?" To be honest, I felt as if I could draw things out of her. And I did. "All right, so, I've been known to sob over random fill-in-the-blank movies." Which was like the most heartfelt thing.

I wonder if we like the same movies, I thought but didn't ask. Instead, I said, "I've only cried over two books, no movies. One was in junior high."

"And the second?" she said.

I had to think about that one. "I guess a year or two ago?"

I could still feel her fingers along my back. "And why was that?"

"I don't know," I said. "It was just intense. And then came that very last page."

"So you cried as you read the last page?"

"I cried during the whole last chapter," I said. "And then I fell asleep."

"Do you read every night?"

"Normally," I said. "Okay, sometimes."

There was a short pause before Logan continued. "I find I'm more emotional at night."

Which I wouldn't disagree with. "I would have cried over this regardless."

"Even in the morning over scones?"

"Do you eat scones?"

"You seem so surprised," she said.

And I could feel my face flush. "Because you don't seem the type."

"What type am I?"

"Black coffee, no breakfast."

She laughed. "You seem the scone type."

"I like them because they're dense."

"And pinchable."

"You assume I'd pinch," I said.

Her brow creased skeptically. "Because you do."

"Doesn't everyone?"

"Everyone who's delicate like you," she said, "reserved."

I sit up, well sort of. "Would you call me reserved just a minute ago?"

"Not a minute ago," she said, grinning.

"And how would you describe me then?"

"On your back?"

"On my back," I said.

"With my face between your legs?"

"Reserved," I scoffed.

"No," Logan said. Then dropped her voice pretty low, though it still seemed bright. "You were rather loud."

"So you think I'm loud?" I said.

"I figured you were just enjoying it."

"Well, I *was* enjoying it."

"Yeah, well," she said, "so was I." There was something in the way she said it, though. Like her voice spoke more than her words. "I love the way you taste," she said indulgently. "I love the way you sound."

"When I'm enjoying it."

"Yes," she said. "You certainly were."

I traced a finger along the warmth of her thigh. "You're awfully sure of yourself."

"Shouldn't I be?"

"And cocky," I added.

"I know where I excel."

"So where else do you excel?"

"That's a tough one," she said, articulating her words cautiously. "You first."

"That's easy enough. Screwing up," I said. "Falling short of my potential. Misinterpreting. Oversleeping—"

"Kissing…" she said.

I glanced up. "You like the way I kiss?" And there's that finger along my back, again.

"And you're awfully good at seducing innocent women," she added.

But I'd been focused too intently on her lips, their shape, their curve, velvety. Recalling how they felt against mine. Memorizing them. "You think I seduced you?"

"Well, yeah," she said.

"And how'd I accomplish that?"

"If I told you," she said, "you'd use it against me."

"Is that how it works?" I asked. "You're that easily manipulated?"

"By you, I seem to be."

"I like that kind of power."

"I bet you do."

My voice softened. "What's that supposed to mean?" But her phone disrupted us. It lit up over there on the table. "Do you need to get that?" And that's when she drew me in. She kissed me, slowly. Soft, slow kisses that seemed to go on persistently, which was not long enough. Teeth tugging my lower lip.

"No," she said, "I don't." There was a laugh in her voice.

"But it's nice to be needed, you said."

"That depends."

"On what?" I asked her.

"On who's doing the needing."

But soon came that exhaustion. "Hey," I nudged.

"Hey," Logan said.

"Tell me," I ventured, "the name of that movie."

"Which one?"

"The one that made you cry," I said, then waited. I could sense the beat of my heart beneath all those jitters.

"Trust me, you've never seen it." It was something I was rolling over in my mind when I heard, "When can I see you again?" And my insides flipped into effervescence all over again.

❖

It's ten a.m., and Logan's gone.

So I'm slipping into a bath beneath bubbles, a bath filled with aromatic salts that make the whole room herbal, my knees peeking up. And all the while, I'm trying to wrap my head around last night. Around everything that's transpired and why, on my first opportunity to take things slow, I've failed so miserably.

Or why I've gotten so tangled up in this—in a moment, in hope, in lending credence—that I've overlooked the clues, the subtle dodge. *The signs.*

Only to be left sorting out a flurry of sensations that all coalesce into a single unavoidable truth, that inescapable reality that Logan's a weekend fling. That none of this is real. That I need to get a grip.

And maybe I'm fine with that. Or at least, maybe I need to be. But the question is, will I be?

As I repeat the maxim *logic over love* while stepping out of the tub and dripping onto the rug, then towel drying and lying across the bed while ruminating in absolute detail over all of those things.

Thinking about what I said. Thinking about what she didn't. Thinking about what we did. Thinking about what I've done. And then I go for a run. Because there's something rejuvenating about this midsummer sun.

And did you know that when you have just the right adrenaline rush, it's not all that bad? It's steady and amped. It's pulsing through me.

Afterward, as I thank the guy who pours me a cup of coffee in the dining area, I glance around—at a marble table held up by a single iron stand. And that vase with white daises. An unopened copy of *The New York Times* and a stack of hefty clay mugs and a bunch of cinnamon-raisin bagels, fresh juice, and a cheese-egg casserole and utensils. Blackberries. And Greek yogurt and Grape-

Nuts in a jar with a generous scoop. And right over there scripted in chalk on the blackboard is today's date and the menu and weather forecast, which predicts a pristine seventy degrees Fahrenheit.

Except nowhere to be seen is Logan. And it doesn't matter that I hadn't expected to run into her until this evening. I still feel disheartened.

So back to breakfast, which I tote upstairs to my room, a room that has been tidied and scoured, folded and fixed in my absence, and where I dine cross-legged in bed while watching a video on demand that's talking about some girls who live in a three-story house on a shady street in Haight-Ashbury, circa 1996—and I'm thinking, I want to live there. In an opulent gingerbread cottage. With swinging hair. Amid blocks and blocks of indie shops. With petal- and pollen-lined walks that lead up to courtyards that are overflowing in Chianti and comradery.

Then I squander the rest of my day in a similar way—channel surfing, caffeine consuming, clothes flipping, and selfie snapping in a moody room that's dripping in nautical light.

It's not until five that the nerves slam into me. Once the sky's simmering and iridescent. Once the bonfire's sizzling, smoke drifting, with distant lights glimmering through dense, salty air. Libations liven the smoky scent of char-grilled and wine-braised, along a sun-drenched shore where we'd planned to meet up.

And where, after trying on three outfits in my quest to find *the one*, I've made my way down fashionably late, or at least slightly, for an evening of fireworks and revelries, having settled on distressed denim and a rather plain shirt that clings, clutching my Baja to warm me when the temperature drops. But still, no sign of Logan. So I text and she pings me back immediately, and we agree to meet up over there at the buffet line.

Which is where I head—filing in as food is being served on cloth-covered tables set up against an odd barn. As the sun wanes.

A small slice, I signal with a pinching motion as I'm handed a plate of boysenberry pie and a cup of fries and a hot dog wrapped in prosciutto, all topped in pesto alongside grilled corn.

But you know how, when you're in a crowd and you're all

alone, how it can tend to feel as if you're being watched. Though I'm reassuring myself that I'm not. That I'm casually conversing or that I'm eavesdropping. That I'm playing it cool. Because, "Small, medium, or large?" they ask. But it's instinctual. That sense that she's beside you. Behind you. Sizing you up as a voice flits up the back of your neck and you turn, still knowing, still hoping to find—

"Logan," I say, relieved.

"I have been waiting for this right here all day." And as I kiss her back, it drips like agony and trickles up the length of my spine.

"Have I missed out on the boysenberry pie?"

"You've cut in just in time for their strawberry tart."

"I'm not a big fan of tart," she says. "But I am hopeless when it comes to pie."

As I catch, in a breeze, her scent, genderless, androgynous. "Which means you have options," I tell her, and we both look up as a gull swoops past.

And she says, "I'd like to hear my options."

"You can either go back to the end of the line," I say, but she bows her head in defeat. "Or," I say, "I could trade my pie for your tart. I'm not a big fan."

"A girl who shares her pie," she says, grinning in the cutest, most foolish kind of way.

And all I need to say about the next however many minutes it takes to get to the end of the line is that it's pleasantly haunting and memorable and dotted in sidelong glances. In shaky voices. In rigid posture. With a reward at the very end in the form of a frosty glass that's layered and stacked. That's blue and red and white, and I'm thinking strawberry or coconut, in a cocktail aptly named The Independent and one that's reminiscent of a Popsicle I used to order from the ice cream truck. We balance all of that on our trays while making our way toward a cute little spot on the porch that overlooks the sea, taking a seat.

I lift my gaze. She takes a drink.

"Well?" I say. "What is it?"

"You won't know until you try."

"Just a hint," I ask and then stir until colors swirl. "Sweet? Tart?"

She chuckles. "You're not supposed to stir." But she's leaning in, which I'm liking a lot.

"Though some things are better swirled," I tell her.

"But you didn't even try." And for a brief moment while I'm watching her sulk, it's as if I've slipped into an abyss. "You do that, and there's no going back."

"Call me a risk-taker," I say, coy. "I am committed to my decision."

"I certainly hope so," Logan says.

"Separate would be extreme," I say. "I like balance. I like a little of each. And, besides, this is prettier."

"It's purple."

Which smacks my tongue. "Actually, it's quite amazing," I tell her, opulent, intense. "And complex. Which is something you won't get unless you stir."

"You like complex?"

"Yes," I say, "I happen to like it a lot."

And in an unexpected, completely divine move, she slips a finger down the cut edge of that pie and reaches over and brings a taste of boysenberry filling up to my mouth, and I suck it between my lips. But we don't say a word about it. She just smiles at me and then glances away—as we eat silently to the clink of utensils against a plate, as the sky chills like a dimming switch into peach, peach chalk, peach creamy, which glows across her skin, peachy cream, softer than her style, which is sharp, edgy, clean, in that coordinated to look uncoordinated way.

"And it doesn't bother you?" she asks me.

"What would bother me?"

"Aren't you curious," she says.

You seem to be, I'm thinking as I glance up. "I'm sure it's like blueberry, strawberry, coconut. Right?"

"There are varieties in each," she says.

"What was it?"

While she sucks that very last bit. "You'll never know."

"I have ways of getting things out of people," I say, nudging her foot beneath the table—and then we just sort of stay that way. A move that sparks something, that ignites something bottomless inside me.

Eventually, though, after they've cleared our plates, she starts telling me about Tanner's birthday and what she'll get, what they'll do. And about some deliveries, about how she likes her coffee, about her apartment. Which feels like life that's been censored down to a few dull books and bad takeout and some shows she saw on Hulu—to our mutual fascination with Ryan Murphy. To this patio weather and sequins. Statement glasses. Which is nice. But it's not last night.

"It was banana pear," she says, adopting a critical tone.

"What, the white?" I say. And she's right. I would've loved it.

It's got to be a good hour later by the time I'm leaning over the edge of that porch railing as she's making her way to that swing, patting the seat beside and giving me a cute, cocked look as if to say *C'mere*. Which I am. I'm taking a seat and glancing up at a few string lights that are threaded through the ceiling beams, my hands trembling.

When I was around seventeen, I was standing in line behind a girl I knew of, but who didn't know me, to order a Diet Coke during a football game. And maybe I'd planned it that way. And maybe it worked. Because we talked and, afterward, she came over and sat by me and we hung out for the rest of the night. The crazy thing is, though, to this day, I couldn't tell you anything about what we said. I couldn't tell you the color of her eyes or how she wore her hair. The only thing I could explain to you in insufferable detail would be her shoes, which were Adidas, paper white with three navy-colored stripes going diagonal down the side, cut in a zigzag with pinking shears. Worn but not smudged, not scuffed, and their soles were a rubbered yellow.

I say this only because as my gaze drops again in tangles over a girl, senseless, it's all that I can see—her shoes. As that mild scent of sea coalesces with woodsmoke, with musk, with androgenous.

As we watch a flurry of cinders drifting and as the sun steps aside to make way for an illustrious prelunar landscape. And I'm feeling that tidal pull when her fingers tickle and curl underneath the palm of my hand, which is the most unbelievable thing.

Smiling irrepressibly, I ask, "so what have I missed? What haven't I asked?"

"Everything," Logan says.

"Why don't you describe your eight-to-five to me, then. In one word."

"In one word?" she says. "But you've yet to ask what I do for fun."

"We'll get to that later," I tell her.

"When I was *so* ready for it now," she says, grinning.

"Were you?" I say. "Good things come to those who wait."

I can't recall if I've ever been given a look that's been this provocative, this seductive. This naturally audacious. "Just one word?" she says. "Demanding." Then she looks at me lazily.

"And what's the most intriguing part?" I say.

"The most intriguing part? About my job. I would have to say that I have it." And afterward, I ask what she means, and she shakes her head in that way you do when you're holding something back. "I guess I don't feel one hundred percent qualified," she says, "to manage or do what I do. But I am. I have for a long time."

"Do you like it?"

"Yeah," she says. "For the most part."

"And what worries you?"

"Nothing," she says.

"Name one thing."

"Politics," she says. "But once you have that down—"

"Do you?"

"It's unsettling," she says, then stops to look at me. Like she won't stop looking at me.

"How so?"

"*You* know."

"I do know," I say. "But tell me."

"It's all about knowing the right people and clicking and getting ahead," she says. "Knowing the right people who can get you ahead. But you have to say the right thing—"

"Would you leave because of it?" I say.

"I'm not there on merit," she says, shaking her head in a sad way.

"You sound a little ambitious," I say.

"Not at all. Just lucky."

"I doubt luck had anything to do with it."

"We're all replaceable," she says.

"Do you really believe that?"

"You take what you get. While it lasts," Logan says. And next is that spark of fear, like she's talking about me, like she's talking about this. Which is weird, how our minds work. "How'd we get on to this?"

"Why?"

She grins warmly. "Because I feel so far away." And next, an arm's on my shoulder. She's drawing me in. "You're not cold, now, are you?" It's just the sweetest thing. Before dropping her voice to a hush. "I'll keep you warm." It's got that calm confidence about it. That reassurance I felt last night.

Not that I share that with her. Instead, I say, "Luck."

"That's me."

"Lucky?" I ask.

"On occasion," she says.

"I like the way you kiss," I say. Since I'm thinking it. Since it's true.

"And what brought that up?" Skeptically as she says it, she's clearly flattered. "Would you like me to kiss you?"

"I'd like you to kiss me," I say.

"Whatever you want, I'll do," she says.

Oh, how my mind reels. "No, you won't."

Then she leans in to me. She leans in and brushes aside some hair and whispers near my ear. "All you've got to do is ask," I hear soothingly. "Tell me what you want."

I must have the stupidest grin on my face. "I've never been asked before."

"How do you get what you want," she says, "if you've never been asked?"

And we settle into it. Into its familiar silence. "How about I get back to you on that?" I say. Which feels so familiar to me. She feels familiar to me.

And I'm thinking, *Don't forget this.* Don't let me forget how this feels. Like, even if it hurts, even if it obliterates me, don't let me forget how it feels.

I can't exactly say how long we sit like this in our silence. Just that it's almost jarring when, unexpectedly, her friend bursts in, squeezes in, crowds in, bright faced and even brighter lipped in that shade of red that fades throughout the day, prompting that hand, that arm, to draw away.

Which is shifting a mood. A mood that, moments ago, felt enormous, felt intimate and weightless. One that now feels shapeless and reckless and wrong.

Overshadowed by that odd comfort you feel when you're invited in, when eavesdropping on talk of a blossoming beach party—about that group down there with their sparklers, those glowing circles in the night sky. Those crisp bright lines now fading into fluttering fragments that float like burnt paper.

And then others join in, sunbaked, carrying icy drinks and wearing suits still wet from their swim.

Before one thing leads to the next, and we, too, are out there on the shore as Logan's arms slip silently around my waist, gently, delicately, facing me when our hips meet. While Tanner's striking a match that makes a glow, makes it hiss. And then there's the matter of this kiss. Which is so deliberate and so decisive that all I can feel are the sounds from empty voices around us, that beat of my heart, this flirting tinge of pain as sparks drop along my arm, with her moves cloaked beneath the ash of night.

❖

As the night wound down, we spent a little longer on that swing, and I don't know, we just had this affinity, which is hard to express. Considering this, we must've seemed irreverent to the others, half a world away, as the air dipped, her toe tapping and tapping to kick off to the soundtrack of a solitary owl.

I couldn't even say how late it must've been once we finally went up. But a night like that shouldn't end, not like that. I kept wondering if she knew, if she could see the effect that she had on me. It had to be the most illogical, unmanageable thing I'd ever felt.

"So," she said in an almost gravelly way, fatigued, pausing affably outside my door as I fished for my key, which was right in my pocket the whole time. But her eyes were studying me. "I guess this is where I head back," as she nodded down the hall. And sure, sure, I didn't want that. Not that I told her this, not outright. Instead, I turned my cheek with a lingering gaze down that tight corridor, which was pleasantly lit in a flattering hue, you know, not wanting to seem rude, let alone presumptuous. Then another couple bumped past us, and I remember thinking *It's late, isn't it?* Those two are going to bed. They're going to sleep. And I've gotten so carried away and a bit delusional, and should I be?

I mean, this can't be everything. But it's not nothing, either. Yet I can't say exactly what it is.

And when have I smiled so much? I kept smiling at her when I was going for something a little more serious, more enticing, more mature. Not cutesy. Not schoolgirl, which is how I felt.

So I turned my back to her, perhaps in a way to hide, then tried to twist my key in that little slot, to do so somewhat competently, when she just sort of grabbed me by the waist and turned me around and said, "I know it's late," in this quiet way as she was drawing me in, which depleted me, but it was just an embrace. And this look on her face just seemed to sweep the world away. Eventually, somewhere inside of this stillness, inside of this should we, shouldn't we, this wavering, she kissed me softly, and it felt like something spiraled inside of me, and maybe I lost control.

It's something that would've felt shallow or empty or

thoughtless or rushed if it'd been anyone else. But instead, this felt like a flight, a fall, the whirlwind of it all.

So why had she loosened her grip, afterward? Why had this shifted? How had she grown so removed—and so abruptly, so unexpectedly that I hadn't the time to adjust? It left me stumbling through a memory of wanting, of wondering.

"I had a really nice night," I heard her say, but her tone had become detached. It had grown polite, uncomfortably so. And I figured, she's leaving. So this was a kiss good night. Which felt oddly right. It was all right.

"Of course," I said. And I smiled with a nod. As I began to edge away.

"Tomorrow," she added conversationally, "is an early day. Not by choice." And of course, of course, of course. I shrugged.

"Why is that?" I asked.

"Invite me in," she said.

And I laughed, briefly, which is my way of letting off steam because this was more than I was capable of feeling. "Yeah?" I teased. And we wove our fingers as she brushed her lips against mine. "I want *details*," I said into hers.

But moments passed and she kept pressing, and I was pressed against that wall. My stomach plunged. "I *want* you," she said. And her voice just ached. I ached.

But you have me. You have me. And there was that dip, that stir, a flutter.

Still, somehow, I was resilient and so mindful of so many things, like her gaze, hopeful, collected, desirous, insistent. When it came to experience, she had that and she knew it well. But wrapped in her confidence peered shyness, a soft dawdling uncertainty. As if she hadn't known what to do. But she does, she had.

Yet the more she withdrew, the more she pulled back, the more I had to have, which is something I think she knew.

"The question is," I'd said, "how badly?" Which felt almost heated or cross, incensed in the way we went about it, in the way I was yielding, as the latch made that clack at my back in a room so blind that it felt unsettling as we moved ineffectually, heels clipped by the bed, as she wedged her jeans between my bent knees, my legs splayed, feet flat on the bed, with the mattress causing me to lean farther into her body.

I could almost imagine the look on my face as those feeble sounds escaped my lips. Just as I could imagine my lying there indecent, stripped down on a bed, my panties hooked to my ankle before I'd flung them to the floor. My pulse throbbing.

Into a cadence that felt like a tickle of sea up my leg, that ache, as all thoughts, all resolve dissolved like honey dripping, slipping. As she lingered *right there, like that,* bracing my knees apart as my mind went blank.

After I came, I curled over, and she walked to the sink in her underwear and, on her way back, grabbed two bottles of water that were stowed in that little refrigerator only to crawl right back into bed, twisting the cap and then passing it to me. And we lay back, disheveled, me wrapped inside her arm. Not asleep, just thinking, just silence, which came across, I know, as silent amusement. Because she asked me, "What are you thinking?"

And I said, "Why do you want to know?"

"Is it about me?"

"I was thinking about this thing I do," I told her.

"What kind of thing do you do?"

"It's just a silly thought I had about shoes."

CHAPTER FOURTEEN

Affaire de Coeur

Logan

Show Tanner a seedy London basement bar at midnight—No, wait. Show her a lesbian in a Stetson trucker cap at sundown just aching to take her for a ride down a country road to an open field to sip whiskey under the stars in the back of her Ford pickup truck, and she's all about it. Show her the perfect opportunity to sleep in, however, like, say, after that all-nighter or now—not so much. Even on weekends or after we'd lost that hour in the spring, and even at the expense of someone who might've needed...

Me: *One more hour.*

Or two. And really, how is it even feasible for someone to be such a night owl and a morning bird all in one, concurrently? It's almost as if her circadian rhythm has grown so accustomed to guzzling insane amounts of Caffè Americano that it wants its fix pronto, not realizing that a few extra z's might just as easily alleviate that insatiable need to get ultracaffeinated in the first place.

And thus explains—

Tanner: *Not today. Wake up, gorgeous.*

As I roll on my back thinking, Why? But there are tangles of hair beside me.

Me: *Trying.*

Me, again: *No, really, I am going to kill you.*

Tanner: *No, babe, you're going to thank me. Profusely.*

As my mind backtracks to last night, to a beach, to sparklers, to that warm taste of sugary rum. And next, I'm vaguely recalling her little arrangement, her ménage à trois.

Tanner: *This is what's missing in my life.*

Except, just beyond the screen of my phone is a figure I could only imagine some hours earlier. On a girl who, unlike me, seems to have no qualms showing it off, I swear to blessed God.

Tanner: *You can hook back up with Kennedy tonight.*

Me: *It's not that.*

Tanner: *So you'll swing by in a few?*

But it's seven a.m. I stare at the wall, then shield the morning's glare with my arm. And all the while Kennedy's rolled to her stomach, heels crossed, elbows smashed at her sides.

I lift my gaze. "Remember how…last night, I said"— recognizing my voice is still groggy, that I sound like a pit of despair—"Tanner needs me," I add, realizing she has never needed me, until now. "Due to some mess, she said, with her ex," I lie.

And this scent, though, what is it? It's like vanilla zest has spilled into a vat of orange petals and surf and warm skin and introspection, sunrise, as she slips two feet off the edge of the bed— and can I mention here the level of confidence, the level of comfort she exudes in her skin, which is absolutely mesmeric. It's an ease I've never felt as I've crossed the length of a room in the nude.

"But you *came* with her," Kennedy's conceding softly as she pinches two panels of curtain until they're sealed shut, less one single blinding streak.

And as she makes her way back, I'm realizing this place is identical to mine. Not slightly, not floorplan, but identical right down to the same framed diptych over two plush chairs against the wall and even that small writing table. Her MacBook sleeping on top. Yesterday's peonies still fresh in their vase. Her phone. And luggage, unzipped, near that shirt I tugged off with prurient curiosity. Our bedding kicked to the floor.

"You look deliriously good," she groans as she's crawling up the length of the bed, up the length of me, before easing her way into the crook of my arm. "How's it possible, first thing in the morning?"

As I trace the curve of her lip, like berries and cream. "Aren't you funny," I say. "Tanner and I, you know, we're not call-every-day, bake-cookies, drink-drinks-on-a-deck kind of friends. It's more like, call if you're in despair." Or on an illogical high after your latest sexual conquest, which is something I'm not about to share.

"Well, we can't stay in bed all day," she tells me in this weak little voice.

I glance at the door. "So you *want* me to leave?" I ask.

"I don't want you to leave," she says.

"So you'll miss me?" I prompt, grinning.

Then we fall into an unusual stillness until all you can hear are those voices coming from the next room over, deep, masculine, muffled. "I'm not saying I won't," she's telling me with fingers that slip beneath sheets, taunting. "But I'm not saying I will, either."

I glance across the room. "Well," I say, "I might." Then I shrug. "You'll miss me?" And by the look on Kennedy's face, I think she might be into me.

"I want to know about your big plans today," I say.

"I plan to get back to those things you've distracted me from."

"So, reading?" I say.

"And other things…" she says in this cliffhanger way.

"Well, you shouldn't expect a girl to leave you," I say apologetically, "this early in the morning."

"Then when's an acceptable hour for a girl to leave after a night like that?" And again, she smiles just slightly. "Would that be ten, eleven o'clock?" Her fingers draw numbers on my chest. "Or do you take her out to lunch right afterward?" It's almost as if neither of us have any idea how to dodge the underpinnings of this conversation, the what-happens-next parts.

I sigh. "You're not making this any easier, you know." As we simply beam at one another.

"You're not being rude," she tells me.

I drop my head. "All right."

"Maybe I'll see you tonight."

"Maybe," I say in more of a maybe, maybe not way.

❖

You try juggling two espressos and a box of pastries up a staircase, let alone knocking on a door with your hands full. Which I do, I have, and Tanner greets me in full-on Hollywood boudoir, a look that should be a mood. Because she's crushing it, collapsed, fanning herself on the sofa, those full lips beckoning for...debauchery.

"That was the best, most mind-blowing sex I've ever experienced in my entire life."

"Which means you have a very low benchmark," I say, then take a seat in a room that's lit in a flattering shade of eight o'clock gay.

"What've you brought me?" she says, flashing a glance that shouts *flattered* as she opens a box of brownies, of maple brioche, of apple turnovers and unknowns, all glazed or crumble topped, along with some spread-on salted caramel cream.

But those éclairs are all for me. "An assortment," I tell her.

"You do this with all your girls, don't you?"

"Only those who matter," I say.

Once it registers, she shakes her head in that don't-look-at-me way. "Am I all yours today?"

"I don't know," I say, filling a plate before taking a seat. "That depends, am I all yours?"

She's spreading caramel cream across the top of a brownie as if it were toast. "Until four this evening," she informs me, saying, "God, I have earned this savage appetite," followed by her semimaternal, "You weren't up when I texted you this morning." Which is usually code for *tell all*. Which I don't.

"Nobody's up this early," I snap, but not in a mad way. Just an exhausted way. Then I lean back and study ceiling tiles for a little while. "So, tell me, is this love at first threesome?" I laugh. "Sorry, that was bad," I add, giggling again because *that bed*, which can only be described as somewhere between erotic ennui meets a romantic balcony of botanicals meets relationship goals. Not that I want to know any of it. I don't.

And after taking a bite, she blots her mouth with a napkin. "I'm not in love." Still, she's dodging eye contact.

"But the question is, are they?" I say.

"At one time," she says pensive. And my gaze, for lack of anything better to focus on, drifts past her shoulder toward that table over there, her round-trip stash of upmarket water, a doorhanger, that wine list, her wardrobe flung and hung as if this was dress rehearsal, paired with that distinct overlay of lemon-sage soap. "Do you think everyone who cheats on their *other* could potentially cheat on you?"

"Why do you ask?"

"I mean," she says, "do you think I should add this little screening question? Have you cheated? Have you been in an open relationship?"

In reality, though, she has no qualms when it comes to breaking in. And that's not to say she's evil per se. It's just that she's right, that jealousy, that other, that interest, can strengthen their own attachment. The minute someone shows interest in what you have, you want them more. Even if you don't even want them to begin with. Even if you're done with them. She'll bring them closer because she's a threat. So in her mind, she's doing those two a favor, given a few days ago, they were at their brink, comfortable, lackadaisical, and losing interest in one another.

"I thought they weren't cheating if it was consensual?" I say, her words not mine. And dear God, this éclair is eight o'clock perfection. "And what would that little disclosure say about you to new suitors—that you caused an affair." I chuckle. "Or are you polyamorous now?"

"I'm not," she says. "I'm definitely not poly. It's fine with me as long as it's their relationship. Not that I could ever stand it in mine. I couldn't have this in mine. I'm far too possessive. Which is interesting." We pause to eat. And, as she licks her fingers, her gaze drifts back to mine. "So, you had a good time."

"What tipped you off?" I say.

"Your hair, always. Not to mention the fact that you haven't changed your clothes. We left you two making out."

"Thank you for that," I say.

"It was a bit much," she says.

"And no," I tell her, "not everyone who cheats at one time will cheat on you. It's situational. Don't be ridiculous. And maybe don't add one more thing to your selection process. Maybe don't screen girls in the first place. And don't let one girl make you bitter."

Then Tanner goes on about that, about the one girl who cheated on her. One time. Literally eons ago. It's like she's never moved on.

"Fidelity is such a fine little fickle line," I tell her. "But you, you're just like them. You always stick around so long that you implode in the end. That you both implode in the end. Just to prove yourself. Just to prove you're right. That you've chosen well. That you're the one who'll fix what could never be fixed." What could never be yours. "And why, because some fools in your life won't accept you for who you are."

"Yeah, well, *you* try fighting a whole squad, you know, just waiting to watch you fail. Just waiting to watch you break. Because, as they'll say, if you can't make it work with this girl…and that girl…and the next, you're *maybe* not gay. That's what they always say. So completely logical." She slices an apple turnover until it's in half. "Because I embarrass them. *I* embarrass *them*," she says, smiling with contempt as she takes a bite. "I certainly hope so. I love that for me."

"But you're smiling," I say. "I didn't mean to upset you."

She swallows, takes a drink, then grins, shaking her head as she does. "Because it was so fucking great last night," she tells me.

"So you've said."

As she slips back inside of herself. "So, this is our last day."

"What's on the agenda?" I say.

"The show, silly. The barn. They're calling for rain."

"As they have every single day since our arrival," I say. Admittedly, I do love to see her smile. "And whatever they did last night—"

"What about it?"

"It couldn't have been *that* great."

"Oh, not at all." She's shaking her head, clearly giddy. "It's just two women using *me* to make the other jealous."

"You're such a pillow queen," I mock.

"Minds and hearts and pussies wander," she says, then takes a long, thoughtful breath.

Tanner is like her own brand of tragedy. "They'll never get over you," I say.

"As if they even wanted me," she says. "They wanted each other, and I was merely a conduit to remind them of that. It's all such a beautiful mess," she says, her fingers glazed, sugared. Lips sucking. "But I'd like to think that, perhaps, I've done a good deed. That they're on the right path to wherever this might lead." As she pauses momentarily to reflect. "They're sweet, you know? They are. I hope they find it."

"What do you think *it* is?"

"I really don't know," she says. "We talked about that."

"So," I say, "you've had an actual conversation?"

"Of course we did."

"And what about?"

"You know, stuff, questions," she tells me. "They asked about me. They wanted to know so much about me." And by now, our sufficiently cooled coffee is impeccable for drinking, as Tanner hides behind a mug, peers up from behind mad morning hair. "The one apparently saw me and lost her mind and asked."

"And she's the one you'd choose?"

"I wouldn't choose," she says now. "They're not exactly available."

I nod. "Right."

"But privately, she asked. She asked if I'd ever felt, you know, a sort of wrong attraction for someone. Because she felt that way for me. *Have you felt something you shouldn't, and how'd that go—or how'd you go about it? How'd you control it. Did you?* She wanted me to say no, that I didn't control it. But the thing is, she won't let that girl go. She made her choice." She rests a hand on her chest. "I thought about what it's like to feel that."

"And what'd you say?" I glance sidelong. "That you haven't?"

"Of course not," she says. "All my attractions have been well within the standard social norms." I set my mug down. "Well, perhaps all but one. One time I felt, like, okay, just shut it down."

Scandalous. "This ought to be good."

She straightens up, stacks saucers, centers her mug—zeroing in on me. "It was kind of about you," she mumbles.

"Wait, me?"

"We were friends, you know?" I drop my gaze, chuckle. "Not now," she adds, haughty. "I know you now. You're way less hot."

"Gee, thanks."

"We had just barely met," she says.

"Well, you should've told me," I say. "It might've been fun."

She smiles at me. And I smile back at her. And afterward, it's like a mess of glances we keep flinging across the silent, uncooperative room. "You brought up way too much food. You know that?"

"Save it," I say. "They might want it later."

She crosses the room, stows that box. "So anyway, that was their demise. Two best friends stupid enough to think *Let's hook up*. And that's what they feel for one another, a sweet saccharine dispassionate friendship."

"I wouldn't call that stupid," I say.

"It's something like that," she says. "And this pretty little box is all for me."

"You don't share well, do you?"

"I share extremely well," she says. "It's just that they're not coming back here tonight. This isn't a thing."

"What do you mean, this isn't a thing?"

"I sent them to their room to make up," she tells me.

"And have you heard from them since?"

"I have. Not that I'll respond." She smiles, meek, and from her phone, she reads, "*I can't not see you again. But for the record, I was their first. And look, it can be very, very beautiful with the right person. With the right people.*" But she's speaking from heartbreak, and heartbreak has its way of making just about anything, including this, feel oddly beautiful.

"Well, I'm glad you're not falling in love," I say.

Tanner sits with a heel tucked beneath her. "Well, I can't say I'm glad that you *have*."

I laugh. "What, fallen in love? You know I don't do those things."

"Logan, you're like that *Casablanca* kiss and *O sweet Juliet*, all full of butterflies and bliss. She'd best be careful with that. She's sweet, and she's clearly into you."

"For a weekend. While on vacation." I shrug. Since we'll be heading back bright and early tomorrow. So I'm thinking about that when Tanner's phone goes off, which she reads, musing, grinning, before she sets it back down on the table. "Your affaire de coeur?" I ask.

"No, it's someone else," she says, offering up the silliest grin. "That girl who started following me on Instagram."

"And how's that going?"

She shrugs, fidgeting. "You know, this place will always remind me of caramel cream," she remarks, clearly sidetracking our conversation. "You remember those candy dots—they're like sugar that's been dipped in food coloring, pastel pink and yellow and baby blue, and you have to pull them off that sheet of paper and the paper always sticks? Those will always remind me of Carri. She's the one who took me to a candy shop on our first date—if you can call it that, a date. I mean, it's never that formal. But I had a craving for Belgium chocolate. She had a craving for dots. And we shared. Remember her? She's the one who broke it off in the morning. Who breaks up in the morning? You break up at night."

"There's an Italian bistro," I say, "famous for its garlic knots, and that's where I met Emily. It's where she worked and I'd hang out and she'd mull around and I'd mess with her during break. Which eventually won her over."

"Exes," Tanner says, "I either regret them or still want them." But I don't regret any of them. Though I don't necessarily want them. "Some girls just click, you know?"

And I think about that. "Perhaps," I say.

"And look what we have in the end. Candy dots and garlic knots. Isn't that the very best thing?"

CHAPTER FIFTEEN

Billet-Doux

Kennedy

There's the door, or is it? And can't they hear…the plumbing, the shower, the valves clashing shut as I reach for a towel, flustered and wishing my heart, now sprinting, would calm down. Relax. At least you've rinsed your hair and aren't coated in soap or shaving or anything like that. In fact, you look good, I realize as I glance past the mirror. You look incredibly good, actually, which I'll credit to last night, to things, this robe offering little more in the form of coverage than a towel. But it's eight o'clock, and who has time to decompress let alone wake up enough for, well. When I answer, it's not even her.

Instead, it's a delightful man in a terry cloth bucket hat, all bronzed up with a pearly white grin as he chimes, "Room service!" only to make his peppy way in, remarkably alert alongside my had-a-late-night aromatic coma. Alongside my wakeful only enough to slip a tip into the palm of his hand.

"But…" Did I order this? I think to myself, and clearly sensing my confusion, he hands me a card-sized note, then sets a breakfast spread on the table, under which I take a seat and pause to read. But it's not typed or embellished or embossed or anything like those business cards you find forked in delivery flowers. And yet, there are flowers, a pale bouquet wrapped in burlap, which feels humbling, energizing as he seals the door shut, departing in a blink. In a breeze.

As I tuck my hair back instinctually to draw it out of my face.

Good morning, she writes. *I was thinking about what you said and wondered if you might want to*... I pinch the tip off a dessert cake that he's left with me. *Because I've tried and tried and I can't get you out of my mind*. Which flips my pulse into some stupid loopy falling-in-love out-of-touch young-dreamer sort of thing until all I can do is lie on my back in wistful solitude as I'm taking every bit of this in amid the virginal flavors of lemon-lavender cake and cinnamon scones and the most ambitious double shot of espresso. My mood composed. Cool. Confident. Clear. Knit in a summer breeze.

Stilled like this in thoughtless concentration for a good hour at least, or until I'm caffeinated and my hair's had time to dry. Which prompts me to reshower in order to get just the right style. Then I settle on this bikini, which complements, under a comfortable cotton shirt and a loose pair of shorts before heading out, wondering whether it's the caffeine or adrenaline that's now causing this rush.

I reach the bottom of the staircase, where the common room is feeling much more in line with my mindset, piquant, white but not overly bright—more subdued—with alabaster shiplap. I hadn't noticed. It's disguising a door that's now ajar to reveal a narrow back staircase. And over there, the subtle drift of a curtain as it balloons, as it deflates. The scent of dark roast lingering with a passing hint of unisex cologne. With a party of four still dining as I walk past. As they're bemoaning such a bad night's sleep while setting their distemper off in air quotes, in side-eye. But that was the weather mostly, they say.

And there's the empty table where we met, or where she sat, playing a game, informal, as if now offering me a midmorning confessional—reflective, introspective. Stealing my attention until a man breezes past, then down those stairs and back up as he busily arranges a buffet, perhaps brunch, clearing plates, slipping jars of yogurt into an ice-filled bowl. And another outside sweeping steps, clearing sand. I smile and say hi as I approach, as I stride past. As I step off into a clear midday sun, the waves rhythmic, consistent. The kind of peace you can only feel when you've left it all behind, that car traffic, that occasional jet as it rumbles, those sirens back home.

Then I take a vacant seat under an umbrella, a towel spread

first, and once settled, I send a quick little text. *Thank you.* One I've delayed for reasons I won't share and one I close with a period thinking anything more, an exclamation, would feel too smitten, too easy—or all of those things I am when I'm with her. That side I try to hide. As I open up my book, the sound of her text chimes in.

Logan: *You're very welcome.*

How is it the simplest reply can feel, I don't know, almost tactile?

Logan, again: *Ignore the note.*

Me, grinning: *How am I supposed to ignore your note?*

Logan: *Please. It's over the top.*

Me: *So you didn't mean it?*

And then there's a lull in our chat, uncomfortably so. One that's so long that I give up on waiting and return to my book.

Logan: *I did.*

Releasing butterflies. Too many butterflies.

Me: *Are you always this moody?*

Logan: *I had thoughts about doing something else.*

Me: *Like what?*

Logan: *Like inviting you over, but then...*

Me: *Social obligations.*

Logan: *Right, social obligations.*

I am smiling so large it's painful. And then guests mingling, voices, the clouds up there now bending, now splitting open to release more heat. The air earthy, sensual, nearly whipping my soul away. As I stare longingly at the phone just waiting. Just wanting her. As she's typing.

Logan: *I was just wondering if that's taken.*

If what's taken?

I always pause a moment when I'm unable to interpret someone's words, someone's text, their joke, when I don't get the joke. Except this feels more fumbling and clumsy, like asking your boss for a raise. Because I can't think of a single thing I can say except, well, laughter always works, an emoji, or I could wait and hope for...I don't know.

And that's when this soft trace of a voice blows against my

ear, and I turn and am caught by a glimpse of her sun-blinding grin, her laughter leaning over my chair, stirrings, a flush, that heat that's rising, that's filling my cheeks.

She takes a seat. "Did I startle you?" she says.

As I dodge her gaze, her lingering on me, which is unnerving, given this is not your basic two-piece suit she's wearing. It's more athletic, more firming, and I apologize, she is just a new level of incredible, isn't she? That gaze—that sweet, sincere, sensual gaze she's always offering up, which is leaning in.

"Are we having a good morning?" I hear, as those words, her voice just brushes against my lips. Deliciously charming this morning.

"What happened to your friend?" I say.

"She's still figuring this all out up there, you know, what she'll wear," Logan says. "It's a process." And alas she glances away and just lies there, she's lying on her back as I gaze down to that dip below her abdomen. And oh, these things I'm imagining. But here we are. "I'm just killing a little time," she tells me. "I hope that's okay?" And there's that rush, ascending. Though our actual conversation is perfectly light, perfectly boring, mundane, and nothing to get jumbled up over, except for its newness, for our unfamiliarity. It's more like, I'll say one thing and she'll say another and we'll laugh. And then she'll give me that look right there, which carries a subtle nuance of *I know what you want. I know what you like.* And she's right about that.

But what does she really know?

As Logan reads the glaring screen of her phone and, after thumbing a reply to whomever, I sense, out of the corner of my eye, that she's nearer. That she's leaning over me, shadowing me, cooling me. Yet all I can discern or distinguish in this is an outline of her frame, backlit, shading me from that heat as it rises—then lips, a tease, but she sinks right here along with me. "God," I can hear her say. Because she thinks I'm so beautiful. She thinks I'm something else. And the craziest part about it is, she makes me believe it. As her mouth presses a smile against mine. "*Mmm*, you're like the hottest thing ever," I hear.

But then she draws back, touching me, my lips, a knee, which is such a small gesture, the subtlest. "I unfortunately need to go." As she's slipping sunglasses up from the tip of her nose. "That was Tanner."

But what has she done to me?

Why have I let her?

"I'll see you later." I smile.

"Six o'clock?" she asks.

As I open my book with purpose, more purposeful, more centered. "Six o'clock." I nod.

CHAPTER SIXTEEN

iPhone Paparazzo

Logan

Tanner's already connived me into joining her for a dip. Mind you, no other guest is actually in the water. They're alongside it, dry. Chaise lounging, promenading, conversing, that coconut water meets grasslands on the dune vibe, albeit seaside. Not that I intend to stay dry this entire time. It's just that, well, this is not Aruba. We're not talking pleasant water temperatures or turquoise translucence.

Nonetheless, she's guilt-tripped me into acting as iPhone paparazzo under the guise of best friendship. Which means a photo of Tanner taking a photo of me as foam assaults our legs. Tanner cavorting along the shore, peering back. Tanner gripping my hand as she guides me into the water—all for the sake of her Instagram feed.

I'm just relieved this whole charade has transpired long after Kennedy's gone up.

And speaking of, I'm not oblivious to the fact that she pulled off her shirt back there the moment I stepped away, leaving little more than two flimsy bikini strings to cover it all up—and little to the imagination. It just didn't help to think about it. Because had I, I would've invited her up to my room without a moment's hesitation. Which wouldn't have been wise.

Since all of this is interspersed with, "Well, how do I look?" as Tanner takes a seat sidesaddle on a padded chaise lounge. That downward gaze. Focused, intent, twisting a lock of hair and then tugging it back coquettishly.

But I can sense my brow crunched. So I switch to feigning engagement. "You look…" How do I put it? Her face partially shaded from the sun. "Posed," I say.

Which does not sit well with her. "I don't want to look posed. I want to look candid. Try and catch me off guard," she's saying in that voice I only hear once she's applied one of those clay face masks, motionless, at least once it's pretty much dry, suppressing any semblance of expression. And in doing so, she's softened her swigging a bottle of Coca-Cola on the shore in matching lipstick vibe with something more, I don't know, somber, moody, cynical. More me. And yet all the while still offering me a robust glimpse of cleavage. "All right," I say, chuckling at our absurdity.

"Stop," she's saying.

"What'd I do now?"

"I'm going for serious here," she tells me in quite the serious tone. "And you're laughing."

So I lean back. "Sultry…" I say.

"Yes, but not intentionally so," she instructs me. "I'm hoping for something more voyeuristic."

"Voyeuristic?" I ask with piqued interest.

"Yes, more documentary. Peeking. Candid." Except it's like a dark curtain's been drawn or a storm's rolling in—fortunate, given this light, almost silver, which is transforming her otherwise pert seaside romp into something more natural, softer, diffused, passé, as if snapped on expired film with just a few slits of rays piercing in as she shifts from jaded to indulgent to a million miles away. "Why am I so tired?" she says, no mention of her late night, her early day.

"You still look amazing," I say.

"Listen," she says, "were you to, say, end a situation, a hookup, how do you normally go about that? I mean, what do you say, you know, to avoid any of that spite?"

"A hookup," I tell her, "ends. It's understood."

"What if it's more casually uncasual?" she insists.

"Does this have something to do with this weekend?" I ask.

She leans in. "Someone's getting attached."

Which makes me chuckle. "Don't say I didn't warn you."

"I don't want to be a bitch."

"Calm down," I add. "Casual doesn't travel for miles."

"But she's willing to."

"Then leave the door open. And don't say it. She can read the room."

"But if the tables were turned," she says, "I think I would want a more direct approach."

"No, you wouldn't."

"It needs to be brutal," she adds. "It needs to. For closure's sake."

"In that case, you will be the bitch," I say. "She won't like you."

And her sigh. "But when it's vague," she says, "I'm left to wonder."

"Ghost her," I say.

"I can't ghost." But just then, the concierge steps in with a tray of truffles—a tray of coffee-filled, of caramel, of chocolate fudge. A tray of options and questions and choices, which we graciously accept. And as he steps away, "I love this place," she tells me. "It's like they offer little trinkets that you don't even need throughout the day."

While I stare at her, absorbed. "You do realize they're only buttering us up to get a good Yelp review." To which she shrugs. "So, hey, what about this? Just fade out, like into that dreaded friend zone. And when she brings it up, you start with something like, where's this going? And maybe we're better off friends. That way, you skirt blame and she won't feel rejected."

"You're astonishingly good at breakups."

Unfortunately. "Yeah," I say. But she's back on her phone, blocking some glare or just secretive. Only thing is, I know this grin. "And why did your mood just switch like that?" Along with this look in her eye. "What's on your phone?"

"This girl," she drawls.

"You met someone?"

"On Instagram," she hurries to say. "And there it is…I know what you're thinking. But it's not some online fling, and don't let me overthink this."

And I know what's coming. *If only I could trust this.*

"You've got to back me on this. Because she's blown my mind away, it's like chemistry, like otherworldly."

And wait, wait. *I trust her implicitly.*

"Logan, it's like I trust her implicitly." I smile, hesitant. "I could stare at this picture all day. God, isn't she gorgeous? And I'm oh-so emotional. And I'm oh-so sorry. But tell me this. Do you believe in"—don't say it—"love at first sight?"

"Absolutely, unequivocally," I say, "not." But do I even mean it?

"Why not?" she grumbles, reverting back to her phone. "I'm thinking I want to know her," she adds, "for just a little while before I…you know."

We lock eyes. "Before what?" I ask.

"Before we're…intimate."

"Intimate?"

"I've never in my life felt this good," she says, gushing. "And that might be the only way to *keep* feeling this good." So I mention purity culture and patriarchy and, and, and. That whole narrative, which we've talked about ad nauseam. And she's like, "We're not getting married, silly." Flippant like that. "I'm thinking three, four weeks is all."

"But what does one ascertain, exactly, during those weeks of self-righteous celibacy?"

"I'll ascertain, as you say, her innermost self." She is so dreamy eyed. "And she will ascertain my innermost self."

"I see. So what I'm getting is you'll talk about the names of every dog she's owned for the past three decades and childhood trauma…and *What's your favorite color.* And bucket lists. And *What'd you eat for breakfast?* And what else, exactly, during your umpteenth puritanical date. Then, once you've ooooed and ahhed over your mutual appreciation for random fun facts, the two of you will virtuously and ignorantly head to bed separately—sexually repressed. And I mean, what if she snores." I shrug, aggravated. "You'll never know. Because you haven't had sex."

"Who cares if she snores?" Tanner snaps, defensive. "It's deeper than that. So, are you done with your jealous tirade?"

"Yes," I say. "And no."

"Too bad it never worked out between the two of us."

"It could," I tell her, "when we're sixty—unless you're frigid like this. And given you're still single." Because this is so not you.

"I can't wait that long."

"But you'll wait for her," I say, crouching in the sand beside. "You'll be a hot sixty."

"I'll be a hot ninety," she says.

I clear my throat. Then we get back to vaguely ignoring one another. Because the point of our spending the day together isn't to stomp on her good time, or her delusional, her written in the stars, her absolute naivety, this bliss—because Lord knows I'm feeling enough of that myself. Instead, it's been to sit things out as she recants every last exhausting detail about this girl, on her good nature. On patience and moderation and persistence—along with more drivel about trust and blah blah blah. When all the while, I'm secretly scanning a text that Kennedy sent, again and again and again—dangerously pondering a random reply from out of the blue when Tanner leans in to peek.

It's not that she says anything about it, though.

"She doesn't want to settle down," I hear.

As I rub the back of my neck. "So she lives in an Airstream?"

"She wants to see the world," she says all singsong. "Isn't that fascinating?"

"And what does she do for work?"

"She *has* a job," she says. "Do you have any idea how much one of those cost? She's well-off."

"Doing what?" I say.

"I don't know. She's a knowledge worker."

"And what is that, exactly?" I say.

"She's not tethered to a desk. She can work wherever. You know, Silicon Valley. Zoom. And, besides, so what—I happen to care more about who she is. I couldn't care less about what she does."

"Or if she does anything, apparently," I grumble. And then it's like my breath is caught because that is Kennedy in that two-piece suit sans cover-up, those to-die-for thighs rubbing one another. Which prompts me to open Tanner's Instagram, then my email, thinking distraction, which isn't working. It isn't distracting, not when she slips her finger beneath the elastic grip of her bikini, widening it.

A view I'm far too obsessed with when Tanner interrupts by rattling those cubes in her cup, swirling. "I love how you pretend to be on your phone while you're really just checking her out," she says. "She didn't even look at you."

I snap back as if I'm twelve years old. "Why does it feel as if we shouldn't be having this conversation?"

"Aren't you cute," she says. And, anyway, upon further interrogation, I get the essentials, or more specifically this girl's one-hundred-character Instagram bio, her favorite hashtags, the color of her old Ford Bronco—which was olive green by the way—her beer preference, and something about mountain therapy and wilderness culture.

And next I'm viewing her photo stream, her latest upload. Her whole conflicted with femininity while still emanating quite a bit of it, that stub of a cigarette lax between her lips. A seventy-proof sort of girl. Think tobacco and suede and axed wood lit by lanterns that are dangling in a deep and dwindling forest. Way more *Brokeback Mountain* than either of us. "She almost reminds me of you," she's saying. "Though you're more classic, hand-waxed leather. More café biker. But maybe that's it." As she sets her phone down. "Listen, this is enough about me. I want to hear about this Kennedy."

CHAPTER SEVENTEEN

Where has this me been all my life?

Kennedy

Minutes into this, into watching those two interact, their passivity, a veiled glance over my book as I read, I get a call from Seth, who opens with something like *Um, hi?* Seeming half-asleep or stalled, make that circumspect, as he proceeds to inform me that Opal's gone missing—which shifts me into a moment of sheer panic, one he talks me through as I head upstairs. In a haze, in an absolute daze.

"So you're telling me you let her out?" I say, which sounds half whisper, half shout as I'm imagining his tattered chukkas traveling in one direction while her vertical tail struts in another.

"No, I didn't," he says blankly. "But thanks." Seth is someone who has the compassion, the consideration, of the Dalai Lama yet not a paternal bone in his body. And not only that, he's not a pet guy. He thinks he's a pet guy. But he's never going to be a pet guy. And right now, he's under the assumption that Opal is incapable of slipping between two legs as he orchestrates a burger delivery from Grubhub, a thought that segues into full-blown foreboding.

Which is totally fine, it is, given I'm going to lose my cat the moment everything else in life falls into place—or at least momentarily, seemingly, I'm thinking to myself as I gesture dramatically into the mirror. "It's this shared custody thing," I tell him. "You should've never taken her home with you. She can sense that I'm not there."

"We've bonded on a very deep level," he says, dead serious, monotone, which I can't help but read in my current state as callous, unfeeling, laconic, though it does center me, admittedly. So I try to explain disruptions and schedules and *territorial* only to have him interrupt me with, "Wow."

Oh my fucking God. "So, yeah, walk me through this, please? Like, where was she, exactly, last sighting?"

"I'm at your place," he says. "I needed to hit the dispensary. For herbs. Then Trader Joe's. For Cajun Alfredo Sauce—"

"Of course," I say. "But it feels as if we're trending off topic right now."

"Right, so, I left her here and ran errands. Went back home. Hit Twitch." Uh-huh. "And when I came back to get her..."

I get a laundry list of possibilities he's quadruple-checked—namely the bookshelf, the pantry, the bathtub.

"Wait, though," I say, pacing. "Not the closet?" Which he assures me he's checked, thus prompting my internal pep talk. "It's where she goes, you know." Then I sit back, regroup, feeling miles and miles from lucid. "My clothes, they comfort her." Then I just start reacting—to this, to that, because he's worried, which worries me.

"So, right," he tells me, "I'm in your closet. And, can I just say, you have some serious type A going on in here. Color-coding? Laundry zero? And hold out because you're on speaker," he shares in this bland customer service tone before ambient noise while he's foraging, rustling, a screech of hangers across a rod, and all the while I'm reassuring myself that she's in there. Somewhere. "She's in your cashmere," he says. Which makes me laugh somehow, though rejoice hasn't quite registered. "Oh my," I hear. "Shit! She's really dug herself in here."

"So," I say, "let me talk to her for a moment."

"Go on," he says and then, "*Fuck*, she cut me."

Okay, so I take back that whole Dalai Lama bit. "Do you miss me, sweet pea? I'm so, so sorry I've abandoned you."

"I know, right? You're always abandoning her," he says in jest. "Newsflash, this is a cat. Who is perfectly fine. Did you not hear the snap of a can? She's fucking ecstatic about her pâté," he tells me. "I mean, I may surprise you yet." So perhaps rejoice is beginning to register. "And how's your stay otherwise?" he says. "In a word. You tend to ramble."

"I don't ramble—oh my God...*stormy*, I guess? With scattered moments of clarity."

"But," he says as if consoling me, "you didn't get lost on your way."

"I'm always lost," I tell him, "unless you're around. And have I mentioned, I think you'd like it here. I mean, the food initially. You'd love their food." *This place really does have a thing for experimental entrees*, I could hear him say. Which is absurd given he'd be logging all of the ingredients secretly on his phone so he could recreate it on his own, passing a spoon as a quiet, silent plea for flattery followed by his humble *Eh, could be better.*

"Feeling lost is just that unpleasant side effect to your being such an introvert," he tells me.

"But two introverts," I say, "might an extrovert make."

"Where's that girl who desperately needed space?"

"She's trying to figure it all out," I say, sinking into a messed-up tangle of thoughts.

"You know what I always like to do when I get to feeling down?" he says. "Visit the nuclear family." And yet again, his sarcasm cracks me up. "Then sit alone at the park. Dwell in my own failings," he says. Which leads to a deafening silence. Because this is what he does. He prods quietly. And he's excruciatingly good at it, at playing tuned out.

God, how many times has he pretended to kick back, engrossed in some stupid video game or Twitch or, say, mincing garlic—paying absolutely no attention to me—and then weeks, months down the road, I'll be talking about something only to find out he'd heard every word? And it doesn't even matter that we're not physically together right now because, even on the phone, it's sucking me in.

Which makes me pause and think. There are things in life that I have to work out alone.

And we can't share everything. He can't know everything. "You're playing Minecraft," I say, "aren't you?"

"I wish," he tells me. "Why?"

"And you're waiting for me to dish on things I don't care to discuss," I say.

"So, what I'm hearing you saying is you're surrounded by couples, and now you need me to be your plus-one," he tells me. "Your wingman."

"You happen to be a decent judge of character, that's all. And it's just a weird, weird situation. I'm in a weird situation."

"Heh," he finally says. "You met someone."

"I didn't come to hook up," I say.

"Listen," he adds, "do whatever. I'm happy for you." Which is really all I needed to hear.

So I smile, searching for a reply. "Well, it's incredibly gay here, which you wouldn't like."

"It's not that I don't like it. Love is love and all that," he says. But the topic always makes him feel awkward. Or maybe he feels left out. "I mean, who hasn't had thoughts?"

"Thoughts?" I say, rather surprised. "What, you mean *you*, like not entirely straight?"

"I can appreciate attractiveness."

"Now you sound like every guy who's tried to pick me up— right after he gets my rejection," I say. "And by the way, I'm sure I could find a pretty boy out here who could help you work through some of those thoughts…"

"Yeah, well," he says.

I know he never would. "It's just nice to spend two days around people who get me, given the whole attitude at work."

"I get you," he reminds me. "And I'm not hitting on you." It's a strange love that I feel for him. In a world where, I would venture to say, platonic friendship is immensely underrated. I trust him.

"And you know the best part? No purses! Anywhere. No cis girl hair. And not one squeaking *God, girl, you're so pretty!*"

"If it's any consolation," he says, "I despise that shit as much as you do. Give me a plain Jane with a brain any day."

"We have everything and nothing in common," I tell him. "Is she purring?"

"She is. I told you. We're bonding," he says. "So, you're back tomorrow?"

"If I don't get lost along the way."

"I'll make you dinner." Cue heartstrings. But after some back-and-forth, some minor protests on my part, "I technically didn't lose Opal," he says. "She hid." I fall back on the bed to cradle my phone. "You buy too much shit online," he adds. "I mean catalog after catalog."

My mind floats over to this note—interspersed with Seth's commentary on White Claw and Bradley Mountain and something about *their fucking cannabis candle.*

"So you totally did, didn't you."

"What?" I say.

"You met someone," he says.

"Kind of," I tell him. "Sort of."

"Legend."

"Not really," I say. "It's doomed. I'm doomed. So I don't want to talk about it."

"Yeah," he says with a big sigh. "I've been thinking about it, too, what you said. About…"

"Asking her out," I say. "That one from work?"

"I'm doomed," he says.

"How are *you* doomed?" I say. "You're simply confirming what you already know."

"What I don't know," he says, "for sure."

"Stop it," I say. "What could possibly go wrong?"

"I could totally get canned for this," he says.

"For asking a girl out?"

"Me Too," he reminds me.

"Then speak in code," I say. "People *do* do lunch. Especially when they're ten months into a budding romance, which has sadly been confined to a stuffy internal corporate messaging forum." And then we get into where, and what to say, and *What could we possibly talk about?* "You must talk about stuff on this forum."

"I guess," he says.

"And what's that?"

"Global warming. War. Marx. Anarchy. Gaming ethos."

"Well," I say, cautious, "if she likes that stuff—"

"She does."

It's not that he's asocial or unattractive in the least. He's just adorably awkward. In that awkwardly charming way. "Then she might be the one," I say. Which makes me miss home a little bit. Our debates over who gets what side of the couch or which bad movies we'll watch—or merlot, pinot grigio, merlot, pinot grigio because pairings and palates and nonsense like that when all we're having is an honest-to-God grilled cheese sandwich, albeit gourmet. Or takeout from the sports bar, accompanied by a podcast or Hulu and Opal—versus more of my late-night e-commerce therapy. It even makes me miss actual therapy.

Which means I really have turned into the UGG slippers variety of queer single girl, haven't I?

Except in this bikini. Because I look *reasonably* acceptable in this bikini. And come to think of it, my hair's seeming just about right. Despite humidity.

Which is maybe the Logan effect. Like, when a hot girl pays attention, and you think you're all that. Take *hot girl* out of the equation and, well, right back to average you are.

Except, maybe not. I grab my key, passing the mirror as I do for one last look. And *hmm.* Maybe I do actually look good. And maybe I *am* all that.

CHAPTER EIGHTEEN

Quit While You're Ahead

Logan

I was expecting to spend the rest of the afternoon with Tanner. But after she's flat out ignored me for the past half hour in an attempt to seduce that lesbian Hemingway online, I find myself nearing Kennedy, who's sunning at the shore. My nerves are in a knot. Not to mention everything I've ever learned about anything up until this point in my life has seemingly vanished into thin air as I take a seat, that smug look of certainty brimming across her face, which feels like a fever, one that's beginning to form across my brow. And minutes in, this has reached a level of inaudible intensity that's, well, more than faintly overwhelming.

But then she gets to talking. And the entire time she's talking, I'm thinking about that mustard-colored shirt she wore this morning and the fact that she doesn't have it on and about her mouth and how it moves and this kinetic quality in her voice. And how her hair's sunlit and the way her cheeks flush as she laughs. And about this scent, which always makes it feel as if I'm groundless or lost in an endless meadow under a kaleidoscopic storm on the most mind-bending date you could imagine.

But you know how, when your skin gets baked from the sun and you need to cool off and finally you get that glimpse of shade and it feels as if that breeze is everything because it's cool like spray or even rain? As if there's electricity in the wind that's able to buoy you up.

Anyway, that's essentially how it blew in, how it hit, like a rush, a blur, an absolute wall of water. A flash in the wind, then a storm. Our hair tossed about. Kennedy's skin slipping against mine. My arm lax around her waist as we ran, as it pelted our skin.

Until we ducked inside a broken barn. Into solace. Into a plump still.

It's hard to even describe how still it can feel as the storm hammers down outside. Once the air's become viscous. I peer back at that rumbling sky then turn to find her sunny, amused, her hair still stuck to her skin. "How long," I say, "before we're found out?" I scruff my hair. And, afterward, I peer up at her and she smiles and I hold that gaze for as long as I possibly can.

I don't think I've ever been in a barn before—or at least, if you call it that given it's not exactly built for sheep. More like marriages and musicals, with glimmers of low light streaming in through gaps which, for some reason, draw my gaze up to that wooden chandelier.

Then I glance at her sidelong, and those drops of rain trickle along her collarbone, wetting her lips. "What are you thinking?" I say.

"I like this place," she says with a harmless shrug.

"Yeah?"

"I'm trying to picture it lit," she says as she's wringing her hair, as water's pooling at her feet. Then, hesitant, "Or tomorrow."

"You're trying to picture tomorrow?" I say.

"Maybe we'll get a rainbow for our departure," Kennedy adds with delicacy.

I settle on her. "For our long drive home."

"Yeah."

I shrink a bit. "But I have you tonight?"

"Yeah," I hear again—only this time with strength.

As for me, I'm thinking about the whole town descending on this place in a matter of hours, or at least those of us who might've converged on Fire Island, on Bear Weekend, on the Castro, on Provincetown's Carnival. And that's not to say we're surrounded by gaiety or glitter. It's more of an earthy, eco vibe. The teak chairs folded, those tables for two topped with beeswax candles and bouquets that are stubby and flat. That stack of stocked wine crates. And a loud illuminated sign that shouts *EXIT*. Overall, though, it's got that flax seed meets blush meets silver dollar eucalyptus vibe, a modest little facade that's failing to hide its defiant disco ball now aching to bend some light.

"An upscale inn," I muse, "in a town so small and remote that it doubles as their queer bar."

"And what song have we walked in to?" she's asking, wandering. "I feel as if I've heard it before."

"It's bittersweet," I say, glancing around. "Like something's over. Or maybe it's just begun. It's like an apology."

"It's not the two a.m. closing-a-bar sad. It's a beautiful sad," Kennedy says. "As if it meant something to someone. As if it was important. Like the last song she heard before she lost the love of her life. The one she'll never get past."

"And what would you know about that?" I say, hoping to prompt a confession. She's fingering her hair, cocking her head. "I would venture to guess that you're rather proficient at the gracious good-bye."

"Is good-bye ever gracious?" she says. "It's usually the most confusing thing after all the rest. Like how'd it come to this?"

I shrug, thinking I must have the most unconvincing smile on my face. Because that's all I seem to be thinking about—good-bye, ours.

So it takes a little while to mull over. "That depends," I say.

"It depends on...?" she says.

"It depends on who you ask," I say. But that's my phone.

Tanner: *Where are you?*

Me, thumbing: *The barn.*

Tanner: *I thought you might've drowned. No wait, is she there?*

Me: *She is.*

"Your friend?" Kennedy asks, which snaps me back.

"Yeah, so apparently, they're all inside in heated towels," I read off.

"Why can't I be in a heated towel?" she says in a voice that's more like thinking aloud.

As I skim the length of her body. "I, for one, am glad you're not," I say.

Tanner: *I'm not a heartbreaker.*

Me: *Guilt doesn't take you far in life.*

Tanner: *But timing?*

Me: *Isn't right.*

Tanner: *I'm wondering if I should give them one more night. To help her get over me.*

Kennedy, out of the corner of my eye, is studying me. "How long," she says, "have the two of you known one another?"

"Ten years," I say, "give or take."

Me: *Good-bye is easier when we go.*

Tanner: *Is that what you're planning to do?*

Me: *As if I ever have a plan.*

This is hard. "So what do you say to someone who's made a very good mistake, one she's planning to make again?"

"Don't do anything impulsive," Kennedy says. "That's always been my motto."

"Is that right?" I touch my lips. "Is this impulsive?"

And while she's going for indifferent, a smile slowly builds on her face. "It could be," she says, clearing her throat.

"Is that bad?" I ask.

"It could be," she says.

"On a scale from one to ten," I say.

"On a scale from one to ten," she repeats, "ten being very, very bad?" And I smile, nod. "That's a tough one. Because who's to say if I like bad things?"

"Okay, let me refine that question."

"Can I ask you something," she says. I nod. "She's not...like, Tanner's not, *um*. The two of you aren't—"

I glance up from my phone. "She's not what?" I say. And this turns into a confusing *Is she asking what I think she's asking* sort of thing. Because she can't think Tanner, that I, that we, "Um, no," I say. "We most definitely are not. If that's what you're asking. We're like family."

"I shouldn't have asked," she says.

I move in close. "Why not?"

"It's too personal."

"Nothing's too personal," I say.

She pushes hair out of her eyes. "Well, I can't say the same."

"What might you be holding back?" It's strange, though, to be spending this much time with a girl I scarcely know. And yet. "I take that as a challenge, you know."

"I'll never discourage a girl from trying," she suggests, inching in, with that hair, a damp sexy mess. Her voice, almost confessional. And I mean, do I continue to play this off or what? Because it's easy to imagine what I'm imagining with a girl this close. "But," she adds, "you're not going to get what you want."

"And what is it that I want?" I say, staring at her.

Her eyes shift between mine. "I don't know what you want," she tells me, but there's a noise, some noise outside like commotion, like someone's laughing or talking about. It's enough to disrupt this tension. "I so wish I had that towel," she reminds me. And it wouldn't even matter now. I want to bring her that towel. I want to wrap her in my arms in that towel.

"I can run out and get it for you," I offer.

"In that rain?" Kennedy says, fidgeting. "Appreciate that. But you'll come to realize that I always want what I can't have." And then we glance away, amused, rain against the roof in its rhythmic dripping, trickling. "So," she says, cautionary, pausing, "nothing's too personal?"

"Try me," I say, but I must have the stupidest grin on my face.

"What's your favorite unfulfilled love song?" she says.

"Oh, that's a tough one," I say. "I didn't expect that."

"You must have that one song," she says, "that you've never assigned to anyone."

"I can't say that I do." I narrow in on her. "And I haven't exactly assigned one to anyone, either."

"All right, so, hypothetically, what I'm getting at is…in theory, if she left you here after whatever happened during that sad song.

After you said good-bye, after it tore your life apart. Because it didn't make sense. And you really needed it to make sense, to know if she was sure."

And all the while, she's taking discreet steps away from me. So I follow along at her pace. "Because maybe she wasn't sure in that moment, but she did it anyway. What would you do? I'm curious. Are you the type to accept defeat? Or do you run after her?"

But it's hard to form a response. Instead, my gaze locks on to hers, as if there was layer after layer of meaning behind her words. "I suppose that's yet to be seen," I say.

And next, Kennedy goes on about something. But that seems to veer all over the place before she comes right back to me. Before she jumbles out, "I wouldn't, you know, run after her."

It's a look that's unsettling. But why? It's the solitude, isn't it? The isolation, seclusion. That's made me tipsy, spinning around dizzy in some sort of loop. "I suppose something like that, some things, I'd just have to chalk up to fate."

"So you're a believer in fate?" she says.

Because she's asking if I'm going to leave. "I don't know what I believe."

She steps away, pondering. "We need music."

I lean against a support beam. "I'm opening the request line," I tell her.

"Don't make it sad," I hear, and next she's rubbing her arms as if she was cold, which I could fix. But I've taken a step away. "Not even fast-danceable sad. It's bad song karma. So what do you like?"

"That would depend on my mood."

"Well, then, what are you in the mood for?" She turns from me, suggestive.

My gaze follows the backs of her thighs as she walks away. "Look, I'm usually a bit more hands-off when it comes to that."

Then she peers back. "You won't give me a little taste?"

And my laugh breaks off. "Not at this moment, no."

She takes a seat at the table. And once she does, I follow

suit until it's just us—until she's leaning in and peering up at me. "C'mon, tell me what you like," she's begging, her smile indulgent. Which has its way of softening me, of tempering me.

I sink deep in my seat. She waits for my reply. "I'll tell you what I like," I say, "and then you'll decide that it's not your thing. And you won't be into me." But she steadies her gaze. "So maybe let's pretend for a little while."

"Why do you hold out on me?" she says, waiting, smiling, triumphant.

I lean back, mirroring her grin. And afterward, in our silence, I scan the room. It's as if my eyes have grown so accustomed to the dark that it feels less empty, less judgmental. And then one thing leads to *one sec* and I excuse myself because, speaking of music, there has got to be some sort of control that manages those lights, that amplifier, that microphone—this whole A/V system they've got going on back here.

And there, right there, it is.

Which is to say, one switch on this panel somehow illuminates the whole enormous place. Then I make my way back. Kennedy's switching her weight from side to side. And her complexion beneath this light, its gleam, it's radiant, unflinching, merciless.

I draw her in, my hand slipping along her curves until I find hers and she grips it. "So why is it," I say, and here come those nerves again, "why is it, all of a sudden, you've left me speechless?" When she turns from me, I swallow my thoughts. As I'm imagining tomorrow and our bags, our tenuous kiss, our cars, and that long stretch of highway that'll lead us home. Then maybe a text, a call, still hopeful, wishful, encouraged until the lure of a local girl— when all of this falls apart.

But what is this she's saying?

I mean, why aren't I listening? Why would I want to?

"I always do," I overhear. "I always get lost heading back." But I'm fixed on a reflection of light now gleaming along the curve of her lip because all she's doing right now is talking, and I'm just really tired of listening.

Since this is all we have. Her waiting kiss. A shadow of a kiss, which is disquieting, much like the air that's shifted, after it's stirred by a storm. And how it sits. Still. In your throat. Not hazy, not weighted or dense. Just vague, just sadly unsettling—like those words. *Good-bye.* But this is not good-bye. That won't hit until dawn.

Chapter Nineteen

Where were we?

Kennedy

Wasn't this something I usually hide? Something I normally shrink about or, at least, glance around about, to see who could see? Yet that cautionary glance would've only revealed a few artfully arranged linens offset by that spark in the air, those tremors, my absolute foolishness, and a tingle of sunburn as she ran her fingertips down the drop of my shoulder, my stomach tight as if braced for what came next.

But what came next was just quietness, just sweetness, that sentimentality. Which I'm beginning to realize is how she is, this hesitance, this virtuous facade she puts on whenever someone else is around. With that tinge of raw sexuality just beneath. Logan who slouch-sits in a two-piece suit just as easily, as securely as if she'd worn a tattered old pair of blue jeans, arresting. Unaware that I'd been watching her. That I'm immersed in her.

It's this carnal effect she has on me. This thing she does, and how I've taken to it—how I've taken to her. When all the while, I'm hoping to play it off as somewhat detached. Though in reality, I think I'm just easy.

Because, like everything else, like every indelicate discussion we've ever tried to have, we inevitably wind up right here. In this shared awareness. With this false sense of familiarity.

And for all intents and purposes, perhaps it was just a kiss. Like, a simple kiss. Not extraordinary. Not breathtaking or enchanting. But in its place, ordinary.

Though I'd venture to say it was not.

And besides, isn't that always how it is? We're always thinking *this* feels more special. More exceptional. That ours is the most magnanimous, the most magnificent. And dare I say, it was. It was the first and only time that I've felt such…excitement, such intensity. Such absolute innocence. Though innocence was never there with us to begin with.

And who could've said what would have happened next had she let it. I couldn't even tell you the placement of her hand until it slipped up my thigh, until I could sense the tips of her fingers slipping inside that thin strip of elastic between my legs. My still-wet bikini. A swelling ache that kept building. Her skin, briny. Our bodies sticking, rubbing. My voice pleading. Because she kept searching for that answer with no intent to find it, but instead, with every intent to deny me, leaving me gutted, pained, and wanting well into the hour.

Since I couldn't stop that want. Which is fine because it seems that whenever I want from her, I lose all sense of control.

And besides, a few hours later, we're back—once the rain's cleared, once we've dried off inside. Once we've showered and cleaned up. During that time of day that they call blue hour. When the shore's making way for high tide, for evening strolls and cold brews amid frothy waves smeared in that salt-stained haze.

But this same space, this same table in fact, at this hour, tells a different story, one costumed in cigar trousers and button-ups. Or at least it is for Tanner, who's set right across the way from us.

And here I am, joining in the midst of their story, and I can't keep up. I can't join in, either. I can't play along or entertain or engage when I'm feeling everything but engaging. Because it's hard to be here, versus where we were before, on this easy breezy evening as Logan listens in, as she grips a frosted bottle of pale ale—one hand at the top of my thigh, high. My cheeks flushed, her knowing smile, and our handful of clueless companions.

As I settle in, I listen in on Tanner as she explains that she'd prefer to be dumped in the evening. "Have I? Unfortunately, yes. Just before sex." A topic that gains momentum as it loops around the table.

It can enhance the experience. Gut-wrenching. No, it's more like a breakup-makeup meltdown. Through tears. Heartfelt. Sometimes, yes.

At one point, Tanner glances at Logan, then at me, then at Logan again, bemused. Before carrying on. "I haven't felt this bad since," she says. "I can't. She's not. I would not be interested in her, regardless. It's just a rabbit hole. *Mm-hmm.* She cheated on me with her. She's really beautiful. But I know how she tastes, and now someone else does as well."

I glance down at my napkin, which is bunched, and then over at a few sugar packets. This hot air blurs into people as they pass plates, hors d'oeuvres. The heavy beat of my heart. A few glasses scattered in various stages of tipsy. While Logan becomes fixated on a few strands of hair that have fallen into my face until she's zeroing in on me as if—

"The menu...?" Tanner's asking. And it's just the fact that she said it.

"What was that?" Logan says, pausing to glance across the table.

"Perhaps the two of you might want to look?" Tanner asks.

And where were we?

Dinner, though I could snack on these all night. So perhaps the only real sustenance I'll need is a little more Moscato. As my finger drifts down the menu. Their craft beer. Pulled pork. Ciabatta. Slow-cooked. Shredded ragù pasta. As I peer over at a roused crowd that's blown past a metal fan on rotation. Eventually my gaze sinks right down to Tanner who, under the guise of taking a selfie, leans into another girl rather voraciously.

And next she's shifting a pepper grinder aside to make way for that basket of warm bread, the kind that's linen-wrapped, along with individual cups of whipped butter. Logan's hand lifts up from my thigh before she's offering up a slice, which I take, slide a knife across.

And listen, it's just that. Okay, it's more than mildly intriguing, Tanner is. They are. You know, in that *I'd never do it* sort of way. Because I think there's something going on right there. "That would be Tanner breaking up with a girl," I hear.

"Are you saying the three of them," I ask, "that they're…?"

Nodding privately, Logan glances at my hand, which has been resting on the menu, adding, "Cheddar latkes, I hope you're ordering those," as I take a taste of this bread, absorbed. "And yes," she adds, "they *are*—in that way." But then she's back to those strands of hair that cross over my face and fall down on my lips. I smile against my glass while a replacement descends on the table. "I took the liberty," she says, then smudges a thumb against my lips until I'm imagining our next kiss.

"So I was taking a lesbian sex survey online," Tanner announces to the table, "and it wanted to know: How satisfied are you with your sex life? Very, mostly, somewhat, neutral, somewhat dissatisfied… or mostly dissatisfied?"

Without reservation, Logan bends across the table. "Can I ask why you were taking this survey?"

"Because did you know that more than forty percent of our fellow lesbians," Tanner shares with exaggerated disbelief, "are settling for somewhat satisfied? I happen to find this bit of information rather disheartening. Sex is important in a relationship, don't you think?" Which yet again builds in force as it circles the table.

But you know, you need to be in sync.

And body issues.

I felt semi-detached.

We've all got baggage.

But you never know.

Except—through another lens, I guess.

Which is quite the flex.

"I want to be absolutely worthless after sex," Tanner adds, inviting advice, analyses. And then meals are served and napkins unfold on laps. Throughout which, they continually carry on.

Love, love, love—it has nothing to do with love.

Which is just a biological function.

If only I were compatible with just anyone. And that's semantics.

But perhaps you could teach her. I tried and broke down and asked my ex.

Versatility. Adaptability. Compromise. Though the last time we talked, you were fine.

The last time we talked, I was curious.

Curious about what?

Whether or not you were fine.

So you're not, now?

I am. There are things I'd just never, ever do.

Yet you do.

Logan whispers in my ear. "I'd like to think of that as a healthy rebound situation."

But the implication being…was I? Which I am not about to ask. "Versus feeling the feelings?"

Nodding, Logan says, "She's not one to take the tough route, though it's made her life more complicated."

"If only there were ways to evade heartache," I say.

"If only there were ways to evade heartbreakers," she corrects me, as I take a leisurely drink.

"It feels as if it's that kind of a night," I say.

"We can only hope," she adds.

As we glance at one another, wondering. "Mistakes will be made." I lift my glass. And all the while, I'm beaming. Beaming like that dreamy-eyed schoolgirl.

"This isn't the song I'd imagined," Logan adds, gesturing.

"What had you imagined?"

"I imagined it would be your favorite song," she tells me.

My glass nearly touches my mouth. "If only you knew what that was," I say. "And how have you evaded this question all day?"

"Perhaps you should try a little harder at getting things out of me." Which makes me pause for a moment. Followed by a vague sense that I need to say something, you know. That I need to broach it, broach the elephant in the room. Tomorrow. Though I wouldn't know what to say and, besides, I'd regret it anyway, I figure, as

Logan peers in seeming agreement. "I'd like to think that some people come into your life for a reason."

"And what would that be?" I say.

"I really don't know," she says. "I wouldn't know yet."

As I tuck away my smile. "Yet you're the believer in fate."

"I don't know that I believe in anything," she says.

"If you believe," I suggest, "I will."

Except panic sets in when I do. "No promises," she says, but her touch is contradicting.

"No promises," I say.

I can feel her finger up my palm. "The last time I saw you—"

"I was soaking wet," I say. "Which I always seem to be."

"Not that I mind," she tells me. And as she leans in, my heart beats hard in my chest. "It looked so hot," she says. As those nerves bubble up inside. "I shouldn't say these things."

"I shouldn't do these things," I add.

And in a voice so subdued, "Why do you?"

I smile away in silence. "I don't know why I do," I say. "And how's that drink?"

"How are you?" I hear, feeling a blush come on. So I glance around at a crowd not noticing, at a crowd not caring as I'm grabbing a fistful of shirt and drawing her in. Until she buries her face in my hair.

CHAPTER TWENTY

Gender Lines

Logan

You can hear that pulse all the way over here, the commotion spilling out from the barn. The echoes of laughter, that beat pirouetting with the sun, so low that it casts an unreal orange-blue glow down its tin roof. Dim lights. Inviting.

Or make that as inviting as a mirage—given Tanner's phone is an uninvited distraction.

"She can't be flipping pancakes over that," I say, chuckling while she's lolling about, oblivious to the obvious, casually swiping across her phone. "One day, I guarantee, you're going to elope with that one. Forgetting all about me."

"And how is that even possible?" she says, ogling back in silent veneration, eternally naive like that.

So, yeah. "Listen, we're getting delivery pizza just as soon as we get back," I say. "Bitch Creek Brown Ale. Some randomly cheesy comedy flick. A cult classic. You name it."

"Such treatment I get when you're repentant," she says.

"Don't act like I've abandoned you," I say, resting an arm across the length of her shoulder. "I do so appreciate you."

"I know you do," Tanner says with the truest grin. "It's just that you also know how I feel about pizza."

As I glance down at her phone. "Unless it's seared over her mesquite flame?"

"Did you tell her we're here?" she says changing the subject.

"Look, maybe," I say. "But how can you *not* like pizza?"

"The real question is, how do you get so many girls," she says, exasperated, "when you top it off with pineapple?"

"They very much appreciate my toppings." I grin. "I guarantee you that."

❖

Inside, the theme is gender lines. So, ruffles and lace and Prada. Classic ties, black velvet, suiting. Pinstripes. Sheer ivory blouses on uber-slender frames. The atmosphere, resplendent. The air moody. The music palpable. With voices hovering like dense fog over closely occupied tables, between which we weave in and out, determined to claim that spot.

And once we do, literally the moment we settle in, before I can even get a word in edgewise, the first to slide in are Ashe, an acquaintance Tanner's adopted along the way, escorted by Elijah, his sculpted boyfriend, who's from Utah, originally. Their faded cologne breezes past, that hint of amber, washed suede, a scent I'd love to own, though I dare not ask. And this opens an exchange that begins with Brigham Young and segues into an enthusiastic *So, where y'all from?*

Not that I need to engage in anything like that. I mean, he's more into Tanner. They both are. And given she's so long-winded and all, well, I check my phone—it's closer to six—then send this off to Kennedy.

Me: *We made it. Front row, center.*

Before scrolling back to her last. And back to her last before last. And so on and so forth until I get this sinking sensation that somehow the table's acquired eyes and they're all on me, or so that weighs while I'm leering up over my phone. "I'm meeting someone," I say.

And listen, I don't mean to be rude. But honestly, I'd rather refrain from sharing my autobiography in the way Tanner has. And that's not a slight on her in any way, I swear. Tanner can be engaging, entertaining even, for those who haven't memorized it all.

Not to mention the fact that my answer will always feel awkward. Because, you know, it's never a single answer like everyone else. It's never a single town or a single place—or even a few. It's innumerable. It's disorganized. It's disjointed. It's broken. And, sure, I get the whole reason they're asking is to get to know me, to find commonality—to say *Hey, I've been.* To say *I know*, but they don't.

And even though they ask, which they always will, it's not as if they care. And it's not as if they'd get that level of instability unless they've actually lived it. And when you try to explain it, that experience, that life with no constancy, no permanency, no trust, they'll inevitably come back at you in the worst possible way. Which only grates on me. Because it's not like that. It's like following a lost soul searching for her fresh start, her clean slate, a new zip code, her perfect life, our new us. Self-acceptance. Contentedness, somewhere. "Nowhere, really," I tell them. "I've moved around a lot." And I'm grateful they leave it at that.

Especially when who's next to slide in but Tanner's fling or tryst or whatever you'd like to call it appearing jovial, cordial even, as I slouch back in my chair, skeptically eyeing their embrace.

And then of course, afterward, predictably, they all get to talking. Except they're not talking to me or even at me. They're talking around me. They're talking among one another.

While I glance back at the door, startled when my phone bings.

Tanner: *Favor?*

Me: *Can you not? I thought you were Kennedy responding.*

Tanner: *She's fashionably late, which is apparently working.*

Me: *What do you need?*

Tanner: *I wanted to make absolute sure that you knew that, even if I run off and get married or do something beautifully wondrous like that, I will love you infinitely more and longer and all that.*

Me: *I was referring more to that favor you mentioned in your first text.*

Tanner: *I need a table selfie, and you being the best paparazzo I know. Which we'll of course sequence later on once your beloved arrives. And last but not least, I'm so here for your pizza.*
Me: *You're so not. We'll make your fondue instead.*
Tanner: *You hate my fondue.*
Me: *We can use it as a dip for salami.*
Tanner: *Why do you hate me so much?*
Me: *For pineapple?*
Tanner: *BTW, tryst just handed me a thing.*
Me: *So you're up for that?*
Tanner: *Why are we discussing fondue?*
Me: *A ring? You don't say. Tryst handed you a ring.*
Tanner: *It's the key, silly, to her room.*
Me: *I mean, was there ever any question? And correction, their key. To their room.*
Tanner: *About tonight, no question. To her knowledge, big maybe. Besides, you know I'm partial to one.*
Me: *But what do you ultimately want out of this?*
Tanner: *A hot hookup, of course. XoXo*
Me: *Then stop holding out. Stop pretending. And make this worth your while.*

Since maybe that's just where I'm at right now. In a mood. As I make a show of sleeping my phone and eavesdrop on conversations now ascending in strength, in enormity, in importance, all around us.

Because that's just the sort of thing that comes to mind, isn't it? Once you dive headfirst into your next, successive, live-in rush of a relationship. Your next rebound is more like it.

Glancing back, then my phone.

And why is that?
This sounds like a loaded question.
No, more like a rumor you heard.
Tell that to your therapist, honey.
And yet, you always do know how to get me off.
But you know, some gays are the exact same way.

Except, didn't she say we'd meet up *on* the hour, which was a good fifteen minutes ago. And my text hasn't even been read. It hasn't even been opened. It's just sitting there waiting, like me, as I scan some flyer they left out on the table that's talking about performers and tracks, about that DJ with her knobs, and all the while, I keep second-guessing myself as to whether, by now, I should be out there and not in here. Given this crowd being so big and all. Which is just what I'm about to do when I glance back and there she is seeming lost or misguided or, what's another way to put it, lucidly out of place. Peering through the crowd, expectant, innocently hopeful, narrowing in on me with a look that's sparked such a rush of euphoria. Disturbing, really, in the way it's affecting me, as if I'm unrealistically alive, outrageously so, annihilated, exhilarated, like anything was now potentially possible.

As she heads my way, sparks implode, like…something, like a flock of nerves taking flight. Over a girl like this, which is, well, it's terrifying, really. And if I think too hard on it, I'm pretty much gone—throughout our embrace and this kiss, one that shouldn't be doing this. Interspersed with handshakes and greetings and, you know, cordialities. "I shouldn't," I tell her, rambling on about how, "I sent you that text earlier and then it got tight and now," now, now her lips are moving against mine, with mine, in this taunting, teasing, silencing sort of way as if time suspended.

And next, I humbly offer a chair, bowing my head. And I guess she takes it. And, as she does, and as I do, and as she's doing whatever she's doing on her phone because, right, that needs to be silenced, doesn't it? So I am doing just that when it vibrates in my hand—

Kennedy: *That kiss just now.*

Which just sort of obliterates me. As I glance at her, sidelong, then play along.

Me: *Can I get you anything?*

Kennedy: *I don't think they'd allow that here.*

She sets her phone down afterward and surveys the table, eventually returning to me, where I'm staring at her pathetically, and

I can't help it. I can't help but overthink this thing. The proximity of her hand near mine. The way she tastes of cherry and citrus or wine. Intoxicating.

"Why on our last night," she says, "did you have to look this good?"

"As if I don't always?" I say, my gaze skimming. But soon, I'm engrossed in our silence. Engrossed in sleeves that are being cuffed. Engrossed in that green wedge of lime that straddles the rim of that glass over there. But eventually, our eyes do find one another once more, and when they do, I mouth *How lucky am I?* as my gaze sinks to her lips, now mashed against a clear glass of water.

Which, believe me, I'm one hundred percent no doubt completely getting into, incidentally, when we're interrupted by *from Utah, originally.*

And in that moment, I lose her to a rather captive audience. "I actually bought a studio a few years back," Kennedy says, so cautiously, so watchfully that it makes me imagine random ex.

"You own a studio?" I ask.

"I do."

So I prompt, "I feel like there's a story behind that."

And as she narrows in on me or at least briefly, "Isn't there always?"

"I'm intrigued," I say.

"Don't be," she says and then shakes her head. And there's a dreamy, wistful quality in the way she glances away before twirling her phone on the table. "We always dream of moving farther away."

"I'm sorry you couldn't escape farther," I tell her.

"I had," she's saying, "only to be lured back."

While I gaze at her in agony. "I'm curious to know what lured you," I say. And then, "Moscato," I tell the waiter who's breaking in before I turn to her, uncertain. "That's your favorite, right?" She wets her lips into a grin.

"It's always the wrong things that pull you back," she tells me. "But what about you?"

"What about me?" I say, deflecting.

"Same question."

"I have not remained family accessible," I tell her. Except I'm oddly enthralled by Tanner, who's doing her thing, who's blushing and preening and casually dropping a napkin onto the floor in hopes that someone might pick it up. And of course, someone eventually does.

"I bet there's a cool story behind that one, as well," Kennedy says.

"Isn't there always?" I say, then smile, reticent. As her drink arrives, well-timed.

And I'm feeling, in her silence, this apprehension, this despondence, this weight, a touch of hesitance, which seems to go on and on. But then, as if some sort of realization unfurls, she lifts her gaze and looks over at me and smiles, withdrawn, pleased, like an understanding's been shared, as if we've communicated inaudibly. "How," she begins to say as she glances toward that wineglass, "did you remember?" Gently like that while staring into my eyes so tragically, so intimately that it's drawing me in, it's drawn me out of me. And don't even get me started on this scent she's worn because it's in her hair, it's on her skin, it's all over me. As we feign interest in their critiques, their commentary. While the space surrounds us and dims, sashays. As my hand slips into hers. One drink spilling into the next, uncounted, uncountable. The table bathed in the most luminous of light.

As meals are served. As plates are stacked and restocked. As conversations rise and wane, unguarded. Until we're slipping out, flustered, forgotten. Past lit phones and loafers. Past stout bottles and cognac bowls. Past half-eaten plates of napkins and cakes and utensils, until we emerge in a haze. Under a silent summer sky. Amid fog grass and lanterns.

"I need you to change my mind," she says to me, but we were talking about… What was it exactly? And besides, what are we going to do when we pack tomorrow and leave? So we need to get some sleep. Which of course she will, eventually, except I'm still that invisible kid already packing up, who's ready to go. So I shut my mind out and listen until I'm here in this, until I can dimly discern her hand, my heart weighted and her skin warm, as if too uncomfortably close.

Have you ever felt safe? she said. *I mean really, really safe. Like nothing could touch you safe. Like nothing in this world could break you.*

I guess so, I said, but I was thinking this, here, now.

And then she asked, *When?*

But I kept thinking, how do we pack our feelings? What do we even do? When it's going…where? When I know where it goes. I know how it ends, how it's going to. So why have I let that happen? As we kissed in evaporated clouds, her fingers comforting mine.

It doesn't matter, I said and, just like that, we were shuffling into the night, into a daze because everything I could see had been scattered, splintered like that haze up ahead, that halo, that blotted midnight window and then up the banister we walked toward the hall, where she fumbled, stalled, a dim light glimmering, the paint thick on the walls as if someone caked it on. And that copious, salted air. Wondering what I should say, because it would be too much—or better yet let's say nothing at all. And instead, leaning against her hips, that kiss, which fell back into her room with a snap, a tug, a pull, a lift, unzip. That shimmied down before lifting up. As her knees were parting, her hands gripping, skin clinging.

I had her. Writhing. Restless. Moaning into my mouth, my fingers thrust inside where she was tight and tense and trembling. Flexing and pressing, heady as she came, quivering, collapsing— limp and damp with sweat.

Her hair knotted as she pushed it back from her face, as I traced the length of her curves like slow fireside kisses. Like that warm gust that chills in the middle of the night, the one slipping over you, straddling you.

Because I can't stop thinking about that. I can't stop *feeling* that. As I listen to strange whispers down the hall.

But she's roused, shifting as I trail a finger down the length of her side, her cunt still wet at my thigh. As if, motionless, nothing was lying between us.

"What were we talking about?" Kennedy asks, her voice still hoarse from our night.

"Nothing," I say, enjoying the taste of her still on my mouth.

"I'm tired," I hear as she's rubbing her eyes. "I can't sleep."

"You were sleeping. I'm sorry. I woke you," I say. "Let's go back to sleep." And soon she is.

CHAPTER TWENTY-ONE

What to Keep

Kennedy

It's such a pale, gray day. Well, I suppose my weather app would describe this as *Cloudy. High 71F. Winds light, variable.* But I much prefer gray. And I'm doing the last thing that I care to do on a gray day, which is toweling off a wet shampoo bottle to fit in my toiletries bag along with a near-empty tube of toothpaste, my electric toothbrush, this Cetaphil, with its pump that won't lock, even after I've pushed and twisted and pushed it down again, which will just need to be packed and transported in some other way, I suppose.

Why is it, though, that influencers and bloggers, those Google links populating my laptop screen as I searched *solo road trip essentials* and *solo road trip female, solo road trip gay*, why had they all painted this out to be so therapeutic, transformative even, the single girl's summer excursion? Arms outstretched in that classic Mustang convertible as you motor off into the sunset, into a tangerine sky or down sweet scenic routes where the air's infused with lavender. At least according to those who've dedicated their days, their lives, to the betterment of tourism, to leisure, to Michelin-fueled adventures because it's all so perfectly explicated right down to the QuickSnap disposable camera you'll just have to pack, to the fleece and The Laundress Crease Release.

When in fact, what I hadn't realized at the time is that they never brought you back. They never took the time to escort you home or actually address any of the real issues you might be facing along the way, like how to pack this still-damp suit or that bottle of cleanser that refuses to latch. The starched anguish. That heartache you've amassed along the way.

So while I'm packing it up, I'm envisioning my therapist in her chair across the way and what she might say and how she'd probably lead off with a few questions. Like *What would you normally do when you've felt this way?* When I've felt remorse or when I've felt loss, when I've felt a desperate hollow emptiness in my chest. When I've felt so heavy and immovable. Followed by something vaguely encouraging like *There is no right or wrong here.*

But even she expects me, trusts me, to draw my own conclusions, to figure it all out—when I'd much prefer that she offer me up some hints to guide the way. Or better yet, just tell me what to do or how to feel, as if I could change that. Or perhaps she might nudge me in the right direction, toward the emotionally healthy approach, or at least through the most difficult parts. Given she's the trained professional in figuring this out. She's the scholar in it. She has the degree, versus me making more of the same dumb mistakes.

I guess I would have to say, after having had my fair share of good-byes and breakups, having left, having *been* left, is that if Logan feels one speck of how I feel for her, she'd *do* something about it, she'd *say* something. She'd throw me a line—I would. Anything to tip that scale. She wouldn't just stand there waving while I motor off. She'd hold on somehow, or at least attempt to string things along.

Versus leaving it up to fate.

As if I've ever delegated anything so important, so elusive, so arbitrary to fate, to some twist of luck, as if blind conviction, lacking action, could actually lead to anything good, to continuations, to more nights like last night—as if highway miles wouldn't matter unless we're committing to it. Unless she's committed to me in some minimal way, to a wait, a sacrifice. To the trouble of seeing it through. Good-bye after good-bye after good-bye.

But is she really, I wonder as I read her note once more, a note that's certain to pin its way onto that cork board just as soon as I get home, which is why I should trash it, why I should leave it, forget it somehow in this room—so I'm not continuously reminded.

But as I wander, as I pack, as I consider this, as I try to convince myself of this, because it wouldn't be out of line, now, would it? It's not the end of the world. Yet as I glance out the window at some low-hung clouds, I resolve to pack it. A choice that I know deep down in my heart is misguided.

And next I'm adding my night cream, my sunscreen, my shoes. I'm hooking my bra. I'm zipping my jeans. I'm combing my hair. I'm choosing a shirt. I'm fixing this stray, my part, my hem. Until I'm wheeling along a narrow hall toward their checkout desk and then cramming it all in the back seat of my car. Where somehow Logan has materialized, has grabbed my hips, has turned me around. Has whispered, "I do hope you enjoyed your stay," inappropriately cute like that. Inappropriately sweet and right and distressing.

"Don't ask me something like that," I say in an almost piteous way.

But she's taken a grip of my hand. "I enjoyed it, too," she says. Meanwhile, I'm backed against my car. "You always smell so good like this."

"It's just shampoo," I say feebly. And this is where I could say something ebullient or playful or heartfelt. But I don't. Instead, I keep things cordial. "I was just getting ready to text you."

"And what would you say?"

"I hadn't figured that out," I tell her.

"I'm sorry I left that way," she says.

"We have to pack up." I shrug.

And next, "Say you'll remember this," Logan says. Knowing I won't hold her. Knowing I won't keep her. Knowing I'm losing her forever.

"Again," I say, but I'm trying to smile, "don't ask me something like this."

Which she seems to be mulling over. "I'm not letting you off the hook."

"Then what do you want me to say?"

"I think deep down," she tells me, "deep down, you already know."

I know my jaw is clenching. "I *don't* know."

"I wish I knew more about you," she says as she's shaking her head.

"When I know so very little about you." And why does it matter?

"So, you're heading out now—already, so soon?" I nod, smile. "I could follow until it splits."

I could follow until it splits. I could follow you home until that highway splits. Until we veer our separate ways. No *Call me?* No *Text?* None of that. So I say, "I'm good. It's all right." I've got this. Until our arms are around each other.

"Why can't I take you with me?" she says. But you can't. You can't. Though I'm easy. It's easy. It could be easy. All you'd need to do is say it—and I'm yours.

But she won't, will she? Since all I get is good-bye, is stepping back, are hands that now dive into pockets. As I put on my prettiest smile and tell her, "Same." Which just feels obligatory, really. It feels customary. It's how you leave. It's what you do. It's what they say. It's what's expected, really.

Chapter Twenty-two

Dreamscape

Logan

The whole way back, because there really is no way around it, is there? I just kept thinking, This is so messed up. You either go through the emotions now or months, weeks down the line, after you've both grown more attached, which is brutal, however long it takes. Even an idealist like Tanner would know about that, that you draw a line. That you get on with it. Before it resurfaces, the issues with distances, the inconveniences. Because it will return. And then what?

Which is why I've been reminding myself of this continuously because, look, it's not as if I could ever dial her up after work and say *Hey, swing by?* It's not as if she's ten minutes away. Try two hundred miles or so out. *But it all comes down to timing,* I'm pretty sure I said. Which I might've believed at the time. Or perhaps I was trying to convince her and, in turn, convince myself. You know, think rationally, realistically, plausibly, much like I always have.

So I didn't say what Kennedy wanted me to say. But I didn't say what I wanted to, either. I didn't say anything, really. Which made it feel sad.

But that's just how it is. There's never a right way to go about it, and there's never a wrong. There's always going to be an unknown regardless of what you choose. There are just too many possible options, and you're only given one.

As for the rest, we'll never know.

And maybe I don't want to know.

Because it seemed in that moment, and even now, like a dream—like the kind of dream you're roused from prematurely, right as you get to the heart of that story, and in the process of emerging too soon, it haunts you, its aesthetic, its potential. You can't step out of it. You're immersed inside of it. It's incomplete.

So that's where I am right now. As if I'm still out there in a dreamy landscape inexplicably drawn to her, that featureless girl, dream girl, a figure embraced by fog. A girl so far out in the distance that I couldn't even distinguish her. But somehow, somehow, I recognize her. I recognize her because I can feel her in a way that hasn't been constrained to the flesh. I feel her in a way that lingers in the hollow of my chest, which is pitiless.

The only difference being, in that dream, I'm thinking and—correct me if I'm wrong but—she shouldn't need to coax anything out of me. She should just know intrinsically. She should know how I feel. Though I'm not convinced that she does.

It's something I've been tossing around all day, and something I've tried to put aside and understand and even justify as I've attempted to cram an entire weekend's worth of running around into a few precious hours—into loads of laundry and bags of groceries—all in prep for Monday.

As I strip out of my clothes and strip the bed and lie across the mattress, which is cool, especially as the fan oscillates across me on what's got to be the hottest day imaginable, as air-conditioners blast. While I'm in the habit of using mine only at night.

Which reminds me of work and working out. And how I haven't. And how I need to. But that I don't want to. And what I would give to just say *fuck it* and stay home and not do one iota of it. But I can't.

So next I'm honing down my grocery list into needs vs. that-can-wait. Given that all I have is one lousy box of waffles, frozen, when I'm plumb out of maple syrup.

Out of everything, really. Because that's what vacations do.

So by the time I get out of the house and start pushing around a cart thoughtlessly, hungrily, I wind up grabbing too much, which is apparent only after I've reached self-checkout, after *Blip. Welcome.* After I start scanning and bagging a shit ton of food I don't need.

And that's when I get this call, because Tanner, and I'm like, *You literally said nothing to me the entire way home.* And now I'm otherwise occupied. While people are waiting. And I'm holding them up. And I can't exactly balance a phone and, listen, she's probably in love again. Because then, she gets mad. *So I'll call you back?* But Tanner can be a real peach if she can't get her way.

Which I try to push out of my mind as I'm bagging the rest of it. As I blip boxes of Lean Cuisine and Jimmy Dean. And as I scan numbers for produce and codes and all that.

Because, after I'd loaded up on frozen meals for those late nights at the office, I grabbed a few other things—make that, something her neighbor made—which is not to say I'm culinary to the extent that he is. Let's face it, I'm kind of a ten-year old in the kitchen.

But I eventually get home and call Tanner, which happens to coincide with unbagging, with dinner. And FaceTime's just easier for that, for cooking on an actual burner.

"Which would not need a recipe," I'm insisting as I'm dialing the burner down given this is already burnt.

So Tanner's offering a hand from my iPad on the kitchen counter. "But why don't I come over?"

"Because you can't," I tell her. "Because I'm fine. It's fine. This is fine." When it's obviously an absolute disaster. "Maybe I just wanted to try," I tell her.

"But what are you trying?"

"I don't know," I say, "I'm trying to make a quesadilla in a pan like this," while demonstrating. "With strips of steak, Monterey Jack, stuff like that—"

"No," she says. "I mean, what's it called?"

"As in officially? I've modified. But this is what is called chimichurri steak quesadillas…with avocado chimichurri? Which I know, I know, needs a better name." But this is starting to feel so interactive, so cooking show, albeit I am not the most gregarious of hosts.

"So," she says, sounding shrewd and facetious, "You're making your own sauce?"

"That would be what I'm doing," I tell her, mashing, mixing.

"Nice."

"I know, right?"

"I'm unexpectedly impressed," she tells me.

"So why are you always surprised at how well I impress a girl?" I ask.

"But what possessed you to make this thing in the first place?" I am wondering this myself. "I was just at the store," I say meandering, "and look, I know I always boast about how I love pizza rolls, but I needed to switch it up." Only problem being, she's not buying it. "She's apparently got this guy," I say.

"She's apparently got this guy?" She says.

"No, no, no. It's not like that. I mean, he's a neighbor, a friend, an amateur chef—as in he actually *enjoys* this stuff." Unable to hide my distain. Because, please. But garlic is calling and next is the matter of cheese...which goes here...like this and—why am I talking to myself? "You are seriously distracting me. It's like, I cannot multitask—"

"Since when?"

"Since I'm actually in the kitchen. You think this is easy? And now look at what you've made me do. You've messed this all up."

"Oh, don't blame me because of some silly smoke alarm."

"Hold on—" I shout because *shut this off*—before blending, it's deafening. "This doesn't seem right."

"Because it's not something you blend," she says.

"As if I own a food processor?" I say.

"So you do have a recipe."

"Not that I follow," I tell her. But I can't help but laugh as I dump cheese all over despite her sermon on measuring.

But, no, we haven't talked. So she's like *Why?* And I'm like *Because.* And she's like *Why?* (Again and over and over.) So I'm about to shout but I say softly, *because.*

And yet, the audacity.

Given it's clearly not something I care to talk about. And yet, she's fished for *this*. She's insisted I do *that*. And all the while, she's dumping terms like breadcrumbing and benching, you know dating terms—and what do I think about that?

Which is excruciating, actually.

But eventually, she gets me laughing. I'm talking the deep therapeutic laughter that only Tanner can provide.

Anyway, I'm at the island, now, on one of those stools. After I've snapped a bottle of pale ale because I need to let this thing cool. Interspersed with *Gordon Ramsay*, and *Binging with Babish*, with *Pro Home Cooks*—who are, and I quote, iconic and cinematic on YouTube, she's saying in a tone that hints that this might be something I'd do.

"You've lost your mind," I say. "Why would I broadcast a disaster of a dish for the likes of YouTube?"

Which brings us back to *virtual* and how she's gotten into it. Into virtual dating, into FaceTiming. And all the while, she's swooning quite visibly over that girl, her new girl, her *next* in line, her mutual on Instagram—and how she cooks. And next I'm hearing about firepits and leeks and charred this and lemon that and chipped dill and finally, after all that, I learn it was fresh halibut wrapped in kelp, which is disgusting. But sunsets and cliffs and coffee in flasks and mornings at coves and vistas and views.

"Such a winner," I say.

"Right?" Tanner says agreeably.

"You're planning on leaving me, now, for months on end."

"I'm not," she says. "We did this thing on FaceTime, though, and she kept, like, staring at me—I don't know."

"Like…you're beautiful?" I ask.

"Yeah, yeah, like that. As if she thinks I'm actually beautiful. But they leave, eventually, don't they? Beauty is never enough. They want some stupid, vivacious personality to go along with it." And soon enough, she's laughing. "But it's nice, you know? And I'm really, really nervous about meeting her," she says as if gasping for breath. "This will be our first nonvirtual date."

"And where is she taking you?"

"Where?" she says, giggling. "I forgot to ask."

"You forgot to ask where she's taking you."

"I'm embracing my sense of adventure," she tells me.

But I've forgotten we're on the screen because it feels like she's in the room. That I'm on her couch. That she's sharing a drink with me. "Promise me you'll text the entire time."

"It's because she's so minimalist, so simplistic. She's reduced her life to essentials, but she has technology. It's like Thoreau, she told me—she's anticapitalist. She's an anarchist in a capitalist society."

"And you're okay with this?" I say.

"I'll cross that bridge when we get there."

"Or so you've convinced yourself."

"Risk is what you do when you're in love," Tanner tells me. "Which you'll never understand until you find it, those flutters. And so," she says, "how was it?"

"You're referring to my poorly named quesadilla?" I say. "It was quite good, actually."

"Quite burnt," she taunts.

"With cheese," I say defensive.

"Right," she says. "Even if it's burnt, it's cheese. And you may get good at this."

"Or never try again," I say.

"You should make it for her," she says, encouraging. "But who's this guy?"

"I don't like him," I say.

"But what is it you don't like?"

"The fact that she does."

"But why would you care if it's over, if *she's* over, if you're so over her?"

"I *don't* care," I say.

"And they're just friends, anyway."

"Which could easily be interpreted as friend zone."

And then, with an air of perception, of sensitivity, of some sort of understanding, she shouts with absolute gentility, "The fuck, Logan," clear out of the blue. "You've gone out with so many straight girls."

"And she's not," I say.

"Precisely."

So I lean across, curious. "And so, what's your point?" I say.

"Figure it out, genius."

CHAPTER TWENTY-THREE

Couch Your Words

Kennedy

I'm in my therapist's office, situating. We've been having this conversation about, you know, endings, Léa, rehashing a bit. I've yet to mention Logan, which is deliberate.

And when she glances my way as if expecting an explanation, because she must imagine I'll go on in the way that I had, as I had last week, as I had the week before, which notoriously ends in tears, I say something like, "Yeah." And I can feel a smile come on, which must seem odd, that I'm smiling. Over endings. Given how perilously we'd left it off.

"Tell me what you're thinking," she says thoughtfully, cautiously, sort of cocking her head.

"I'm thinking about a lot," I say. "It's not one thing per se."

"Though you're smiling," she adds as if pleased. Except she has this way of turning my moods around, always.

"I think something in me has clicked, decisively. So we don't need to rehash Léa. Like maybe it switched. Like maybe it's off. Or perhaps I've hit rock bottom, you know? I do feel as if I've simply had enough." After which, she doesn't respond or prompt or anything like that. But it's not as if she believes me. She's just sitting over there listening to air as it blows through a vent. "I don't like endings that are quick like that, that are blunt—that aren't gradual. I don't like it, or maybe it's because I don't understand it, when someone cuts me off, just shuts me out of their life for good without the courtesy of a warning. It's too extreme." But she's already decided that this emotional pivot of sorts has more to do with escapism—with last weekend—and less to do with actual progress. "I much prefer to live in a gray area for a little while where it's ambiguous. I mean, who doesn't need a buffer just to process it, a seismic shift like that? God, even the smallest shift, though I think this was significant—perhaps not in longevity but intensity. I guess what I'm trying to say is that I need a transition phase, like that pretty little cross dissolve you get between scenes in a movie."

There's a lengthy gap after that before she responds. "Why is that?"

Which I ponder. "I think it's because there's an aspect of forgiveness in it. There's an aspect of sacrifice. Of compassion, which I thought we'd had for one another. Reciprocity among two who might've been experiencing"—I shrug—"a similar pang. An adjustment. A reconciling of what comes next. And, sure, she's the one leaving. And I'm the one left. But it is easier to leave. This *can't* be more difficult for her." I smile as I shake my head. "And even if it is, hypothetically, I'll give her that benefit of doubt, let's say she's heartbroken after losing me, which she herself caused, wouldn't we understand one another the most? Couldn't we work this through, you know, together, process our ending together in much the same way that we'd processed the good? Though I guess I'm in the minority here. Because it's not as if I've ever been given that courtesy," I say, avoiding her gaze. "It's not as if anyone has ever had the decency to stick around until I'm strong enough, let alone capable enough of letting them go. So I guess that's what I want," I add conclusively. Meanwhile, this hilarity's bubbling up inside, this amusement. "Which I'm never going to find because how do you foresee something like that—how she'll end it? How she'll leave."

I'm listening to myself, though, and I can't help but think that I might be talking myself in circles. Or that I'm starting to sound like one of *those* girls, with their bottomless bitters, their baggage because they'll never get past it. Their victim, victim, victim. With barriers and rules and criteria for all the fools who step into it. *We're only talking*, she'd say. *We're only expressing thoughts, here.* And in doing so, I remain open, right? Because I can't let this narrow my view. I can't let this turn me bitter.

In any regard, she seems to get me. She's been sitting over there motionless. Sitting over there thinking I'm still thinking and talking about Léa. "You say it's hard to explain," she says. "Why don't you try."

"I don't think she's someone I want anymore," I say sensibly, rather pleased with my newfound stoicism. Or numbness. An ability to clamp things down. "Which is not to say I don't *want* her. I do. But she's not right for me…or good for me. She's not *the one* for me—she can't be, not when she couldn't even afford the smallest act of courtesy, that out." But verbalizing this does hurt, and it's that deep sort of hurt that rises up and weaves and tugs at you like a river edging a bend, one weighed in exhaustion. "I've said so much before, though, haven't I? I've felt this numb before, this indifferent, this beat down and over it? And then," I add, dismissive, "for some ungodly reason, I flip right back."

But here's that other catchphrase she always uses. "Tell me something." After which I can almost feel its ellipsis hanging in the room. "Tell me about flipping back."

"You mean why?"

"How do you feel," she says, "when you do."

"I feel love, an overwhelming sense of love. In its purest and truest form."

"Okay…"

"It's *so* hard. It's *so* hard letting go," I say as I'm subtly shaking my head. "And then I'll remember happy and it's like, Why am I happy? She's gone. So that can't be right. I can't feel *this*. And then there's guilt and remorse. There's shame and blame. There's jealousy and fear—it's alarming. I'm in this never-ending conflict, a pendulum."

"Yeah…"

"Even when she's hurt me terribly." And there you have it. There it is, but how does she make me do it? How does she flip an otherwise bubbly day into some sort of cry-fest? I've never understood. "I suppose all I can feel is contempt, you know, contempt and regret, because I'll never have her back, at least not in that way—not in that pure, idealistic, untainted way." I think that's what it was with Logan, that pleasant sense of connection, of disconnection, of reading me, of reading into me, of seeing me, and that transparency. Except now every muscle in my body is stiffened, it's cramped.

"Something's happening," she says.

"Yes."

"Can you tell me what's happening right now?" she says.

"I'm thinking about how you'll never love the same way twice," I say. "And how it's individual to that person. How it's attached to that person."

And while I'm not able to see her face at this angle, I can sense her straining to hear. "Stay in this for a while," she tells me gently, coaxing.

I grasp for a deeper breath. "I was wondering along the lines of…others." Because I am pathetically missing Logan. "It helps when I don't get too fixed into concepts like all or nothing, right or wrong, beginnings and endings, into absolutes, as if there was one right and one wrong way to think about this, which is unbending, unforgiving, unchanging," I tell her. "When life is changing constantly, and it's always surprising us. It's never what we'd imagine. It's never what we'd expect. Yet I do have that tendency to think that it has to be this or that. That she's either in love with me, or she's not. And there's never an in-between. And that right there has become such an immense burden, because that means it's all on me to be right. To stop her before it's gone because gone is irreversible. And that's a hard stop." She looks at me dead on. "I think that's why I cling—illogically so. I know. Or maybe I'm jumping around, which is what I need to stop, stop worrying so much about what's been said or misread or is this enough?" But my therapist doesn't nod in agreement. She doesn't shake her head, either. She doesn't do anything. "Because this can't happen—I can't be *wrong*. I can't be that mistake, that reason, the cause, that oversight, a misunderstanding. I feel like saying, *I don't want you to leave. But if you have to—you need to go on for the rest of your life knowing that this was all on you.* That I never wanted to lose you." I pause in hopes that she'll speak. "How do I give that up?" I ask. "Or better yet, how do I trust fate? Is that what you think I should do?"

"It's important for you to feel some sort of control over a situation."

"Because I have control," I say.

"But you don't."

"And how do I let that go?"

"That sense that you might be the only one holding on to what's right," she says intentionally. "That you're what's holding it all together."

"I want to let go," I say.

"Does this remind you of something?"

"I know where you're going with this," I say. And I don't want to go there. I don't need to go backward. But she won't respond. She doesn't need to.

"You laugh, but everything you've described to me when it comes to your mother was…"

"Terminal. She went nuclear, and she couldn't care less about me," I say, emotionless. I am emotionless. "Which messed me all the way up, right?"

"I think you should stay in that gray area," she says, "in nonabsolutes."

"So can we talk about something else?"

"We can."

"I feel uncomfortable," I say. "And I could barely get out of bed last weekend. So I called Seth, who swung by and made me dinner and made me eat. Then we cried over a bunch of dramadies," I say. "Wine might've been involved, not that I need wine to cry these days. I seem to be doing *that* pretty well on my own."

"What'd he make?"

"Seth? He made quesadillas. I mean, he made dessert, too, buñuelos, which were, oh my God, so good. Which is so weird because, for the most part, he bores me. But at the same time, he intuitively gets me. And we can talk about every boring thing you could imagine, and that we did—right through the entire movie.

And he's right, you know? He's like, it's all an illusion. Love and hearts and all that sap. Because when you fall for someone, they transform into some sort of fantasy. Because you'll *only* see what you want to. You'll only hear what you want to. You'll read meaning into meaningless words, into meaningless moves, as if she was your happily ever after. Making shit up as you go. Confirming your bias. Thinking she's the one to end in that scene, the one that won't come because we change or she changes or life changes us. So maybe I'm reconsidering. Because maybe I'm starting to realize that I hadn't stepped back from that intensity. That we hadn't slowed down enough to see. And I think that right now I kind of am more discerning, judicious, observant," I say. "That I'd made every bit of her up. And anyway, then we got to talking about something else."

"What was that?"

"Predestination," I say. "He's super weird that way."

"How so?"

"It's so antithetical to everything he believes. He's more of a fatalist, really, except karma, causality."

She smiles at me. "You'd like some meaning in life."

"In life, yes," I say. "It would make life so much easier if we had meaning. If I could believe in something. If I could hand life over to fate. If I could do no wrong. If I knew that somehow this universe had a hand in my destiny, which is where? No matter what we did to sabotage it. No matter how many things went wrong. Except, it's just unbelievable chaos." I smile at her, relaxing into this couch.

"Did something happen while you were away?" she says. "If you don't mind my asking."

CHAPTER TWENTY-FOUR

Typing and Deleting

Logan

I don't care what Tanner thinks.

Because how I see it—or at least what I've learned over the past thirty-some-odd-years is that if you can just face up to it now and not distort it, if you can circumvent it versus forcing life into a blindly hopeful box, into a game of *Let's stay in touch* when you know you won't, you can't, you never have—if you can just accept reality versus diving headfirst into miles of mileage and for what, for sex on a random night after an hours-long commute? Into juggling long distance with my job, with every day, with life, with hers, with all that's wrong with this. With putting life on hold or, worse yet, with diving way too deep into something way the fuck too soon.

Because it's never going to work.

And shouldn't one of us acknowledge that fact, acknowledge the obvious. That it's best if we leave it at that. As opposed to promises and lies—as opposed to I-love-yous. Only to wind up where in the end? Not moving in, not marriage—not after a few lukewarm showers in her room during a brief holiday away. Because every road, as I see it, leads us right back here to this. Or at least, eventually.

To *I didn't think this through.* Which is all I'm trying to do, to not text, to not call—to pour myself into everything but. Into agile, into Zoom, into *Corporate needs this by when?* And then it dissipates.

It's how you forget. It's how you sink right back into everyday while maintaining some semblance of sanity, of sensibility, responsibility.

Stability.

Because once you do, once you break that pact you've made with yourself, the moment you type those broken words and click send and she responds, it's all over. I crumble.

Which is why, come Friday night, I'm back on a stool at Rue B slumped over a Vieux Carré intent on having a good time. In Tanner's absence, that would be, given she's wildernessing, she's trekking, which I know because I'm following her stream, her Instagram stream, where she's on an actual stream. Getting knocked about. In dangling woods. With their cowboy grill and jugs and jugs of wine.

When I notice, over there, a girl, cute, midtwenties, that sort of European meets delicately athletic vibe but pretailored, the type of girl who's on the verge of becoming *something*, of becoming someone else—someone sensible and dependable, but not tonight I hope, as she slides her drink beside mine.

With a look that says, well, "Nice night." She smiles, blushing.

And we both look at each other. "Full moon," I add.

"Yeah," she says dreamy. "I'm all about moon cycles."

I cock my head. "Is that so?"

And then silence settles in. "Listen, this may sound a little weird," she says, "but can I ask why you're here alone?"

I laugh. "Why are you?" Then I bow my head.

"Those two over there"—she's whispering—"they've been hounding me."

I slouch, subtle, then tent my hands. "What, those scrawny little guys?" Because scrawny, they're not. More like brats on pledge week, all branded in Greek, broad and brotherly. Her gaze traveling to one, then to the other, before settling back on me.

"I'm sort of here on travel," she says with a sweet all-American grin. "All right, so, I'm couch hopping. I'm visiting friends."

"Enjoying yourself?"

"I wish." She smiles, leaning in. "I needed to get out."

"Oh, I know how that feels," I say. But why'd I say that? I can't exactly relate. "I travel only to dull, windowless conferences where they serve bad sandwiches for lunch."

Then, with a lost look in her eye, "I'm visiting family." So I nod. "Is that what you do—corporate, travel, and such?"

I shake my head. "Not much. It's not a good time."

"Tell me about...I don't know," she says provocatively, leaning in. "What's your idea of a good time."

But I'm thinking about travel. I'm thinking about last weekend. And I'm thinking about where Kennedy might be tonight. I wish I knew. "A good time," I muse. She smiles then laughs, settling in. "Listen," I say, "I'm not one of those guys."

"What do you mean?"

"I mean..." You don't need to play those games. You don't need to come on strong. "Never mind," I say. I take a drink, peer at Princeton, then at her. "Don't worry. I've got you."

She smiles, big. "You know, I've kind of been into past lives lately."

Which raises a brow. "Is that right?" I add diplomatically. "I can't say that I've ever actually thought about that." I feel put off, no thanks to this drink, which is now most absolutely, unquestionably kicking in.

"I'm a Leo, by the way. And wait"—touching her lips—"Virgo, right?"

I grin. "Why do you say?"

"Leos, they're observant," she informs me. But why does she seem so giggly, untameably so? "Analytical." It's cute, though. "Which you seem to be, with that look you had just a minute ago, scrolling your phone...as if you were a million miles away."

"I guess I should pay more attention."

"When were you born?" she asks. "I mean, really."

"And next you'll be emptying my bank account." But I like how she's doing that. I like how she takes my hand.

"And imagine how much fun we'd have," she says.

Still, I'm questioning whether I should be alarmed or flattered. "March," I tell her. "March twelfth, to be exact."

"So you're a Pisces," she says.

And I can't believe I'm asking this but, "What does that mean?"

"I click with Pisces."

"And why is that?"

"Our signs are strangely compatible. They are perfectly in sync," she says. "Like really really—"

"You don't say?" I add, cutting her off. But why am I feeling so short? Perhaps I'd just like to be alone. Perhaps I should've stayed home. "I suppose that's good to know." But my drink and only my drink will slog me through the next however many minutes of Elements and Air 101—of pseudoscience, of her ex, of his grandiose delusions. *But don't let me get started on that,* as she slowly sips her drink. *Don't get me thinking about that because, you know, he's too moody, too sentimental, a Pisces, too, and so deeply connected with—*

I glance down the bar sidelong, catching her eye. "The music in here is nice," I say.

"It is," she says. "Thank you."

"For what?"

"For shutting me up."

I laugh uneasily. "I'm not shutting you up." So she delves into fashion—but not in a gay way. More in a circle of friends way. An overheard at the gym way. The designer shades and makeup counter way, which I happen to mind. "Like this one here," she says, posturing.

And look, maybe I'm just done—with being their first, with being their coach, with saving this girl from heterosexual hell. "I mean, you look very nice," I tell her. And I mean it, sincerely, because I also know that it has its short-term advantages.

As she drops her head. "Have I mentioned," she says, unsteady, "that I've started this new celery diet? Which might not have been the brightest idea."

"Why is that?"

"This drink," she says.

As I peer at that glass. "Hey, listen," I say, "are you okay?"

"No," she says in a voice that's as empty as her drink. "No, yeah, I'm good, for sure," she tells me. But I order a glass of water amid her pleas, her apologies. And listen, she's not the most helpless I've met. But she's damn near close.

"I'm going to take you home," I tell her, "and get you *in* bed—" Shit. "*To* bed, I mean, *to* bed."

"You. Are. Adorable."

"No, I'm not, really." But she's nestling into me and, "I'm going to call an Uber."

"No," she whines, pouting. "Won't you take me home?"

And, no, just no, I won't. Instead, I pay her tab and mine and I see her into the cab, a female-run cab I've requested, with directives that she get back safely. Add this spiffy little Styrofoam container of takeout as we nod congenially. "Text me the minute you get home," I say.

Which is when it hits. Not the drink, just the shaky, silly.

Relieved, alone, weak-willed. Anxious. Panicked. Unfurling. While staring at the glow of my phone. Because I'm unlocking, thumbing, scrolling.

Assuming. Supposing. Remembering. Reading.

Typing and deleting.

CHAPTER TWENTY-FIVE

Three Little Words

Kennedy

Before I get too carried away or full of myself or twisted in a knot over one unexpected text, let me preface this by saying it was the smallest and most miniscule of gestures Logan could've possibly strung into three little words. And, no, I haven't texted back. I haven't even composed myself enough to compose a response. Especially when phrases like *beck and call* and *at her whim* come to mind. Not to mention the time stamp, which read eleven p.m. In other words, that time of night when a text is meant to enter the void with the assumption of a tomorrow reply. Or when it's being sent with a side of regret, pinging me like an alarm after I'd scarcely dozed off only to leave me inappropriately energized and in my mind. So remarkably so that I could almost feel her presence in bed alongside me—the weight of her body, that slight depression in the mattress, her hand as it slid up my shirt, and those fingers amusing my skin until they slipped inside me, leaving me achingly aroused.

Then I fell back to sleep. Assuming this morning I'd feel more rational, more reasonable. More clear-headed, perhaps. Which I am not. Instead, I'm barely lucid enough to snap a can of Nom Nom as Opal prances up, clanking its tin against her bowl and then dialing Seth up, who's still in bed. "I'm not asking for your advice," I tell him.

"That's good," he says inside a yawn, "because I'm not offering any."

"Good, because I'm not taking it."

And next, a stretching sort of groan. "I'm not exactly a wise sage for my age, you know?"

Though he kind of is. Or at least he's a bit more sensible and impartial alongside my gush and gush and sigh. In response to a three-word text: *How are you?*

"That's all she said?"

"That's all she needed to," I say, reeling, "prompting pure, unbridled butterflies."

"Hold on a minute," he tells me. "I'll need to think this through. But don't you think you might be getting a little carried away? I mean, this type of thing could sway either way. She's chosen a classic move. She's good. But let me dissect. Over coffee." And with that, I make my way to the window, where I watch someone else's turquoise television screen through a glaze of speckled drops of rain that adorn my window.

It's sort of a quasihypnosis that leads to imaginings. It leads to daydreams. Until, after an immeasurable spell of silence, I ask. "Well?"

"It could be anything," he tells me. "It could be nothing."

"Then why'd she text?"

"How would I know?"

"It's nothing, then?"

"All right, not *nothing*. Just a girl who might've been having a rough time given your whole cut and run," he says. And then, the audacity, he laughs. "Even I'd reach out, say *hey*. Check in, ask *How've you been?* And don't take this wrong, but it might've been her way of lightening the blow."

"I don't think you fully understand this situation," I say.

"You're right. I probably don't," he tells me, but his tone... "For all I know, she's harboring doubts. It's different for a guy. And when you're gay, as you always say."

It all makes my heart sink. Then flutter. Then sink again. "You do this." While that little voice inside keeps urging me to call because what have I got to lose that I haven't lost already? "You tear me down," I say, "then talk me up," as I stare placidly out the window. "Are you telling me to call, which could very well end in *Good to hear* period, end of story, case closed? Or no response at all."

"I never said call—"

"But I should," I say, lulled by a faint drip, a slow percolation, on the other side of the line—the type of hypnosis you experience when huddled over a counter as a carafe fills.

"*Tomorrow night. My place. Eight sharp*," he says.

So I groan. "Be serious."

"I am serious," he says. "It works."

But I'm laughing at its audacity. Its spunk. It being so not me. "It works on a hookup app."

"I'm quite the catch," he tells me, "for straight-oriented girls."

Steam swirls up from my mug. "But when will you realize that?" I say.

"Come on," he pleads, "you're so willing."

I know, I know, I am, and that's my problem. "So if you were me…" I say in earnest.

"You mean infatuated and forlorn?"

"And sleep deprived and really, really tongue-tied."

"I'd leave it up to her."

"And how do you suggest I do that?"

"Play the ambiguous card," he tells me. "Leave it up to interpretation."

"You're almost good at this," I say, intrigued.

"You don't need to convince me of that," he says. "So, *Good, and you?*"

"Just *Good, and you?*" I ask. Why are guys so blah that way? "That's the text?"

"That's the text."

"It's positively, absolutely indifferent," I say, and I love it.

"As opposed to *Where do I begin.*" he says.

Adding under my breath, "Who would say such a thing?"

"You have," he reminds me.

"All right then," I tell him. "Don't ask why, but it's officially sent. Verbatim."

"Why do I feel so afraid for you?" Because he should be, and he knows it.

In any regard, I take a muffin over to the table, where I caffeinate, pinch its cinnamon streusel, more caffeine, more streusel, while listening, like the loyal friend that I am, to his entire corporate potluck play-by-play, to say nothing of his discourse on casseroles versus kebabs. And next he's tossing out icebreakers, introductions, the team-building stuff they used at that ridiculous office event— beginning with How should success be measured?

"They actually asked you that?" I say.

"Keeping in mind," he says, "that's my boss over there."

"So, I hope you said *take-home pay*?"

"Yeah," he says, "we're not supposed to mention pay."

"As if you're there for anything but."

"We're *family*," he scoffs.

"Of the dysfunctional type."

To which he offers a trite, "I said something about meaning and purpose."

"Aren't you an incredible suck-up."

"Which is how you get ahead," he tells me.

"And what came next?"

"Which on-hold music," he says, "would be your theme song?"

"I don't know, maybe something like Martha Argerich," I say, "something like that."

"And let me guess, another *so sad, never moving on* song."

"She's a pianist," I say aghast, "perhaps the best female, and not even female, the best pianist, period, of all time. So it could mean anything. It's instrumental. It's open to interpretation, as you say, which may be my approach to life going forward."

"Therapy has made you way too emotionally stable," he says. Then he pauses to take an endless drink of coffee. "So, next they asked...If you were a candy bar, what would you be?"

"They didn't," I say. "And the object of your affection said...?"

"Payday."

"Ah, so *she* can mention pay?"

"In a very different way," he says.

"And you, no wait, no wait, let me guess—Goobers. Mr. Goodbar. Big Hunk." I giggle. Before I go full-on orgasmic, "Oh Henry!"

"5th Avenue," he says apathetically. "I wanted to seem ambitious."

"Without seeming ambitious," I say, rinsing my plate. "But wait, you didn't say—what's yours?"

"My what?"

"Your theme song."

"I passed on that one," he tells me.

"How come?"

"Don't you think that's a little too personal for work?"

But *I know* he knows. I know he has one. "Fine, then…between me, you, and the wall?"

"Yeah, let's not."

"I told you mine," I say.

"You know exactly what it is."

"Okay, then, let me guess. 'Wish You Were Here'?" I ask.

"David Gilmour, Roger Waters," he says, "collaborating."

I cradle my phone. "I got it on the first guess," I say. "I love you so much."

"Heh," being his way of saying the same. Because you've got to read into it. It's all in the tone. Anyway, I catch myself smiling in silence out the window. "She seemed interested," he says.

"Your coworker, I take it we're back on her," I say, "was interested in…?"

"The dish I brought. I'd like to call it nouvelle American cuisine."

"So I hope you're making more for her," I say, taunting.

"She offered to stop by," he tells me.

"Wait," I say. "What?"

"This afternoon," he says.

"So, you're saying people actually do this?"

He chuckles. "If you're referring to cooking dates."

"No way." So how can I be polite? "I guess it's a nice thing to do, right? The couple who whisks together, stays together."

"Once those spaghetti noodles set on fire, it was all over for you, eh?"

"You don't submerge the tips," I say.

"Unless the flame is so high that it licks those tips."

And, listen, I get why you wouldn't scale a mountain on a first date unless you were at least buff. Not to mention those harnesses aren't exactly flattering. But cooking?

"Haven't you ever watched a girl eat?" he adds.

"Don't tell me that turns you on?" I say.

And he's like, "It can."

"Personally, I avoid food dates. Especially when it's my first," I tell him. "And if I can't, I will always slip away to freshen up."

"I doubt this'll lead to a kiss," he says. "We're working on a project together."

"It could," I say, preoccupied by my text, my phone. "And anyway, I haven't heard back."

"You will," he assures me.

Still, I tuck my knees up, feeling more than mildly concerned. "Or maybe Logan's starting to regret what she sent."

"Or maybe she's taken aback," he says.

"By what?" I ask.

"Your ambiguity. She might've expected more."

"God, maybe she wants something casual," I say. "You know? Like a hookup."

"And would that be a problem?"

"It hadn't been," I say.

"So why would it matter now?"

"Yeah," I say. Why would it matter now? "I wish there were rules—a baseline, a boundary. This is so much easier for you."

"Think for one moment what it's like to be a guy."

"I mean straight, your culture, conventions," I say. "Maybe... can I rephrase that to say something about guys growing up with the expectation of rejection. Whereas, we were not made for this. We are not good at it, especially when you put two women together."

"How little you know of me," he says, "if you think that's true."

"I think you are, sort of, the exception," I say. "Not like the guys who push and push. It's always like, back the hell away from me. I always have to be rude."

"As you should be," he says. "Guys are fucking pigs."

I laugh big. "Generally speaking, though, in your culture, it's like guys make the move, you know? He asks her out...he pays...he drives...he initiates sex..."

"Women initiate sex," he tells me. "They initiate a lot. You act like it's 1950. Like I order her meal. Like I help her on with her coat." Then, under his breath, "Though I *do* open doors."

"Aren't you the gentleman," I say. "But, you know, there are gender roles. And the thing is, for us, there aren't any of those roles, those expectations. We make this stuff up as we go. And with each new girl, it's different."

"And there's a freedom to all that," he says, which segues into his caffeine-fueled lecture on feminism and intersectionality. On Christian feminism, on anarcha-feminism. On postfeminism. On antifeminism. Yet somehow, somewhere in the midst of this, once I've apparently zoned out, I glance at my phone.

And my head spins. "Logan replied," I tell him.

"She replied?"

"My hands are quite literally shaking."

"What'd she say?"

"*Call me.*"

"That's all she said?"

"Which is good," I say, "right?"

"It's good," he says.

Only problem being, my idea of *good* is *promising*, whereas his is more akin to *eh*. "Am I allowed to gush now?"

"Just channel your inner guy," he says. "And don't get carried away. She might think you could be friends."

"But I don't want to be friends," I say.

"Says the girl who always wants to remain friends."

❖

Calm down, calm down, relax. Just think about something else. Like, I don't know, poetry, art, anything, nothing—the gentle torment of dialing her up. As I'm imagining our whole interaction, some laughs, entranced. My muscles clench as it rings.

And then she picks up.

So I'm like, "I hope I didn't interrupt." My heart racing, my palms clammy. Whereas, she acts as if nothing's happened. And this becomes circuitous—cautious, tempered, a sort of give and take that combines two parts avoidance to one part divulgence. As I feign indifference, because I'm not about to ask why she messaged me. And she's evidently not about to say. Which is not to say I haven't stopped wondering.

So when I tell her about my week, reluctantly, what I really want to say is *Why? Why'd you call? Why'd you leave? Why now?* And when she tells me about hers, which sounds enchanting, what I'm actually thinking is I like this. I like you. I want that. But what do you want from me?

And then I think, Take it.

Which becomes *Take me.*

Try me.

Torment me.

Until I feel as if I could weep again. Until I'm drifting so far from *elated girl* into someone who's calmly incensed, unsettled, and oddly inarticulate.

To say nothing of the fact that, to Logan, this shift seems to spring out of nowhere.

"So, work was good…your week?" she asks.

"It's fine," I say calmly.

"Is this something you don't want to talk about?"

"It's just not that interesting," I tell her.

"And you made it home okay?" she says.

"I got lost for a little bit," I say. "Some summer construction, rerouting."

She laughs. "You always get lost, you say. I hope you enjoyed the rest of your day."

"Oh, I did, once I got home," I tell her. "Seth made a really fabulous dinner. We had a good time. So now I know everything about this girl, this Stephanie, he's been working on some project with," I say, pacing. "They've arranged for a cooking date." Which sounds almost chipper.

"Is everything all right?" she says.

"Yeah," I say, "why do you ask?"

"You just seem so…"

"I need to wake up, that's all," I lie.

"If you'd rather not talk," she says.

"No, no," I say. But why is she being so nice? "I'm happy to talk." Which feels almost conciliatory.

"Well, it sounds like a perfect date," she says.

"He's pretty psyched," I say.

But next comes the longest pause. So long, in fact, that it's a little unsettling. "What would be yours?" she says.

I snap the top off a can of diet soda. "Are you asking my perfect date?"

"I guess," she says. "Yeah, I am."

But then, this flash of losing her forever. "It wouldn't matter."

"Why do you say?"

"It's more, you know, the person." As I stare out the window, blank.

"See, for me, there's always this thing that I've wanted to try."

"And what would that be?" I ask.

"I've been building up the nerve all week to ask you out," she says.

Cue uncontrollable angst. Because it's like she's here with me again. It's almost that close, in the way she sounds—in the way she says it. It makes me remember too much. "I don't understand."

"Is that a no?" she says.

"Are you planning on driving up?" I say.

"I thought we could maybe meet up," she tells me, "over FaceTime. Someday. One day." And then, "I know, I know what you're thinking."

And that very well might be true. "So, what am I thinking?"

"You're thinking about telling me *no*."

"God…why, just why," I blurt out, "do you do this to me?"

"Why," she says, "are you mad at me?" But I don't respond right away. Instead, I lean over myself and let my eyes lose focus, which seems to intensify our silence. "I'm really, really sorry," I hear as I sink against my phone. "I guess I felt overwhelmed," she says then laughs. "I guess I *still* feel overwhelmed."

But there's something about *I'm sorry* that makes me soften. "Thank you for sharing that."

"We don't have to talk about it," she says.

"But we could," I say.

"I didn't want you to think you had been used or anything like that."

"I don't mind being used," I tell her.

"Well, that makes two of us," she says. But hearing Logan's voice like this, it does something. It's like a weight, a lightness, an endlessness, one I wish I could stop. One I hope would go on forever. "You're complicated," I hear her say, and my mind empties.

So while I finish my soda, I think about sharing *this*. About admitting *that*. But I don't. Since she's already making a joke. She's already making me laugh. She's already moved on. Since maybe she already knew.

Chapter Twenty-six

Low Power Mode

Logan

Kennedy's voice couldn't be softer or more inviting when she says, "Ask you anything?"

"Anything," I offer. But dialing her up like this after a morning's reception that was, well, that wasn't as warm as expected, and listen—I was mortified, though I hope I didn't come across that way, that I felt like running away. That I felt like staying that way. But it's as if I'm tethered to her, powerless in a sense that wants to flee, wants to fly, but not in the way that I had the entirety of my life. Instead, I want to run *with* her. Which is not possible when listening to her feels like plummeting from ten thousand feet only to land smack-dab on top of a cloud. On my knees. I wouldn't have the strength to.

"I'd like to know about your day," she says. "What'd you do?"

"After a week of not talking," I say, "that's the best you can do?"

"And why is that," she says, "we haven't talked?"

"I don't know," I say. "I wouldn't be surprised if you're angry."

"I'm not angry with you," she tells me. And it's not unfriendly the way she says it. It's not meandering either. It's not bending. "Why'd you text me after you said it was over?"

I laugh, which I don't mean to do. But I do. "I can't answer that," I say.

Which leads to an unnerving period of silence. "Of course you can."

"This is not even remotely feasible, is it?" I say.

"It's not," Kennedy says, which hurts. It hurts deep. "But you contacted me."

"When you hadn't thought I would," I say. And I can hear the disappointment in my voice, which means she must hear it, too.

"I'm just wondering what it's about," she says, "that's all." Dismissive.

Which concerns me. I'm concerned I've pushed too far. I'm concerned I'm unforgivable, irredeemable. "I enjoy this," I say, holding back.

"Except what *is* this?" she says. And there's something poignant in her voice when she does.

"Us...talking, interacting."

"Then walk me through your day," she says.

"I did laundry," I say.

"I hope you squeezed some fun in there?"

"Did you?" I ask, playful.

"You first." But her voice is weaker now, blushing, like the effect of fine champagne.

"That answer would require a droning tour of my place. Which, come to think of it, I could offer so much easier on FaceTime," I say, admittedly baiting.

"We have all night," she says, which is making my mind reel. "So why not walk me through. Like this. I'm dressed far from video-appropriate."

"How are you dressed?" I ask. But she laughs, deflecting. And disappointed as I am, I won't stop trying. "If you insist," I say. "Cue boring tour."

"Did you find mine boring?" she says.

"Nothing you say is boring," I tell her. Only to be left filling this unexpected void with, "In case I hadn't mentioned, I have a fourth-floor apartment in an old brick building, which is frigid in the winter, by the way—its sole downside. So imagine an 1800s mall, were it located somewhere in the midst of Harvard Square, that Ivy League, rowing, quadrangle vibe. Only it's not a mall. Though it used to be, well, sort of. The ground floor used to be a dry goods store where, as I'm told, the town's housewives descended to purchase...I don't know. What'd they need back then? Fabric to sew? Flour to cook? Tobacco to, you know—"

"Smoke," she says.

I sink deep into the couch. "What's that I hear?"

"I'm pouring a glass of wine," she tells me. "And that was the cork."

I sigh audibly. "I wish I could join you."

"Why haven't you?" she says. But I physically wish I could. "If you don't, you'll begin to think I'm laughing too hard at your jokes."

"What, you don't find my jokes naturally amusing?"

"You don't tell jokes," she says, "not deliberately. And yet, you amuse me."

"I'm glad that I amuse you," I say, which slopes into a longing stillness. Longing, at least, on my part.

"So," she says, "you were saying..."

"Yeah, well. Now I'm wondering"—looking around—"what they had up here. Like, maybe offices, desks, some filing cabinets. Though it's way too big for that. And with no separations, no walls, aside from my bedroom, an en suite, but that's a new wall. And there's a glass partition between the living room and kitchen, square mottled blocks, which I bet has been here forever. And they just sort of built around it." I know that I'm muddling through, but Kennedy's giving me cues, like audible cues. Like that audible nod. "Anyway, that's not really a division."

"Is that where you're at?"

"I'm not in the kitchen," I say. "I'm on my couch."

"But you can see your kitchen?"

"Partially, peeking, a galley kitchen, an island, metal stools. I put a painting up."

"Then what are you facing, now, as you sit on the couch?"

"I'm facing a massive window," I say. "I snatched a coveted corner unit. So light is bathing in. But the walls are a dark...I don't know what you'd call this color. And at night, when you look down, you can see cafés, patios, and string lights are draping. It's like little fireflies in trees, the lights."

She swallows, weak. "Over your small-town downtown?"

"A bustling small-town downtown," I say, relaxed, alas. "But this is as urban as I get. And it's peaceful, quiet, as long as you keep your window shut. Well, aside from the occasional summer night, which can get a little rowdy. Tourists, you know? And New Year's Eve, as you'd imagine. But right now"—I ponder, squinting into its light—"the sun's about to set." I take a drink.

"With a suggestion of a moon."

"Yeah," I say in agreement. "You can see it?"

"Yeah," she says, so beautifully. "What'd you wear today?"

"I wore jeans," I say. "And an old button-up."

"And when I called, where were you?"

"This morning? I was at that island. On a stool," I say. "Drinking coffee. I'd just woken up."

"Hot," she says.

"Not," I say, a slight uptalk turning it into a question. And as I head toward the fridge for another, I catch my reflection grinning in the mirror like an absolute fool. So I laugh to myself.

"And after that?" she says.

"Let's see," I say. "How would I describe this? If you make your way down three flights of stairs from here, it's this wide U-shaped staircase that seems to go on forever, or you could hop the elevator, you'll eventually reach the first floor, which is more hardwood flooring drenched in shellac. And there, you can sit all day, for hours, at least, if you'd like, as they serve pastries and local roast, espresso, and, later on, Reubens that are so amazing at this place…What's it called? It's kind of like an al fresco, a sidewalk or pavement café, indoors. And that right there is my thing. On weekends, at least on Saturday. I'll head down and hang out with a bunch of tatted-up hipsters, my fellow coffee addicts on laptops, their custards and pastries—you'd love their pastries—because I never have food in the house by the end of the week."

"I was thinking about you," Kennedy says, "when your text came in."

"I'm always thinking about you," I say, morning, noon, and night. And with a hefty dose of humility, of graciousness, I add, "I could take you there, one day. Perhaps." But her receptive silence says everything. So I carry on. "I had their ham and cheese croissant."

"When was this?"

"Around ten in the morning," I say. "The shops won't open until eleven. On the weekend."

"So what'd you do?"

"I read the news," I say, "people watched."

"People watched?" she says. "As I recall, that's how I met you."

"That was my lucky day," I say.

"I bet you've met lots of girls that way," she says. But our conversation has grown increasingly silly, tipsy, and less accusatory.

"Would that bother you?" I say.

"Were you looking to?" she says.

"I was not."

"Yes, it would," she admits. "It would make me pause."

Which is fine. I might like it. I might feel the same for her.

"Which would mean I'm redeemable?"

"That depends," she says.

"On what?"

"On *why*," she tells me.

But the affection I feel for her makes it impossible to respond in any way other than impulsively. "I haven't felt this."

"But what is this?"

"Overwhelmed," I say.

"I felt overwhelmed, too," she says, "but I wouldn't do that."

"Do you want me to go?" I ask.

"No," she says.

Then in the purest, most humble way possible, I say, "I am very, very sorry."

"You're very good at apologies," she tells me.

"That's not exactly a compliment, you know."

"But it is, you are," she says, "Most people won't do that. Most people won't say that, ever."

"Apologize?"

"In my life, no. They don't. They just carry on and pretend as if nothing's happened. It means a lot that you do." Then, when my hand combs through my hair, it just sort of stays there. "I didn't say that, anyway, to get an apology out of you." In a room that dims under slow-moving shadows. "I do like talking with you," she says.

"Thank you. Very much," I say, grinning painfully. "Are you making progress yet on that book?"

"I'm on to another," she says.

"Why are you laughing?" I ask.

"It's not something you'd like."

"Tell me," I urge.

"Maybe, maybe," she says. "I'll need another drink. So, finish your tour."

"But where was I?" I ask.

"You were people watching," she says.

"That's right," I say, "when everything was closed."

"What's everything?" she says.

"The first floor," I say. "The shops. A wine shop, small, which is, I guess you would call elitist. And an odd bookstore with a cat wandering around. They take him home at night."

"How do you know this?"

"I asked," I say. "It's the owner's cat. It gets lonely at home all day, so she brings it in."

"And what else?"

"This place that sells gourmet cheese," I say. "A men's clothing shop, more tailored. A shop that sells nothing but soap. And a florist, if you can call it that. It's more like white buckets they fill in the morning. Those refrigerated coolers. It's fragrant. I like the cafés."

"For all of those times you need a last-minute bouquet?" she says.

"Or sixty-dollar soap," I add.

"And after that?"

I shrug. "Laundry, groceries," I tell her. "Where are you?"

"Why?" she says.

"It's quieter, different."

"I came into my bedroom," she says.

"Thank you for sharing that."

"Well, I finished that glass of wine," she says. "So maybe I'll read some, a passage. It's short."

"From the book you're reading now?"

"Yeah," she says.

"So what's it about?"

"You'll see."

And I listen, motionless, dropping my gaze to the floor, at that touch of trepidation in her voice. But then she goes on. And as she reads, tepid, tiptoeing at first, I can't help but feel as a priest would while he's listening to a woman confess something like this. Self-conscious and secretly lustful.

And let's see, this begins roughly at a residence, a dinner, a couple, a few women, which dips into conversations, into nothing, into something. Into a bedroom. It's the sort of thing that begins in your mind and then just sort of builds from there, intensifying. The sort of thing that travels into every fiber of your being. And it's not even the content of the story that's making me blush, although it *is* risqué. It's more the fact that she's sharing this with me. That she's chosen this. Albeit intolerable to hear when we can't exactly reenact it.

In any case, she pauses to take a drink, which is when I do. But it's this thing she does without knowing, I think to myself, as I head toward the window, catching that reflection of my smile, which is shameless. Because we've been talking like this for hours.

Eventually though, "My power's low," she says, followed by, "I need to find my cord." But after some time, "Can I call again, later, maybe tomorrow?" Because the cord's too tight, she tells me, tethered. And that's fine, tomorrow.

So I lie on my back in bed thinking about alone. Thinking about her. Thinking about how alone I feel when I don't have her. Which I haven't felt. Until we'd met. When, in reality, wasn't I?

Chapter Twenty-seven

Text Bomb

Kennedy

I woke this morning in a deep fog, dressed in my underwear and covered to my waist in a sheet, bemused and not quite alert and having forgotten. Half with it, half somebody else. Detached and relaxed and alone as I scanned the length of the room to that moss-colored lamp on the table right next to a succulent, who's tossed herself off the ledge like a string of peas, only to circle back to the waxed ash bookshelf on the far-off wall. And that's when it all came back. That blinding belief in faith. That sense of enoughness. Then the emptiness of hanging on. Until everything breaks apart.

And you know, you know, you never want to follow those rules. You never want to play those games. But they forge ahead, written or unwritten, taught or learned or passed down or flat-out misgendered and heterosexual, it's what they preach, that sooner or later you'll realize that the only way to keep her from running away is to give the girl a chase.

So that's what I've done, haven't I?

When the battery died, I scrambled and couldn't connect or even try to recover, as if fate had shuffled her way back through my door once more to instill that will, that resolve, that innate sense of control I've never quite had with her.

Which is fine, right? Because who wants to be her prize, her prey? I'd rather be her do-anything head-over-heels in-a-cloud loop-de-loop all-out dream of love. That never-leave-me love—that infallible one.

Or at least that's what I've been battling out in my head for the past half hour as I lie on my back with my phone overhead, rereading some of Logan's texts she sent consecutively overnight. In all of this unlikelihood. In its arc of impossibility. As I envision her asleep or half woken or showered and smelling of sea salt soap. Looping over and over in my mind.

Which is something I should be doing as well, getting ready to start my day, as I attempt to wrangle this in, this fix, this hold she has over me. And maybe then I'll have the strength to text her back.

But after some time, I slip out and onto the terrace in my robe and distract myself on socials, tapping their obligatory likes beneath dusky skies before they rise. Which is so befitting my mood. The sky with its air of wants. With its bird's eye-view of every romantic spectacle you could imagine. Of every irrational love. Of every giddy first. Of the rawness, the sweetness that makes strangers pause to reminisce with a revisionist's brush of nostalgia. Of the kind of love that lures you wildly and blindly behind headlights, into shadowed thickets, beneath brilliant pastel skies, celestial blues, our laughter, giggling, to static and radio waves because they've just begun playing our song.

Anyway, it's with this foolish sense of eagerness that I text her back.

Me: *Are you awake?*
Logan: *I absolutely am now.*
Me: *I've woken you.*
Logan: *I was up. So tell me about your night?*
Me: *How are you?*
Logan: *Good, actually.*
Me: *And your night?*
Logan: *I've had better.*
Me: *From the looks of my bed, I have, too.*
Logan: *And here I am, wishing I could've improved that.*
Logan, again: *How long have you been up?*
Me: *An hour, maybe.*

Logan: *And you waited that long to respond?*
Me: *I'm sorry.*
Me, again: *See, I can apologize, too.*
Logan: *Don't be.*
Logan, again: *Can I ask you something?*
Me: *Sure, give me a call.*
Logan: *I want to text it first. And then, if you reject me…*
Me: *Which I couldn't.*
Logan: *Which you could.*
Logan, again: *Because you no longer trust me.*
Logan, again: *I want to see you.*
Me: *You want me to come up?*
Logan: *Yeah, maybe I do.*

It's a conversation that carries me through my day, elusive. Relentless, she is. We are. Because I'll be toweling off after a shower, and just as I snap that little hook around my bra, while I'm standing at my closet pondering, a text will ding on my phone. *Am I distracting you?* Then thoughts of her will engulf me.

Later as I'm jogging along late-season tobacco fields, harvests that gleam in green, her next will slide in. And I'll pause to read, smiling at my naivety. As I'm taking a seat on a bench, skin flushed, hair knotted in a tie pulled loose where I snap a photo of myself to send and, as you'd expect, she reciprocates, which becomes the first photo of her on my phone.

It's hard to say how many hours, how many exchanges have passed before I'm talking with Seth, who's knocked on my door, though it does persist. His talking. My texting. And this quite honestly surprises me, that he hasn't asked. That I haven't said. Not that I'm *not* thinking about it, about mentioning it. How it feels a tad bit rushed. As if we've skipped over, skipped ahead, skipped under some caution tape along the way.

Or perhaps I'm overthinking it. Perhaps I've already forgotten to care about it.

It does feel as if I've forgotten just about everything around me. Which might be why he interjects in this way. It snaps me back. "Do you think it's a good idea?"

But I haven't been paying attention. "It's your decision," I say offhand, invisibly smitten.

"I think I should wait," he tells me. "For personal reasons." As a glut of guilt consumes me. This being the guy who's agonized and philosophized with me over breakup bowls of Baskin-Robbins and kettle chips. "Can I come in?"

"Of course," I say. But it also feels like...you know how, when you're out with a girl and you come across some of her friends and you're just standing there, listening—because you can't join in? So eventually, you just tune out. Which is not to say you're *not* interested in what they have to say. You're just far more engrossed in watching the way she moves, the way she talks, the way she interacts with someone else, cordial, friendly, guarded, which is so remotely different from the way she acts with you, soft. It's like that, like you've kept that little secret. Like you have a secret to keep.

"I could really do something more," he's saying. "But if you're going to get involved with a coworker..."

"So you're involved?" I ask.

"Not at all," he says. "Strictly business."

But he hadn't framed it as *strictly business* before. He framed it as a date, potentially. "I know very few people who are as committed to their work as you seem to be—and she seems to be—to actually want to meet up on Saturday to go over it."

"Well," he says, and with the same flat tone, "We're that committed. This is a fucking huge project."

As I search his face for an answer. "Can I get you something to drink?"

"No," he says. He's agitated.

"Soda?"

"It's fine." We're seated across from one another, my phone dark on the table. "I keep thinking about how, one day, life will prove me wrong."

"How do you mean?"

"I just need it to stop rotating in a circle," he says. "Or at the very least, turn that into a spiral. So I can go up."

"You are way too existential for me today."

"I think I deserve something like that, though. I deserve a bump," he says. "I can't sit in park with my foot on the gas, revving up. Like, honestly, that's a huge thing for me." Mm-hmm. "You get up, go to work, do your thing," he says. "Get up...go to work...do your thing. I've turned into the Folgers variety of the best espresso."

"I happen to think you are the best espresso," I say, "with that little cream heart on top."

"Heh," I hear, which means *thank you*. "Yeah, well, I'm glad for that. But girls see that as bland, unappealing," he says. "They want the Italian loafers, the black suit, the super successful."

"But what do you want?"

"I want a promotion," he says. Imagine someone twisting a towel between his knees. That's how he seems.

"Which you'll get," I assure him.

"You know, I hate, I hate that," he says.

"What?"

"I would never let myself."

"Move up? Why not?" I ask, perplexed. "It's a sure thing. You keep saying this. You went on and on the other night. That's the whole point of taking on this project."

"Of course it is. There's a promotion in this. For *one* of us."

"What?" I say. "You think they'll give it to *her*?"

"No," he says, aghast. "They'll give it to me. Of course. I'm their golden boy."

"So what's your problem?"

"What's my problem? Are you kidding me? That's flat-out sexist if they do. I mean, she's the brain. I'm just some, you know, spokesperson. I'll sell it. She can't...So I have to wonder, why am I wasting so much of my time pumping up some project that won't even land me a promotion?" He meets my gaze, intent, then bows his head.

"Are you saying you'd turn this down?" But there's so much tension in this room that I want to slice it. "You're really into this girl, aren't you?" And I wish he'd answer. I wish he'd say something. But I guess that's all he'll give is this silent nod. "Well then," I say, regrouping, "how was that nouvelle American cuisine?"

And alas, a subtle grin. "I have leftovers," he says bashfully. "I'll make some."

I glance at the clock. "Cool."

"What," he says, mocking. "Don't say you have plans."

"I have a date, sort of." I shrug.

"Didn't you just break up with that girl?"

"She broke up with me," I say, "and she's back. In a way. I guess?"

"So it went well," he says, getting up. "In that case, I'll let you go."

"No," I say. "I have time. Please. Stay." This is a very good distraction to have. But not only that, he needs me. He never, ever needs me. I can't believe this.

"I'll just heat some up," he says, flattered.

But the thing is, I'm the one who's flattered.

Chapter Twenty-eight

Meanwhile, Said My Intuition

Logan

There's just something about Sundays, don't you think? It's for football people, for brunch people, for those hands-in-the-air Lord's Day people. Except those are not my people. Because I am what you'd call too preoccupied. So I'm kicking back on this couch where I can bury my heart in a beer.

Correction, I'm lugging this immovable chair over there, so it's facing a broad window, testing out some light.

Truth is, I don't know what the hell I'm doing. All I know is that I've convinced Kennedy into doing this virtual whatever you want to call it, which comes highly recommended by Tanner—you know, the sort of thing you do over FaceTime. Which wasn't very easy to do, the talking her into it part, since it's a whole ordeal or so she says. Not that I don't loathe video chat myself. It's just that this isn't work or Zoom. Nor am I presenting to an audience of zoned-out faces in boxes while fielding a flood of remarks and questions along the adjacent screen, most of which I find highly irrelevant.

To the contrary, this will be just the two of us, which I'm trying not to freak out about. I'm trying to just chill. Not helping matters is the fact that I'm ready to go with a good twenty minutes to spare. So I'm having to wait. All because she needed a little more time to do her thing and said this would give me time to do mine, which is basically dinner. Then add a quick shower.

As those nerves begin to kick in. So I've been entertaining

myself with a little catching up by text with Tanner, who's currently in that souped-up Airstream en route home after her extended date in the woods—which isn't creepy at all. So call me skeptical when she says they had an honest to God decent time, a respectable time, mm-hmm, a didn't want to leave sort of time.

Hence, their ensuing cohabitation—or, more precisely, adventurer is staying the night. Except you know as well as I do what this means. Because one night is going to morph into a week which'll morph into a sticky situation, which I've politely forewarned her about. Thanks to some putrid fish she caught on the lake in that rickety boat, which is a surefire way to win a girl over if you ask me—set up camp on an empty shore only to row her out into oblivion while demonstrating the finer points of casting a line and reeling it in, as if Tanner wasn't already adept at the latter. And in true courtly form, adventurer offered to manage all those fishy chores Tanner deemed unseemly.

The shit we'll do for a girl, I swear.

Certainly not topping that doughnut-themed wedding reception I attended with Emery, one that looked more like an edible game of ring toss, after two short weeks of hooking up, sampling every fucking variety of icing and sprinkle and cake as opposed to, say, real substantive food—because sugar shock goes extremely well with those bottomless flutes of champagne, preceding several photographs of us, the un-couple, later on display in their wedding album for all of eternity.

And while I'm reminiscing, who could forget that flight attendant who somehow managed to get me out to Jackson, Wyoming, to meet the extended family because *What was I thinking?* I should've ended that weeks ahead of time. But she was hot. I'm talking insane levels of hot. Hot enough to accept, and wear on our return flight, a gift of matching holiday sweaters. Which proved yet again that Daisy Dukes and cowboy boots could, well, convince me to do just about anything in my twenties.

In any regard, that's as far as I got with Tanner, that they fished and skinny-dipped and then something about cast iron and her cowboy grill. So, needless to say, she is blooming.

In the meantime, I'm just now beginning to realize that I am not the biggest fan of the twenty-minute wait. Shorter, fine. Though longer might be better. Since this just so happens to be that unsavory point at which you're prevented from doing just about anything productive. It's like you literally cannot do a thing aside from sit and worry and wait. Thinking relentlessly. On this rearranged chair facing out as I watch zoomers and millennials at street level purchasing hemp oil and ethically sourced greeting cards or sipping sunset martinis. When it dawns on me: What am I going to do when I lose all this light? When this place gets so doomy and gloomy that I can't even improvise. Not that the lighting in here is *bad* bad. It's just moody bad, which happens to be the whole point when I'm bringing a girl home, just not like this. Given it's not exceptionally flattering, cinematically speaking.

So anyway, after I've set up a few lights and opted for this button-up, casually cuffed, as opposed to a graphic tee, and after fixing my hair in the mirror for the umpteenth time, it's about two minutes till. So I'm like, "Hey, Siri, FaceTime Kennedy."

Talking to my iPad, which I've set up on one of those walnut tablet stands with a groove. Whereas she's apparently on a laptop. I only know this because she's now agonizing over preferences and options and technical things. You know, keyboard things. Given her sound's out.

Whereas I've apparently fallen into some sort of a trance over this narrowly focused and magnetically engrossed girl on the other side of my screen. But in any regard, as soon as I grow vaguely aware of this, I broaden my view—gathering a glimpse of her one unadorned wall, that antique fireplace off to the side, its manly black giving off that Members Club meets Boston Public Library vibe.

Her voice like a breath breaks in. "All right, so, this should work." And she's cupping a glass of wine. "My AirPods earlier," she adds, "that must've been the issue. Or maybe it's something else," she mutters, slowly moving her head from side to side as she's grinning at me, since I've been gawking, until she reclines back into fabric, that lucent complexion, her fixedness alongside my recklessness, despite my lack of patience moments earlier and everything else that's compiled throughout my day, a bleak standstill of a day now whirling and outstretched and boundless as miles and miles of steep panorama and transcendent endlessness.

"Give me a second, all right," I say, getting up to get a grip and, once I do, I'm lost in an onslaught of flighty, of forgetful, of flustered. Of overflowing ice and water in a glass in my last-ditch effort for playing it cool, and then, just as soon as I find my way back, she's asking a question. Or make that asking if she can ask in this needing permission way, which I've noticed about her. To which I guess I've responded in an *interested in whatever you have to say* way.

Because she's begun with, "Oh wow, so…" while I'm settling into my seat, as I'm settling into this look, which is stifled, I'd say, ambivalent. "I'm afraid to ask."

And then that sinking feeling again. "Tell me," I say, leaning in.

"So, this is the infamous apartment?" she says.

"One view of it."

"The couch where you called?"

"This morning," I say. "How was your day?"

"I kept thinking about being with you."

"Why aren't you?" I say.

"Don't be ridiculous," she says, despondent. "I'll arrange it." Then raises that glass to her lips.

"So why is it," I say, "you look as if you're about ready to back out on me?"

"That's not the case," she says. "It's just hard. It hurts a little, now. But it's that strange kind of pain. That wanting kind. And I'm dreading how this'll end," she says, dodging my gaze. "I'll have to compartmentalize."

"I'll back off," I say.

"I don't want you to."

My voice drops. "I'm not thinking about an end."

"Then what are you thinking?" Kennedy says.

"I'm thinking about how much I want you."

"You want me"—she shrugs—"because you can't have me."

"Is that what you think?"

"At some point you're going to have to choose," she says. "*We* are," I say, which comes out before I'm able to think about what I'll say. "Or we could do this for the rest of our lives." And as I say it, it's like I don't believe it, but I do.

"It's frightening how much I trust you," she confesses as a long bout of silence settles in. It's not off-putting to hear, though I can't say why. Since it should be. It should terrify me, and maybe it does. Though it's not as if I've responded either way. That said, why would I need to? Given I have reacted, I've smiled, which is encouragement. It's reassurance. So please excuse my ensuing shrug, which might seem out of place, I do realize. It's just that, it's *not*. Well, maybe it is. Since this is quite literally the most irrational thing I've ever done in my entire life.

Anyway, this goes back and forth, amusingly, for quite some time. Her talking about nouvelle American cuisine, about music. And me, well, nothing of real substance. And next, I'm hoping to camouflage this ridiculous grin on my face with—

"Show me your place?"

Because that's what you do, isn't it? It's evidently what I'm doing, what we're doing—is offering an awkward tour of, let's see, one riveting butcher-block countertop and this cabinet, a chaise lounge, my view, as evening sets in to an eggplant blue. A tour that has—admittedly and coincidentally, okay accidentally and quite fortunately—finished up in our bedrooms.

Where she's suggestively fingering down the length of her neck, backlit by the glow of a lamp now gleaming through sheer translucent cotton. "It's oppressive heat, isn't it? But they say it'll cool off overnight," which is why I've opened a window, a steady breeze drifting in from over there. Where leaves are rustling in trees. As the crosswalk bing-bings. Accompanied by *Wait. Arbor.* In the distance. *Walk sign is on to cross Arbor.* Sounds too faint to distract me from this. From the moisture above her lips. From envisioning her beneath me, gripping me, weakening me, wet—the way she gets when she's just about ready to come.

And then I decide to ask, "Have you mentioned this to anyone else?"

And she answers immediately. "I mentioned it to Seth," she says, "which was a mistake."

"Why," I say, "wasn't he happy?" It's not a jealous thing. I'm not suspicious, either. "I'm just curious."

"I mean, he's supportive. Don't get me wrong. It's just that I should not have disclosed so much. I knew better than that."

"What did you say?"

"He's protective," she says. "It's fast, it feels fast, that I have strong feelings for you. *How do you make that work?* is what I said. Just hoping to get advice."

I twist the switch on a lamp and reflect on that. On its undemanding light. On its lemon-meringue glow. On my chest. On weight, wait, weightlessness. On noise and noise—white noise. "I think we make this up as we go," I say. Then I hold her gaze, and she holds mine, which feels like a dash of heaven alongside that very small trace of hell. "It's hard for me, too. I try not to think too hard on it."

But she is voracious. "And what could I do to soothe you?" I nervous laugh. "C'mon, tell me."

"I'm going to regret this, aren't I?"

"Yes," she says, "you will, I will…as if I wasn't petrified enough."

"But I think you like that," I say. And there's that knowing grin. "Don't worry," I say. "I'm not about to lose you."

"Well, that's good," she says, "because I'm not about to lose you, either."

"Yet you barely know me."

"But I'd like to," she says. I drop my gaze. Because this is incomprehensible. That I even trust this. That she trusts this. As I rub the back of my neck. And after some time, she says, "I bet you always get girls to come on this strong," her smile widening. "You do, don't you?"

Then she almost laughs, starts to look me in the eye. And I can't stop watching. "God, you look incredible."

So, eventually I hear, "Thank you."

"It's like when I met you," I say, "and I couldn't wait to kiss you."

Kennedy's messing with her hair. "Because you assumed, of course, that you would."

"Well yes, I assumed of course that I would." She smiles briefly, silently. "And for the record, I do enjoy when you come on strong."

So she says, "Tell me what else you like."

Which makes me pause in this settled, unsettled sort of way. "I like how this feels."

"And what else?"

"I like how you looked when you first noticed me, as if you were surprised to see me. And when you bury your face in my neck. And when you straddle me. And how you told me about that song."

"I play that song on loop," she says. "It helps me feel you."

"If I could only get my mind *off* you," I say.

"And what is it you think about when you do?"

She's been fidgeting some more with that sleeve. "Look, I'm just saying. That lamp you've positioned right there, it's more than revealing." Which, I can tell, she's thinking about. I can see she's smiling about. Which segues into a should I, maybe, I think you should sort of thing. "It's distracting me."

"Well, I could fix that," she says, which I'm going to urge on. I'm going to ask and ask and ask, again. And she's going to, or rather she is…she's lifting her shirt overhead. While my smile dives into a pillow, deep, because this is beginning to get interesting.

"Do you have any idea what I'd like to do to you right now?"

But after a moment, "Maybe you should describe it," she's saying, settling back in a shadow of sorts, wearing a trace of sheer mesh, indifferent to it all.

Which feels, for me, like that lick, like that first sense of desperation rising while you're unwrapping a Popsicle stick because you just need to stop that drip. "I wish…"

"What do you wish?" she's saying.

"I wish you were here," I say.

Then in a distant, inattentive way, "But you're here, right

here," she's whispering as she's reaching beneath or between and below the screen.

As I reflect on that. On that expression and her mouth and soon the heaviness of her breath—on a breath that's yielding into a moan. "Tell me," she's saying, "what you'd do to me. What would you like to do?"

Words that roll over me, the air thick, hot. "The other night," I say, "as I was attempting to fall asleep, I could imagine you like this." I can almost feel my hand up the crease of her thighs, that sticky, balmy, those straps slack along her arm because they keep slipping, as if we were jostling our way toward the bed. "The elastic bound low at your hips." Flushed as I bent you over. Because I've memorized that mark on your skin. Your breath at my mouth. Your sighs, your tired and faint. Your slipping, sliding rhythm. Your silly reckless restraint. "Then pinning your knees apart. All wet down my hand."

There have been times when I've wondered about this, when all I could do is follow the sounds of her moans, the sounds of her smoldering, whimpering. Knees limp, spread as I kneel between. And her pleads while she comes against my mouth. Then throbbing, quivering, clenching. Heady and restrained. Her steady, rhythmic sighs.

Shivering in stillness.

Morphing into our silliness.

And now I know. Though who could describe this?

It reminds me of that flick of a whip, that ache. That last-minute swerve, that fright, as you veer to the side and slide. On that last lap. At long last. That last gasp.

Never knowing where that turn might wind up.

Chapter Twenty-nine

So It Went Like This

Kennedy

And there you have it. Logan would reel me in only to sit back and watch as I'd unravel. As if I was some tightly wound spring that only she could uncoil. Meanwhile, I'm trembling inside, slowly growing aware of the lengths that I could go just to please her.

Which is all I've been thinking about as I make my way along this sun-drenched highway en route to her place, my insides tied in a knot. "I'm almost there," I tell her.

"As in where?" she's asking. But her voice is missing that soft, affectionate quality it usually has when I have her on the line like this. In its place is a brazen loudness that's been picked up by my car's speakers.

"About twenty minutes out," I say. Then she starts in about landmarks, about markers, about this turn I'll need to make.

But, yeah, she's right. It *is* rather bucolic and very much out of the way. Or at least, once I find that turn she's been talking about. Because this route is all about pedestrians. It's about weathered crab apple trees, the splendor of snowdrops, snapdragons. It's about neo-Gothic chapels and lost tourists and luxe shops and unexpected crosswalks. It's a route that arcs into a rather interesting stay— because things happen fast.

And you know, there's something always so brooding, so soothing in her embrace and the way it consumes me wholly, exclusively. The way she conceals me and protects me from their hustle, their bustle, their insignificance. Their lack of importance. As her breath follows the length of my neck, which I'm beginning to feel all the way up my spine.

But then we step out of it.

And when we do, I pan around at that crowd now forming at the quaint indoor café she'd been telling me about. Their glassed-in display with neatly crammed bagels, croissants, muffins, that proud spider plant just past, a dangling elevator sign. As a patron dips a white plastic spoon into a cup of yogurt.

But seeing it now after having imagined it, after having imagined her having coffee in that very same spot, feels oddly removed yet connected at the same time. An unsettling. A settling in. Interrupted only by a firm grip. And in it, a modest little bouquet. Which I can tell makes me blush. So I drop my head and she leads the way, staring at me the entire time.

To put it in perspective, the whole scene is giving off that prep-school privileged Ivy League academy vibe. Even inside as I wander the length of her space. Her scent ubiquitous, since maybe it's on me. But I'm remembering, now, how I pictured it, or at least that small glimpse of it as she toted her iPad around this space as if narrating the first scenes of our documentary. Even though nothing could've prepared me for the sheer grandness of it. The tallness of it. Its presence, and her presence in it. Not big in square footage, mind you, but lofty, all of which I'm luxuriating in. In its privacy, despite large industrial windows that span the length of two walls, warped and distorting my view.

It's where I've set my bags.

I should probably set them in her room, but I don't want to ask. And she hasn't exactly offered to show me around. Though we do wind up there, eventually. We wind up there because I've asked if I could take a shower after that long drive, given the traffic, delays, a few breaks along the way. Which has left me drained in that artificially alert way.

Until the ambiance in her bathroom, nostalgic and fresh, has semirevitalized me, its calm light giving off an opulent appeal—

with sheen or gleam that reflects off white subway tiles and Carrara marble. That's where I am, at the sink. Unpacking my comb, a tube of leave-in conditioner, before pausing to reflect for a moment, and when I do, her fingers weave and lock across the front of me. And next she's clinging to me, my heart secretly pounding as if, in some incomprehensible yet recognizable way, she's always been here. She's always been with me, and I've always belonged with her. As if she was my one in a million.

Though it's not as if I could actually admit something like that to her, how one simple touch can make me feel all looped up and giddy inside. Because here's that little voice inside my head that's always holding me back, that's slowing me down. That voice that keeps reminding me: This is not the time.

Which all works out in the end because, within the span of time it's taken me to wander around in my mind, she's slipped away. She's slipped out of the room and has saved me from making a regrettable mistake, only to return with a stack of towels as I undress, as I unsnap the hook on my bra, as it slips down the front of me, as if this was the most natural thing in the world, me undressed as she makes her way in, which is almost companionable.

Then eventually, once I step into the shower, or at least once the water's comfortably warm and I'm dousing my hair, Logan joins me. She steps in and slips her hand up my spine and things transpire from there. Until we've toweled off and I'm naked on her bed, balmy and spent. Consumed in our breathless silence.

Because she's gone back into herself, and so have I. Or, that's to say, I've fallen into some sort of flushed meditation that coincides with the rise and fall of her chest. Reflecting on the scene just moments ago, as my hand dripped against steamed glass, her wet soapy grip. Her fingers inside me before she got down on her knees and spread mine.

But had I braved that confession moments earlier, would we still be lying here like this wrapped inside unbelievable closeness? But you'll never feel this unless you give a little, I remind myself, unless you open up. Then I roll off her and onto my back. "I doubt I could move from this spot."

And she rolls against me. "I doubt I want you to." But her hand's between my legs, and it's turning me on.

Which is why talk of Grubhub and DoorDash ensues. Along with *What do you like?* and *What do you have in mind?* Then, once it arrives, we dine cross-legged on her couch on plates that we balance on laps while listening to good music and sipping summer wine until the sun's as edible as creamy lemon meringue. Or orange Creamsicle pie, its hazy light flowing up her walls and gleaming along the floors as we talk and joke lasciviously.

As we clean up.

And as she rummages through a kitchen drawer and pulls out a brass Zippo, which she dips into calf-high candles, their flames mirrored along that broad window, against the acoustics of an indigo sky. Which is when it dawns on me that I've been staring at her. I guess I'm wishing she would kiss me.

I suppose I could just as easily kiss her. But I don't want to. Even though I seem to be preoccupied by it, preoccupied by her as she sets that lighter on the table after having twirled it in her hand for quite some time. So I've been thinking about that. I've been thinking about her hands, as well, gripping. I've been thinking about that song she put on. And I'm thinking about her lips and the way they move and how she talks and what she says—and what she doesn't say. And what she might say next. And what I might. And then I'm back on that lighter and how it's worn and etched with the word *Godspeed*. And I'm wondering what that means. As I slip my gaze toward those glasses of wine now empty—to hers beside my phone. And when I follow that line to her hand on her thigh, I cover it with mine.

And, that's how I get that kiss.

Logan exhausts me. And I don't mean that in an unwelcome way. I mean that in the most sublime keep me up way, as if I was winding around a hangover, tipsy—were hangovers insular, poetic, or somehow suspended in time. Or if they could make you experience so vividly the sensate pleasures of an infinite freefall.

One that's plunged me into the grips of insomnia, or at least that point at which sleep deprivation can charm and delude and woo you into believing your mind's lies, its dialogues, its projected exchanges, its fascinations. In that imaginary playground that always leads me into a reticent *I love you*. But in the end, that's all they really are—thoughts.

Perhaps there's always going to be some aspect of wanting her that's going to invoke some pain, some fear—fear, excitement, exhilaration, whatever you want to call it. Maybe it's all the same.

I reach for my water, then slip back into the recesses of my mind, into its darkness, into this void, this hollow, empty, chaotic frenzy of a mind. Into *Where could this lead?* Into *What do we do?* Until I'm reminded by a stirring, a shift, that she's in this void along with me.

That she's somehow buoyed me up.

It's a thought that lulls me to sleep.

I only know this because I've awakened to the aromas of something sweet, something roasted. Scents that seduce me out of this bed and into the kitchen where sun is angling in, mirroring my soul, which is bursting with light—the chirping, a sparrow—and Logan with her back toward me at the stove, rakish, clumsy, clenched again in concentration. So absorbed in what she's doing, however, that she's oblivious to the fact that I'm right here beside her. "What are you doing to me?" I ask, and she smiles back indecisively.

"I believe I'm trying to impress you," she says. And later, as she's serving—french toast, cider syrup, whipped butter—she's explaining to me that she's substituted whole wheat for sliced brioche.

And that's how the day wears on, leisurely and greedily, quietly, conversationally, through a sultry afternoon and into a starlit night. "You always impress me," I whisper to her as we're lounging in a lush matted field, on a blanket beneath a calm summer sky, eyed by a voyeuristic moon, beside a pair of lanterns that light the way, her gaze as uncertain as mine in the way it lingers, amused, admiring one another, her hand brushing up against my thigh before looping in mine—my heart brimming in suspense.

Which is when we get carried away in that blundering, vaporous sort of way, a hand approaching then broaching my waistband before unbuttoning, pulsing, thrusting—before she's eased me into a languid, dreamy ecstasy.

The next time we glance over at one another, it feels quieter, unbearably so, and I'm back to wondering what she's thinking. As it rolls over in my mind, again and again, silently, exuberantly absorbed in it. The projection of it. My silent reckoning with it. But as I do, as I ponder, I realize that I've actually said it this time. *I love you.* And she's added that *too.* And then it's over.

We haven't mentioned it since.

Though it's danced me into our last day, into our pulling things together, our rushing about, our passing glances. As we bumble along and then head out for a morning walk—in part to stall good-bye and in part to say it. A walk that has reminded me that there will always be some sort of a good-bye with us. A coming apart, that faint fear of falling apart, and then a coming together.

As we stroll solemnly amid the distant hum of traffic, the scent of wet earth, dew rousing the morning grass, as I tip my head and say, "I love road trips," sentimentally, as if this might lighten the mood.

And through a smile, she says, "Don't know if I could say the same."

"Well then," I say, turning to her, "I'll have to come to you."

"As if you could keep me away?" And then we pause beneath that white birch tree, her gaze permeating. "When I'm about ready to follow you home?"

"But you wouldn't," I say.

"I couldn't," she tells me.

"And therein lies the problem," I say.

But she keeps drawing me in until I can't read her face. "But you couldn't either," I hear.

"But I will miss this," I tell her. And after a few salient minutes, "I'll pretend that we're still together. I'll just think about this."

"But we *are* together," she says.

Which I let marinate in my mind. "All right."

Still it wasn't until she said it a second time that I actually heard it. That I felt it. That I could touch and hold it. Or perhaps it was a matter of her kiss, which coddled and constrained, skimming, teasing.

I couldn't even tell you how the rest of that morning went aside from the filling of mugs, the folding of shirts, the reticent zipping of bags, the sunglasses, the cables charging, and that last long stroll along the hall until we stood at the trunk of my car. And its slam as I glanced back.

Then her clinging, her falling against me. Her scent surrounding me.

It's still hard to comprehend that I'm *that* girl. That I'm her girl. Those words melting off every ounce of despair and filling me with hope. "Call me just as soon as you get home," she said while I was tugging at her belt loops.

But how would I feel back home? How would I feel come Monday? When I couldn't even say how I felt right then. Would I be gutted? Or, like this—invincible, unbreakable, alive.

The only thing I can tell you with absolute certainty is that all along that drive, it feels so intense that I think it might crush me. I think it might swallow me whole. And I love it.

I love it so much that I sob in the car. But then it passes. It passes and proceeds. It loops and recedes. It rushes all the way through me. But it's not grief. It's not even bleak. I'm thinking all this could be is beatific.

About the Author

C. Spencer grew up in Southern California during the 70s and 80s—watching Disneyland fireworks off her balcony and ditching school to hit Tower Records and thrift shops on Melrose Avenue. She spent two years as an art major in college only to switch midway to English literature, which led to her unnatural obsession with Hester Prynne, Lady Brett Ashley, and Henry David Thoreau's lifestyle of resistance.

After graduating, she packed her car and moved to Burlington, Vermont, sight unseen, living in the land of maple syrup and snowboarding for the next ten years. She currently resides in Western Massachusetts. She's worked as a freelance copywriter and editor since 2001. In 2013, she began writing fiction on the side.

Books Available From Bold Strokes Books

Lucky in Lace by Melissa Brayden. Straitlaced stationery store owner Juliette Jennings's predictable life unravels when a sexy lingerie shop and its alluring owner move in next door. (978-1-63679-434-1)

Made for Her by Carsen Taite. Neal Walsh is a newly made member of the Mancuso crime family, but will her undeniable attraction to Anastasia Petrov, the wife of her boss's sworn enemy, be the ultimate test of her loyalty? (978-1-63679-265-1)

Off the Menu by Alaina Erdell. Reality TV sensation Restaurant Redo and its gorgeous host Erin Rasmussen will arrive to film in chef Taylor Mobley's kitchen. As the cameras roll, will they make the jump from enemies to lovers? (978-1-63679-295-8)

Pack of Her Own by Elena Abbott. When things heat up in a small town, steamy secrets are revealed between Alpha werewolf Wren Carne and her human mate, Natalie Donovan. (978-1-63679-370-2)

Return to McCall by Patricia Evans. Lily isn't looking for romance—not until she meets Alex, the gorgeous Cuban dance instructor at La Haven, a newly opened lesbian retreat. (978-1-63679-386-3)

So It Went Like This by C. Spencer. A candid and deeply personal exploration of fate, chosen family, and the vulnerability intrinsic in life's uncertainties. (978-1-63555-971-2)

Stolen Kiss by Spencer Greene. Anna and Louise share a stolen kiss, only to discover that Louise is dating Anna's brother. Surely, one kiss can't change everything...Can it? (978-1-63679-364-1)

The Fall Line by Kelly Wacker. When Jordan Burroughs arrives in the Deep South to paint a local endangered aquatic flower, she doesn't expect to become friends with a mischievous gin-drinking ghost who complicates her budding romance and leads her to an awful discovery and danger. (978-1-63679-205-7)

To Meet Again by Kadyan. When the stark reality of WW II separates cabaret singer Evelyn and Australian doctor Joan in Singapore, they must overcome all odds to find one another again. (978-1-63679-398-6)

Before She Was Mine by Emma L McGeown. When Dani and Lucy are thrust together to sort out their children's playground squabble, sparks fly, leaving both of them willing to risk it all for each other. (978-1-63679-315-3)

Chasing Cypress by Ana Hartnett Reichardt. Maggie Hyde wants to find a partner to settle down with and help her run the family farm, but instead she ends up chasing Cypress. Olivia Cypress. (978-1-63679-323-8)

Dark Truths by Sandra Barret. When Jade's ex-girlfriend and vampire maker barges back into her life, can Jade satisfy her ex's demands, keep Beth safe, and keep everyone's secrets…secret? (978-1-63679-369-6)

Desires Unleashed by Renee Roman. Kell Murphy and Taylor Simpson didn't go looking for love, but as they explore their desires unleashed, their hearts lead them on an unexpected journey. (978-1-63679-327-6)

Here For You by D. Jackson Leigh. A horse trainer must make a difficult business decision that could save her father's ranch from foreclosure but destroy her chance to win the heart of a feisty barrel racer vying for a spot in the National Rodeo Finals. (978-1-63679-299-6)

Maybe, Probably by Amanda Radley. Set against the backdrop of a viral pandemic, Gina and Eleanor are about to discover that loving another person is complicated when you're desperately searching for yourself. (978-1-63679-284-2)

The One by C.A. Popovich. Jody Acosta doesn't know what makes her more furious, that the wealthy Bergeron family refuses to be held accountable for her father's wrongful death, or that she can't ignore her knee-weakening attraction to Nicole Bergeron. (978-1-63679-318-4)

Tides of Love by Kimberly Cooper Griffin. Falling in love is the last thing on either of their minds, but when Mikayla and Gem meet, sparks of possibility begin to shine, revealing a future neither expected. (978-1-63679-319-1